TROY
CHIMNEYS

MARGARET KENNEDY

With a New Introduction by
ANITA BROOKNER

PENGUIN BOOKS – VIRAGO PRESS

PENGUIN BOOKS
Viking Penguin Inc., 40 West 23rd Street,
New York, New York 10010, U.S.A.
Penguin Books Ltd, Harmondsworth,
Middlesex, England
Penguin Books Australia Ltd, Ringwood,
Victoria, Australia
Penguin Books Canada Limited, 2801 John Street,
Markham, Ontario, Canada L3R 1B4
Penguin Books (N.Z.) Ltd, 182–190 Wairau Road,
Auckland 10, New Zealand

First published in the United States of America by
Rinehart & Co. 1952
First published in Great Britain by Macmillan & Co. 1953
This edition first published in Great Britain by Virago Press Ltd 1985
Published in Penguin Books 1985

ISBN 0 14 016.112 0

Printed in Great Britain by
Cox & Wyman at Reading, Berkshire
Set in Imprint

CONTENTS

INTRODUCTION

TROY CHIMNEYS is a disconcerting novel. It belongs to
Margaret Kennedy's later period, when her plots became
more complicated, sometimes excessively so, and her early
rebelliousness was becalmed into a quite perceptible long-
ing for goodness and honour in the conduct of life. Both
these characteristics are probably carried to their fullest
extension in *Lucy Carmichael*, arguably the most popular
of her last works and a book which carries a charge of an
ordeal endured and a resolution vindicated which continues
to impress even today, when the comparatively pellucid
moral climate of the 1950's has become clouded to the
point of obscurity.

For these late novels of Margaret Kennedy, like those
which Elizabeth Taylor was writing at the same time and a
little later, are about virtue. They are virtuous novels written by essentially right-minded women, and it is a tribute
to their sophistication that they are by no means as simple
as that point of departure would seem to indicate, for
virtue does not triumph, patience is not rewarded, people
do not receive from the author their just deserts. One
might then quite legitimately ask how these novels are to
be perceived as virtuous. The answer, I think, is to be
found in the pain the author feels that moral conundrums
cannot be resolved and the result presented like a cheap
diagnosis of a chronic malady. Margaret Kennedy (and
here Elizabeth Taylor resembles her most closely) is a
serious woman who is content to translate her concerns
lightly into the traditional forms of the English drawing-
room novel.

Her distaste for formulae can perhaps be deduced from a remark made by one of the characters in *Troy Chimneys* about the novels of Jane Austen.

'That lady's greatest admirers will always be men, I believe. For, when they have had enough of the parlour, they may walk out, you know, and we cannot.'

The speaker is Caroline Audley, a lonely thoughtful woman of high intelligence and integrity who is in a position to observe that Jane Austen's life in the parlour concealed a certain abdication of passion and risk, and, more interestingly, a certain collusion with the traditional male activities of getting and spending: her heroines, with their curious appeal, are essentially gamesters for whom everything comes out right in the end. But for the serious woman (and I do not for a moment compare Jane Austen and Margaret Kennedy as writers) the end can be sad or disappointing or merely inconclusive. Mrs Kennedy does not offer nostrums in the form of easy solutions, and in this it can be seen that she has concerns over and above bringing her story to a neat conclusion.

Troy Chimneys is an exercise in all these negative modes, and at the same time it is not what it seems. The title would seem to promise one of those soothing panoramas of English country life in the middle to upper income range, for Troy Chimneys is the name of a house, and a very idyllic house it would appear to be, somewhere in Wiltshire. It is the house that serves as the main vehicle for Margaret Kennedy's nostalgia, for it represents peace, happiness, withdrawal from the murky concerns of fortune hunters and politicians, and the reward on earth for all the hard work that men have to devote to their careers, sometimes against their better nature. Yet Troy Chimneys also represents an unattainable goal, for the hero of the novel, Miles Lufton, who buys the house as a guarantee of the time when all his conflicts shall be over, dies before he can ever live there. And despite the really quite complicated and occasionally puzzling arrangement of the novel, it is the image of that house, silent, peaceful, and yet eternally out of bounds, that stays with the reader.

Yet Troy Chimneys, the house, is merely a strand in the background of the book. The foreground is occupied by Miles Lufton, the almost self-made politician who labours half-heartedly in the England of the Napoleonic and post-Napoleonic period. Should this promise an agreeable exercise in the higher reaches of Regency tosh, the promise is again unfulfilled and the reader discomposed. For Miles is a very complex character. He has apparently all the gifts, loving and virtuous parents, handsome and agreeable brothers and sisters, a country parsonage for a home, good health, a fine wit, no great fortune but an enlightened perception of where his interest lies and a determination to devote his energies to his own advancement. Indeed this perception strikes him early on in his career as something that might lead him into an inferior mode of behaviour, and he resolves to treat himself as two distinctly separate people: as Miles Lufton, a man whose native goodness has not been finally extinguished by self-interest, and as Pronto, the all too available extra man, diner out, weekend guest and flirt who sees all social gatherings as occasions for advancement and who never refuses an invitation because it might lead to useful contacts. Lufton and Pronto combined add up to an extremely plausible public figure: agreeable, even desirable, company, possessing the instincts of the rat pack, yet with a keen memory of original goodness to temper his appetites.

But the interesting thing about the Lufton/Pronto character is that nothing goes right with him. His generous impulses fall short of effectiveness. His passions can be seen to be all too moderate. He cannot carry anything through to fulfilment. And when he finally considers himself to be in love—with the authentically serious Caroline Audley—he cannot see that he has turned the possibility of loving her over in his mind for far too long, has left her to grow older, has in fact ruined her life, because of some flaw in his nature or his character or his outlook which prevents him from making any clear distinction in the moral order of things between the imperative and the merely beguiling. Even his death is a sort of accident, although the occasion is a duel, the proceedings reported by an interested witness, and a great deal of the evidence suppressed.

The story is an oblique one, and is rendered even more oblique by the manner in which it is told. The main body of the narrative is a limpid memoir which purports to be written by Lufton himself. This memoir is sandwiched between two sets of letters written by descendants of the Lufton family who are initially attracted by this colourful ancestor and then prudishly distressed by his example. It is the method used by Benjamin Constant in *Adolphe* and it would appear that Margaret Kennedy took it from that source. If it is a method which marries uneasily with the tradition of the English novel as practised half way through the twentieth century, then it must be allowed that Margaret Kennedy cannot be relied upon to give her readers what they think they have been led to expect. She is disconcerting in her preoccupations, disconcerting in her methods, and technically more learned and experimental than many of her successors in the 1980's.

Anita Brookner
London, 1984

PROLOGUE: 1879

PROLOGUE: 1879

I N letters and journals of the Regency occasional reference is made to a person called Pronto who is generally mentioned as a fellow guest in a country house.

Conscientious researchers have identified him with a certain Miles Lufton, M.P.; he sat for West Malling, a borough in the pocket of the Earl of Amersham, and he held an important post at the Exchequer during the years 1809–1817. He spoke frequently and well in the House, in support of Vansittart's financial policy. Nothing else is known of him save that he could sing; in the *Bassett Papers* he is reported to have been visiting Lingshot in 1813 and to have delighted the whole company one evening by 'singing like an angel.'

At the age of thirty-six he wrote a short autobiography. This, together with a kind of diary that he had kept, came into the possession of his sister, Susan Lufton. She took them with her to Ireland when she went there to live with another sister, Lady Cullen, of Cullenstown, Co. Kildare. She subsequently married a Mr. Lawless and sailed for India, leaving the Lufton Papers behind her. They lay forgotten in the attics of Cullenstown for thirty years. They were then removed to the library by a Miss Honoria Cullen, who had taken it upon herself to sort all the papers in the house because she had nothing else to do. They were not read at that time, and they remained undisturbed in the library for another thirty years.

The Cullens had no motive for perusing these faded pages. They had little interest in their Lufton grandmother or in any of her family. The Luftons, who came from an obscure parsonage in Gloucestershire, were, by Cullen standards, 'nothing much.' Only one of them, a Eustace Lufton who became an admiral, was worth remembering. But the papers were eventually taken from their drawer in 1879, and sent to Brailsford in Warwickshire, at the request of the Hon. Frederick Harnish, brother-in-law to Sir James Cullen. This was not on account of any sudden interest in 'Pronto,' but in connection with the following correspondence between Harnish and Cullen.

Brailsford, Dec. 3, 1879

Dear Jim,

I think Emmie once told me she thought you had some old papers in which frequent reference is made to our queer relative, the Chalfont whose collection of pictures, etc., we now have at Brailsford.

I wonder if you would do me the great favour of letting me see them? Convalescence is such a bore that I have been amusing myself by going through his letters, and am getting very much interested in 'Cousin Ludovic' as he is still called. He left boxes upon boxes of papers, all in the wildest disorder. I don't think they can have been touched since he died in 1830. He never succeeded to the Amersham title; my grandfather was his first cousin and that is how we came in.

I want to know more about him. I had always heard that he was a lunatic. But you know our family! That is what we *would* say about a man who bought pictures and did not hunt. We have a portrait by Opie, which looks decidedly mad, and there is a secluded suite of rooms, still called 'Lord Chalfont's Rooms,' in which we, as children, imagined that he had been confined with half a dozen keepers. Emmie, who was the bravest of us, was the only one who dared go there after dark.

He must have had lucid intervals. The first papers I looked at were all about the Elgin Marbles, which he seems to have admired when nobody else did. He was one of those who supported their purchase by the British Museum. And I have found a couple of letters from Wordsworth, dull in themselves, but not, obviously, written to a lunatic.

As evidence on the other side there is a portfolio of drawings by the poet Blake. Only a madman could have drawn them or bought them. You never saw such things ! One cannot even be sure whether the figures are clothed or not.

There are no letters written by him. Have you got any? He must have written thousands to have got so many replies, and he seems to have kept every scrap of paper ever sent to him. A good many are solemn records of his dreams ! He wrote down every dream he had, as soon as he woke up.

It is very difficult to get information about what went on thirty years before one was born. That is an epoch about which everybody shuts up. Family skeletons ain't respectable for at least a hundred years. My chief source of information about that period is our old neighbour, Sir Mervyn Crockett, now well over ninety. He was no end of a buck in his time, and full of anecdotes, — seldom of a kind which I can stomach. Some of them, in fact, make me feel quite sick. The squalor of their jokes is un-believable and so was their brutality. He remembers nothing of Cousin Ludovic save that they 'roasted Chalfont at Eton in 1796.' I thought this to be some kind of slang, but it is literal. They hung the poor little boy up before a very hot fire for several minutes ! Crockett chuckled when he remembered it ; to him it was a capital joke.

Do, my dear fellow, let me see those papers, unless they

are private and confidential. Love to Emmie. Tell her that I am getting on famously and hope to be well enough to visit you all in the spring.

Yours ever,

F. H.

Cullenstown, Dec. 10, 1879

DEAR FRED,

We have found the papers you mean and sent them off by parcel post. They have been kicking about in the library as long as I can remember. I glanced through them and see that they are full of references to a 'Ludovic' who must, I think, be your man.

What you say about family skeletons is very true. I know nothing about the great-uncle Miles Lufton who seems to have written these papers. I once asked my mother about him and she protested that she didn't either, but with a little blush which she always sports when she tells a fib. I believe she does know something and that he was *not quite the thing*. She hates anything shady.

I don't see why he should have vanished into complete obscurity like this. I only took a very hasty look at the papers, but, by his own account, he seems to have been very much the thing, an M.P. and all that, went everywhere, knew everybody, and cut quite a dash. And he owned some property too, a house in Wiltshire called Troy Chimneys. There were one or two letters about it, along with the papers, which I have not sent because they cast no light on Chalfont. They are merely about leases and repairs, etc.

If you see Crockett again, do pump him. Ask him if he knew anybody called *Pronto*, for that seems to have been my great-uncle's nickname among his fellow bucks. And pass on anything that he may let fall, the more disreputable the better. Emmie agrees with me that there might

be some mystery.   When my mother comes here after
Christmas I will try her again.

Emmie sends her love and tells you not to keep your
nose in dusty papers all day long, for it can't be good for
your cough.

Yours ever,

JIM

Brailsford, Dec. 15, 1879

DEAR JIM,

How very good of you to send the Lufton Papers.
Tell Emmie that it *is* good for my cough.   When people
ask after me, my family say : Oh, he is so much better
that he is writing a history book !

How curious that your great-uncle once owned Troy
Chimneys !   I think I have seen it.   At least, I have seen
a house in Wiltshire answering to that odd name, and I
can't believe there are two.   A local antiquary told me that
it is probably a corruption of *Trois Chemins*, and three
roads do certainly meet at its front gate.   I saw it when I
was staying at Laycock, and we all agreed that it is a pity
such a striking old house should not be properly kept up.
It is a mere farm-house now.   There is a manure heap
by the front door and half the windows are boarded
up.   I remember it chiefly for a very pretty stone dovecote and a great old mulberry tree in the rough grass in
front.

I saw Crockett yesterday and tried to pump him about
your great-uncle.   The name *Lufton* stirred no memories,
but *Pronto* did.   He burst out laughing and said that of
course he knew Pronto.   Everybody knew Pronto.

He remembers no good of anybody, but I am sorry to
say that he could not produce anything very disreputable
about Pronto, or tell me what became of him.   He described him as ludicrously determined to get himself on in

the world, out to please, especially where the ladies were concerned.

He claims to be himself the author of the nickname. *Signor Pronto*, he says, was a character in a popular farce, — a most obliging person who always turned up in the nick of time to arrange matters for everybody. The catch word of the farce was : *Pronto will manage it !* Some great lady was lamenting the difficulties of arranging charades at her country house party; 'But,' she cried, 'I expect Mr. Lufton tomorrow and he will manage it for me.' At which Crockett, who was present, said : 'Oh ay ! Pronto will manage it.' After that they all called Lufton Pronto behind his back.

I must catch the post with this. Love to Emmie.

Yours ever,
F. H.

THE LUFTON PAPERS: 1818

THE LUFTON PAPERS: 1818

To The Rt. Honble. The Earl of Thame
Copley, Northamptonshire

The Parsonage, Great Bramfield, Gloucestershire
May 20th, 1818

MY DEAR LORD,

I have the honour to inform you that I mean to be your guest at Copley towards the middle of July, — for how long I cannot tell. I will engage to quit Northamptonshire as soon as I have secured a more agreeable invitation elsewhere. Had I been able, this year, to arrange my usual succession of summer visits I should have done my best to avoid your lordship's hospitality. But my affairs are somewhat confused; I am out of a place and mean to give my acquaintance no peace until they have done something for me.

I therefore find myself obliged to depend upon a sort of invitation issued by Lady Thame, in the autumn, which I choose to construe into a firm engagement. She may have forgotten it, or believe that she has not absolutely committed herself in the matter, in which case you will be so good as to inform her that she has, for I intend to come, little as you both may desire my company.

I believe, however, that I shall be tolerably welcome, since guests at Copley are shy birds. In autumn you shoot them, in winter you ride over them, and in spring you let loose your pedigree bulls upon them. July, so I have heard, is as safe a month as any.

I need no assurance of your lordship's concern for my health and happiness. All my friends have been, these

11

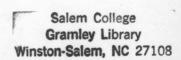

six months, so anxious to know how I do that they have ventured upon no enquiries, lest they might learn that my accident, last November, proved fatal. They believe me dead, I suppose, and are very sorry for it. Most of them were at Gracedieu when this misfortune befell me. Your lordship witnessed it and was so good as to inform me that I had broken my neck. 'By God, Pronto!' said you, 'I believe that you have broken your neck.' 'By God,' said I, lying in the ditch, 'I believe that I have.' But you were gone on by then, and killed, so they told me after, near Ulverscroft. Some cottagers came to my assistance and carried me on a hurdle to my inn. My neck, as it turned out, was safe, but I had broken a leg and three ribs.

You were all gone next day, but I lay perforce for three weeks in that inn, doing my best to die. In addition to my injuries I had got a fever from lying in the rain, untended, for so long. I must have an excellent constitution for I began to mend and crept off to my father's parsonage, an earth to which I return when wounded in the chase, but about which I keep pretty mum at other times. The fever has at last departed and I can hobble about. But I doubt that I am perfectly recovered, for this letter won't do at all. It is scarcely in Pronto's style.

Pronto, however, is not dead. He sleepeth. Another week or so may see him out of the wood and he shall then write a prodigiously civil letter to your lordship, securing his invitation to Copley. In the meanwhile,

I have the honour to be,
    With great insincerity,
        Your most obliged and faithful servant
            MILES LUFTON (Pronto to you, old boy!)

May 21st

I thought that I had torn up my effusion to Ld T: but here it is in my desk! I shall keep it as evidence of my reviving spirits. A week ago I should have found no amusement in composing it. I wish that I had the assurance to send it!

But I have torn up another letter which I began and never finished, — to Ludovic. *His* neglect I cannot overlook. For the rest I care nothing. I know that they value me only as I am useful to them. My vanity was wounded when I learnt how easily they could forget me. But I thought, I believed, that Ludovic had a real regard for me. Our friendship is now of many years' duration; he knew me long before Pronto came upon the scene and I have ever been a loyal friend to him. If he were to be near dying, I should not treat him so. He *should* have written. He should have showed some concern.

I must remember that he never does write letters unless he is riding some hobby horse. His concern is all reserved for the muses; he will weep at a poem but not for a friend. I have always known him for a heartless little monster. But life here is such a dead bore that I wish somebody would write to me.

Sunday

I hobbled to church this morning. It is the first time that I have got so far. I was in pain for most of the Service and could not sleep as all the rest of the world did. George preached today as my father has a touch of his lumbago. Only Macbeth could have remained awake when my brother preaches and I doubt if even he could have listened. My eyes were open but I can recollect nothing save the text: *The children of Israel brought a willing offering unto the Lord* (Exodus 35, 29). He preached for an hour but it would have taken him less than a minute to make his point: Those who will not pay tithes in full must certainly expect eternal damnation.

Sukey and Anna slept with their heads sunk forwards

so as not to crush the feathers in their Sunday bonnets. In my sister, slumber was excusable; I would have joined her if I could. But Anna should have stayed awake; a wife should listen when her husband preaches, however tedious he may be. In the Park pew, over against ours, I heard a rumbling like the Severn Bore. It was Cousin Ned snoring. I spied on him through the old knot hole in the wood; when we were boys we poked marbles through it. He had some half-dozen of his children there with him. They gaped and picked their noses. I wonder he don't teach them noughts and crosses; that used to be the great game in the Park pew during sermon time, in the old days. But not in ours; any levity would have distressed my mother. We sat to attention, all seven of us, and I believe that we were not a little proud of my father's sermons.

Mrs. Ned was not at church. She lay in last night, so they say, of another boy. I suppose we shall have the bells ring out this afternoon.

The monument that they have set up to my mother is the most frightful I ever saw. It is a *bas-relief* representing one of the pyramids of Egypt. At its base, beneath a willow tree, sits, or rather squats, a disconsolate female. But they have done better in the text that they chose:

> Strength and dignity are her clothing
> And the law of kindness is on her tongue.

The law of kindness!

Is it a blessing or a curse to have known no other, through the first years of infancy?

'Nothing that you do, my dearest Miles, can make me in the least uneasy, so long as I am satisfied that you feel as you ought.'

I had been stealing green gooseberries and she found me ready to vomit in the kitchen garden.

'Our feelings,' said she, 'must ever be our best guide. How do you feel, my love?'

'Very bad, Ma'am.'

'That is conscience, Miles. Conscience will always torment us when we have done wrong.'

I have never doubted it, and got rid of conscience as soon as I could, behind the potting-shed.

There go the bells! What a busy fellow is Ned, to be sure! I forget how many he has got, but Mrs. Ned lies in every year about this time.

In the old days my mother would have been off to the Park this afternoon with a little crock of our rum butter. It was incomparable, and it went to any house in the parish when a child was born. But we don't make it now. Sukey has forgotten the receipt, — she is the least housewifely of my sisters. As for Anna, she never knew it; my mother was dead before Anna married into the family. We don't take presents to our great cousins at the Park nowadays, nor do game and peaches come from them to us. All those pleasant customs are quite gone over. Though, in justice to Ned, I must remember that he did come to see me when I was ill. His appearance put the household into quite a fluster, for no Chadwick had crossed our threshold for close upon two years. He sat for half an hour beside my bed, breathing heavily, and looking as if he wished to say something cordial but getting no further than a gruff enquiry after my bowels. He was not quite sober, but nowadays he seldom is.

I continually look out of my window as if I expected to see my mother set off with the rum butter. I could have followed her course for quite a while, across Parsonage Lane, through the little gate, and among the trees in the park. She had her own way of walking; she neither sauntered nor hurried, but sailed onwards with a smooth easy motion, like some handsome ship gliding over the sea. Wherever she went, she always seemed to be expecting a pleasant end to her walk.

Wednesday

Spirits at zero this morning, although I feel a great deal better. If I have to remain at Bramfield much longer I shall run mad. That is the worst of recovery, — one grows more observant. It is all so dreary, so unutterably dreary here now ! When I reflect upon the past I can scarcely bear it. Not only is the loss of my mother daily, hourly, felt, but my father is but the shadow of what he was. His mental powers are failing and his temper is very uncertain. Of the seven children who grew up here, one is dead and three have found other homes. Sukey, George and I are melancholy survivors, nor is the addition of Anna likely to raise our spirits.

Have made a resolution to be kinder to poor Sukey. Her peevish, spiteful ways are very provoking, but her lot is hard, — penned up here. She has no amusement, no distractions. George is an affectionate brother, but he was always a dull dog and his marriage extinguished the last vital spark of sociability. Six months of George and Anna are too much for me ; no wonder Sukey grows sour ! I wish she could get a husband. She used to be a pretty girl, but her bloom was short. It might revive if she could but get away. If Harriet would invite her to Cullenstown, for a month or so, she might recover her spirits, even if she did not get a husband. Have I not cause to know what havoc such a life may work upon a woman's heart ? If *another*, far more amiable than Sukey, had not grown hard and bitter I might now be able to call myself a happy man. To live unloved, disregarded by others, is to become, in the course of years, unloving and censorious. We deride old maids, but they cannot help their narrow hearts and spiteful tongues; life has made them what they are.

What *could* have induced George to marry Anna Cotman? That thought was uppermost in all our minds when we assembled for the wedding. I remember Kitty's explanation:

''Tis all the consequence of Mamma's death. Poor George was very lonely and wretched and Anna was by. Sukey is to blame. She should have tried to be a more cheerful companion to him.'

He had just taken Orders and was doing the duties for my father at Stokehampton. He was wretched and Anna was by. That must have been the way of it. But Anna had always been by; we were united in wishing that she were not. Mrs. Cotman lived, with her five daughters, in The Red House, just beyond the village, upon the Tewkesbury road. She was the kind of woman whom one cannot imagine as a wife, — only as a widow, as born wearing weeds. Most of the Cotman girls were oppressively lively, but Anna had the spirits of a slug. I think that a determination to be dismal is the most positive trait in her character. My mother always exhorted us to dance with her at children's balls; each boy must stand up with her at least once, because 'poor little Anna' never could get partners. George, in those days, objected as loudly to this kind of charity as did Eustace and I. We felt that Anna preferred to be slighted.

Little did we think that we should all be trooping to church one fine summer's day, triumphant Cotmans, disconsolate Luftons, George with hay fever, and Anna, awkward and aggrieved as ever, in a prodigious white bonnet and a Brussels veil which (so like her) she contrived to catch and tear upon the latchet of the church door.

All through that ceremony we thought of death, for it

was but six months since we had gathered at my mother's grave-side. And I perceived then that home was home no longer. It was *she* who had made it so. She had bound us all together, obliging us to love one another because she did, so tenderly. She wrote continually to each, giving news of the rest. When we returned nothing was changed, and the old days were there to welcome us. But gone now for ever, — the children finally scattered, bound only by ties of memory. We buried our childhood in that grave. Bramfield Parsonage was thereafter merely the house where our father lived and where, when we paid him a visit, we might scan 'the marks of that which once had been.'

I cannot recall the day, the hour, when this stealthy door closed for ever behind me. I was at Bramfield in October. I suppose that I said goodbye to her and rode away, unaware that this was the final farewell, — that I had weighed anchor and set out upon a voyage from which there could be no return. But whether it was a Monday or a Tuesday I know not, or if it rained or shone, or if I turned at the corner of the lane to wave to her. The leaves must have been falling. When we buried her the snow was on the ground.

Thoughts of that inclement day, when we stood in the snow about an open grave, were so strong upon me during the wedding that I was amazed, coming out of church, to see the lilacs in bloom. Thrushes were singing and the glebe meadow was full of buttercups. Clocks had ticked. The earth had rolled round to summer. But we had been left in the snow.

KAI CHRONOU PROUBAINE POUS !

I forget who said that. I must ask my father. He will like to be asked ; I shall do so at dinner. It may give us a little rational conversation and protect us from the eternal bickering of Sukey and Anna.

Thursday

I did ask, and might as well have held my tongue, for any hope of enlivening the dinner-table. My father was in a very ill humour, which is not to be wondered at, for the dinner was abominable. I wish it could be determined whether Sukey or Anna is mistress here. A dinner ordered by either would scarcely charm the *gourmet*, but we might at least have some consistency in our discomforts. As it is, each insists that it is the other's province. Nanny, our cook, does her best, but I sometimes suspect that she procures our meat from a knacker.

'*Kai chronou*,' says my father, '. . . never heard of it! Pray Sukey, what d'ye call this?'

'Mutton, sir.'

'Mutton? I'm glad to know it. I had thought it might be old shoe leather.'

We champ in silence until an indistinct mutter is heard from Anna about a hare-lip. One can never be quite certain of what she says, but I gather that the midwife told Goody Wellbright, who told Nanny, who told Anna, that Ned's new infant has a hare-lip.

'*Not* very likely!' snaps Sukey.

I foresee a controversy which will outlast a night in Russia. We shall inspect the child at the christening, but that will settle nothing. An idea, once lodged in Anna's mind, is a tenacious guest. George supported her, in conjugal loyalty I suppose, for he can know nothing of the matter. Copley, and Thame growing maudlin over his wine, would be Paradise to this.

After the women had gone my father became more genial and asked what my Greek line had been.

'And the foot of time advanced . . .' said he. 'Let me consider . . . I fancy it is to be found in Aristophanes. But I believe that it may be a quotation from some other poet.'

After some cogitation he went off to look up the passage and finally pronounced it to be, in his opinion, a quotation from one of the lost plays of Euripides. Being once got on to Euripides he grew quite cheerful, and discoursed for some time upon the merits of this neglected poet. Later he showed me some translations that he has made. I am glad that he should still have the spirit for that sort of thing. His verses are scholarly and elegant, as is all his work; I used to admire it immensely but I have lately come to think that he translates the *sense* only. Of the sentiment there is little indication. *Does* a woman describe her probable rape thus ?

Perforce the hostile alcove to ascend !

When bewailing her murdered infant *does* she say :

Alas ! Still starts th' involuntary tear !

I do not believe these lines sounded so to the Greeks, when pronounced in their theatres. It is the *sound*, the heavy tramp in the syllables, which has taken so strong a hold upon my fancy in this line about Time's foot. My father can see nothing remarkable in it. I sometimes wonder if he really believes that there were such people as the Greeks, although he has spent a lifetime in deciphering their literature. He refuses to believe that there can be merit in Ludovic's great dote, the marbles which poor Ld Elgin brought back from Athens. He has not seen them and Humphs ! and Pshaws ! at any suggestion that they can bear comparison with some acknowledged master-piece, such as the Apollo Belvedere.

'Are they not great clumsy, barbarous things ?' said he.

I said my piece, learned from Ludovic, that they are intended to represent gods rather than men.

'And how,' asks my father, 'may gods differ from men?'

'Were they not immortal, sir ?'

'Why, what nonsense is this ? You don't suppose that

there ever were any such individuals, do you ?'

'No, sir. But the Greeks supposed so.'

'The more fools they !'

Saturday

George gone to Stokehampton. When he goes over for the duties he sleeps at a farm.

We have suffered all day from a superfluity of icebergs. My father can talk of nothing else. He has been reading an article upon the Arctic Regions in *The Gentleman's Magazine*. It appears that an iceberg exposes but one-tenth of its bulk above the surface of the water, concealing nine-tenths below, for the inconvenience of shipping. Since I never intend to visit the Arctic, this peril does not appal me.

I had letters yesterday. Ludovic wrote, sending a song for Sukey. There is no direction on his letter but I imagine that he writes from Brailsford. He says of the song that :

All the women are singing it. The words are striking and you may guess to whom they are attributed when I tell you that T. Moore sang them at Ly Dysart's one day, and would not name the author, — since when there has been a scramble for copies, and no album is complete without one.

He says that Harding was asking after me and said that I could not be in town, for he never saw me anywhere.

I told him that you are very well, for you always are, an't you ? I assured him that you must be somewhere about.

After raving over some new purchases, — half a dozen drawings by Ingres and David, he suddenly remembers that his sister told him, not long ago, of my death in Leicestershire.

She says you broke your neck, hunting at Gracedieu. Did you ? My father is quite put out ; he says that you should have informed him of it immediately as Clancarty wants your seat for somebody. An M.P. has no business to die in this hole and corner fashion.

Then, after an airy finish, he changes his tune in a post scriptum.

I begin to grow anxious! Pray let me know *immediately* that you took no harm from this fall. I shall not be *quite* easy in my mind until I hear from you.

I shall pay him out for his long neglect by not making him *quite* easy for a week or so.

My other letter was from King, about Troy Chimneys. He wants to renew his lease for a further five years. I cannot make up my mind. He is a good tenant; if I refuse he may go, and I shall be at the trouble of finding someone else. But five years is longer than I like. I have not given up all hope of living there myself before I am forty, although every dearer scheme connected with it is destroyed for ever.

Sukey tried over the song: *They Say that Hope is Happiness*. I daresay it really may be by Byron, although, if he is responsible for every set of verses handed round nowadays as his work, besides what he publishes, the poor fellow must have writer's cramp. But this is in his vein, — a good dismal song which reflects my present mood.

Sunday

Icebergs again for supper. George had to hear about them. He is returned from Stokehampton in a vile temper. The people there are perfect heathens, little better than Dissenters. It was the Sunday for the Sacrament, but no person there except himself and the clerk. The celebration could not have taken place had not George, who is a persistent fellow, gone out and given sixpence to an old woman to make up three.

They were still upon icebergs when I came upstairs. The night is so warm that I doubt if I shall sleep. My chamber window is open and not a breath of air comes to disturb my candle as I sit writing. There is no moon to be seen. All is wrapped in a stifling darkness and silence, though I heard an owl hoot, a few minutes ago, far away among the park trees. I daresay it will thunder before morning.

A human being is uncommonly like an iceberg. Only a tenth of him is apparent to the world. But, in most cases, all is, I believe, pretty much of a piece. We can guess at the submerged creature by that portion of him which is visible above water. Perhaps I am mistaken. In my case it is not so. Do most men carry a Miles and a Pronto about with them? I hope not.

Miles and Pronto don't converse. That is the trouble. They are formed, I think, of different substances. Pronto is member for West Malling. Miles is still wondering how the devil that came about.

I have a whimsical notion that I should like to write a short life of Miles, while Pronto is out of the way. It will give me an occupation, which I sorely need. If Pronto goes up in the world, which he means to do, he will have his biographers; whereas nobody will put in a word for Miles unless I do.

I think that I will begin tomorrow. For the life of Miles is now quite concluded. He had a blow, poor fellow, which finished him, last summer. Some months before Pronto fell off his horse, Miles took another and a graver toss, from which he can never recover. The foot of Time will advance, and Pronto will go with it. Miles waits by the Styx.

THE LIFE OF MILES LUFTON:
1782–1818

Theodosia

A MEMOIR of this kind should open with a guarantee of respectability, both upon the paternal and the maternal sides. There should be property somewhere, a baronetcy (at least) in a collateral branch, loyal endeavours, a bishop or two, and all that sort of thing. The Luftons, unfortunately, are deficient in this respect. The Chadwicks are rather better connected, having got hold of Great Bramfield at some time or other. But there is nothing very striking to report until Dr. Aeneas Chadwick, the eminent antiquary, breaks his neck while scrambling about the ruins of the Baths of Caracalla in the year 1775. He leaves many debts, a widow, and three daughters, — Augusta, Theodosia and Amelia, with whom I must principally concern myself in this chapter, since my father, for the greater part of the time, is still at Cambridge, a humble and industrious Sizar. Whereas the Chadwick females, abandoned by their natural protector in a foreign land, were far from humble.

Evidence of their disgusting independence may be found in many houses throughout these Isles in the shape of a picture, which hangs upon some dark staircase or in a lesser bedchamber. If examined closely, it turns out to be an indifferent copy of a Reni or a Luini. The master of the house will explain that his father, or his grandfather, bought it in Rome forty years ago. And he will wonder why Pronto peers at it so closely.

Pronto is looking for a little scratch in one corner which will tell him whether this sad daub has been the work of his Aunt Gussie.

People who make the Grand Tour must bring back some evidence of its effect upon their taste. Squire Bumpkin must prove that he has travelled further than his neighbours; a picture will do very well, and it won't cost him much, for there are painter fellows by the score, in Rome, in Venice, in Florence, who will sell him one for a few soldi.

Miss Augusta had been at this trade for some years before her Papa broke his neck. She took to it, in order to support the family, when it became clear that he had dissipated the whole of his fortune. Her appearance, for she was a handsome girl, brought her custom. Set up with her paints and her easel, in some old church, she was a striking object, — she attracted the attention of travellers. Her situation was interesting and her fluency in the English tongue gave her an advantage over the foreign painter fellows. Not that her English would now pass muster in polite society; the only specimen of it known to me, which I will quote later, does little credit to her breeding. She must have been the true daughter of her mother, an Irishwoman of no discernible family, disliked by all the Chadwicks, whom the antiquary met and married at Avignon.

Blood is thicker than water, and some effort was made on behalf of these unfortunate women, when news of Dr. Chadwick's death reached Bramfield. Provision of a sort was offered, if the family would return to Albion, fogs, roast beef and genteel dependence. This generosity was rejected, with marked incivility, in favour of sunshine and *risotto*. Miss Augusta, who wrote the letters (and I am sure that they were lamentably ill spelt), protested that they might all manage very well in Rome upon her earnings as a she-painter-fellow.

The affronted Chadwicks were thus able to wash their hands of the whole set, and would have done so had not a very pretty letter from Miss Theodosia reached Bramfield, shortly after the arrival of Miss Augusta's scrawl. This revived a preference which had always existed, for poor little Dosie had been a favourite, in spite of her disagreeable family, ever since a visit which she had paid to Bramfield when she was eight or nine years old. I don't know what convulsion in the antiquary's household had caused her to be deposited there for six months, but she seems to have won every heart in a very short time. They would have liked to keep her for ever, but she was eventually snatched away again by her black-haired Irish mother. They have a crayon portrait of her, up at the Park, which was made during that visit. The artist has given her, not only the rosy Chadwick complexion, which is well enough, but the protruding gooseberry eyes and the lithe proboscis of the Chadwicks, which I am sure she never had. There is no trace, in this simpering little miss, of the angel whom I knew; I don't covet the little picture, and Mrs. Ned is welcome to it, though anybody else would have offered it to us, when my mother died.

Dosie's letter abolished all resentment, so far as she was concerned. It was felt that she had been overborne by her hoyden sister, — that she would have come to Bramfield if she could. Not that she uttered any complaint. She wrote simply because she wished to thank her uncle for his kind offers, and to express the gratitude which her mother and sisters ought to have felt. She, alone of the family, seems to have perceived that these offers were, in their way, pretty generous. He had a numerous family of his own to support; to take in four extra would have put him to considerable expense. And he had proposed coming himself to Italy that he might wind up their affairs and escort them all home. This, for an old gentleman who seldom stirred out of Gloucestershire, would have been a formidable undertaking. Dosie was grateful for such a proof of amiable solicitude and said so. She thanked him warmly and furnished him with fuller particulars of their situation than Gussie had vouchsafed. In conclusion she sent affectionate messages to all her young cousins, desired news of them, and declared that she would never love any place so well as Bramfield.

Calculation was ever foreign to my mother's disposition. Upon this, as upon every other occasion, she *felt* as she ought and therefore *did* as she ought. She was genuinely grateful and sincerely attached to all the people at Bramfield. It was but natural that her enquiries should embrace the whole neighbourhood, for she had found a friend in every house. Old Dr. Maxwell had given her lollipops when he examined her in the Catechism ; why should she not remember him ? I can see no justification whatever for the construction which certain minds have chosen to put upon these artless letters. For she wrote several times. A pretty regular correspondence sprang up. The Chadwicks were anxious for more news of her, and eager for an excuse to get her away from Rome. No opportunity occurred, however, until after her marriage. When, at last, they got her back to Bramfield, she came as Mrs. Eustace Lufton.

My father, meanwhile, had quitted Cambridge, taken Orders, and got himself a noble patron with whom he went a-travelling. This bored him mightily but offered a short-cut to preferment. Of his travels I know but little ; he never speaks of them and I don't suppose he cares to think of them over much. Anybody acquainted with the late Lord M——'s reputation might well be surprised that he should choose to travel with a clergyman. But he had his reasons. He desired to be married, as soon as possible, to a lady who was also of the party. She was about to present him with an heir, and it was of great consequence to a number of people that this child should be born in wedlock, but nothing could be done during the lifetime of the legitimate Lady M——. She was, however, dying as fast as she could; the melancholy news was daily expected, and Lord M—— intended to waste no time. Prudence might have kept him in England where word might reach him immediately; foresight of another kind took him out of it since, at a pinch, a little juggling with dates might be necessary. He wanted no witnesses save of his own choosing.

That my father should ever have consented to play such a rôle I must believe, since many circumstances bear it out. But, when I reflect upon the uniform respectability and piety of his life at Bramfield, I am stunned. He never perhaps fully understood the circumstances, or supposed that he would be expected to perjure himself, should the heir turn up too promptly. A poor man cannot afford to be over nice. It is even possible that an excessive unworldliness trapped him into a course from which a baser mind might have recoiled. He was a scholar, desiring provision which would enable him to continue his studies in peace. Ample provision was offered, if he would accompany a nobleman upon a six months' tour of Europe. His travelling companions may have been so totally uncongenial that he took very little notice of them. He may not have observed the lady's condition. He may not even have observed the lady. I like to think that he did not, though she was certainly present upon the momentous occasion when his lordship encountered my Aunt Gussie.

I should have known nothing of all this, had I not fallen in with my Aunt Amelia, in Paris three years ago, when I was there immediately after the victorious conclusion of the Brussels campaign. She turns out to be an amusing old fellow, gouty and raddled, but very good company. The *salon* in which I met her was not of the choicest kind, there was not a woman of character in the room, I imagine ; it was the kind of half-way house which we don't have over here. Upon hearing my name she immediately claimed me as a nephew ; I called upon her afterwards and she told me all about Gussie and the old life in Rome, — everything, in fact, which I had long wished to know and despaired of ever finding out. I could only wish that she had been as communicative about her own history, which must, I am sure, have been lively. Upon that subject she was mum. She calls herself the Princess Czerny.

To her I owe all this information, including the sole specimen extant of Gussie's English. Gussie was copying an altar-piece in an old church when she heard voices behind her, raised in unfavourable comment upon her performance. Lord M—— and his party would not have quizzed her so loudly had they supposed that she could understand what they said. But she was black-haired, like her mother, and her dress was in the Italian style. Nothing was to prepare them for a sudden *volte-face* on the part of the Signorina, as, fine eyes ablaze, she administered the memorable reproof :

'Fools and weans shouldn't see things half done !'

Explanations and apologies ensued. Have I not said that Gussie was handsome ? His lordship's opinion of the picture took a most favourable turn. He grew anxious to buy it, as a means of pursuing the lady's acquaintance. Unluckily it was bespoke, but Gussie could offer him many others, if he would call at her mother's house by the Spanish Steps.

Here came an intervention from her ladyship designate, who did not above half like Gussie and her eyes. Mr. Lufton, said she, might do the calling, had better do it, since he was fond of pictures, whereas this appeared to be the first evidence of such a taste in his lordship. Mr. Lufton might go to the Spanish Steps and select a canvas, since there was very little else, at the moment, that he could do to earn his keep.

Mr. Lufton called in due course, caught sight of Dosie, and then it was all over with Mr. Lufton. Not for an archbishopric would he quit Rome without her. When Lord M——'s party moved on he remained, throwing all ideas of preferment to the winds. One hopes that some other, more accommodating, parson was secured in time. Pronto is acquainted with the present Lord M—— and has been at pains to discover that he was born in Naples, but there is some obscurity about the date.

My parents became engaged in the teeth of severe opposition from Miss Gussie and her mother. Theodosia, whose beauty was remarkable, had already irritated them by refusing several excellent matches. That she should throw herself away upon a penniless clergyman was a piece of folly which estranged them for ever.

'*Claire de lune!*' sighed the Princess Czerny. 'But then you know Dosie was an angel, and they did not do too badly neither, since our uncle gave him the Bramfield living. *Il paraît qu'une ange porte le pain sous le bras.* If Dosie had not been an angel they must have starved.'

This is very true. I have witnessed, again and again, the effect of my mother's charm upon all around her. All were sensible of an impulse to please her, to oblige her, to say agreeable things to her, to strew her path with flowers. Kind offices sprang from any encounter with her. My own place in College at Winchester was got for me by a gentleman who once stayed for a se'night at the Park and only saw my mother at church.

The living was not vacant when the young couple first arrived in England, but upon the death of Dr. Maxwell, a few months later, the gift was a settled thing, — a clever scheme for keeping Dosie at Bramfield for life. My father was well enough liked by all the family, but this provision was made for her sake. I am certain that Uncle Chadwick would have done nothing of the sort for any other niece, but angels do generally receive the treatment that they deserve.

To Mrs. Ned, of course, the whole business is incomprehensible, though she knew my mother, received endless kindness from her, and professed, at one time, an excessive regard for her. She, so I understand, has never ceased to grumble at Ned's grandfather, and to wonder at the doting folly which could thus dispose of a valuable property. Sukey is my informant upon this point; she has it from the Chadwick girls. They should not have told her and she should not have told me, but we are all in a sad way, now that our angel has returned to her own dominions.

I learn that Mrs. Ned admires the discretion which prompted so young a girl to keep upon good terms with her rich uncle, when the rest of the family had offended him. She wonders at the prudence which demanded constant news of Dr. Maxwell's health. She applauds, as a bold stroke, a marriage which took place so soon as that health was reported to be failing.

Mrs. Ned, in short, believes my mother to have been uncommonly sly.

Eden

WHAT is good society?

Pronto could answer that question without a moment's hesitation. But for Miles it must ever be a matter of debate. He has been dragged by Pronto into company of all kinds, but he questions whether any satisfies him half so well as that which he knew first of all in his home at Bramfield Parsonage. Greater elegance, more of worldly polish, he may have encountered elsewhere, but always at a cost, — always with some sacrifice of sincerity and genuine refinement. Greater luxury he has bought at the expense of simple comfort. In the best houses they hide your breeches and bring you tepid shaving water.

How can any society be *good* which does not contribute to happiness? How can a man impart felicity when he does not possess any degree of it himself? Happiness is the first ingredient. I cannot be content among peevish people, though their inward poverty may be concealed beneath a polished exterior. The rational melancholy produced by sickness or bereavement I can excuse; I don't ask that my friends should be in perpetual spirits, but I do ask that they should be capable of enjoyment.

My parents were singularly happy. They were devotedly attached to one another, they enjoyed an income sufficient for their modest needs, they were esteemed and loved by all who knew them. Their children were born into a climate of perpetual sunshine.

My father, I imagine, never knew how to be happy until he came to Bramfield. The study of Greek had ever been his ruling passion, but he was continually called from it by the necessity of advancing himself, since a curiosity concerning Euripides puts few guineas into a man's pocket. At Bramfield he had the means and the leisure wherewith to pursue his favourite study. He learnt also to appreciate blessings of which he had hitherto been quite ignorant. He became aware of what he ate; he began to enjoy his dinner. Taught by my mother, desirous of loving all that might be dear to her, he perceived the beauties of Nature. The awkward, shy scholar

became very good company, — warm-hearted, well informed, a fluent but not an overpowering talker, with all
the ease of manner which springs from genuine content-
ment.

For her the change was equally benign. She had
always longed for England and for Bramfield, yet I cannot
feel that her early travels in France and Italy were entirely
wasted ; to natural good breeding there was added experience of the world, and manners above what one usually
finds in a country parsonage. During her father's lifetime
she had been used to meeting distinguished people. She
liked to read, although she was no blue-stocking. She
possessed that power to be continually interested, even
in the commonest objects, which is one of the marks of a
truly superior intellect. She loved a country life, yet had
no trace of rusticity.

The society in which they moved, however, was nothing
above what might be expected in such a place. *They*
were superior ; their neighbours were not. I think that
I must have perceived this very early, and I therefore
took it for granted that I was a great deal more fortunate
than my cousin Ned Chadwick, who had no such parents.
I was sorry for him. Although I gradually came to learn
that the world thought him more fortunate than myself,
I continued to be sorry for him until we were one and
twenty.

He is the nearest to me, in age, of that family, though
he is an eldest and I a second son. There were seven of
us ; Eustace, Caroline, Miles, George, Catherine, Harriet
and Susan. Our cousins were more numerous, but given
to dying in infancy. Only five of them survived. Perpetual funerals were one of the many disadvantages for
which I pitied Ned. He was for ever wearing black for
some little brother or sister, too young to be of consequence to anybody.

We were all handsome children and our cousins were extremely plain. I suspect that my mother's faith in green vegetables and fruit may have something to do with our advantage in this way. Her notions of diet were continental and she dressed many dishes at which our neighbours stared. Cabbage, for instance, which she cooked with sour cream, was a great favourite with us ; in this country it is reckoned as only fit for cottagers. She set great store by sour cream and buttermilk, which our people throw away or give to the pigs. Nor would she suffer the gardener to send in those prodigious peas and carrots which are thought becoming to a gentleman's table. She would have them small and tender. As for fruit, which is often forbidden to children, she gave it to us daily. My Winchester fare of beef, cheese and beer distressed her ; at the beginning of every Half she would give me a guinea, with strict instructions to lay it out, not at the pastry-cook, but with the apple-woman. She believed that fruit is good for the bowels. And it is a fact that we seldom needed the *black draught* which was daily administered in the Chadwick nurseries. My sisters' complexions were the boast of the country and we all had the bright eyes, the glow of perfect health, which is so particularly prepossessing in young people.

I once asked Harriet if she was not, as a child, very sorry for the Chadwicks.

'To be sure I was,' said she. 'And am still. Only consider the size of their noses !'

'Ah ! You are thinking of the girls.'

'And the boys too. Such a nose is a misfortune to anyone.'

'But did you not pity them upon other grounds ?'

'Yes indeed ! Everything at the Park was always so flat and spiritless. They had no notion of fun, or picnics, or schemes, or anything. They were good-natured enough, not cross or peevish, but they could not enjoy themselves as we did.'

'Did it never occur to you that they were richer than we ?'

'No ! Why should it ? We kept a better table. My mother was beyond comparison the best housekeeper I ever knew. And our dress was always far more tasteful. Their Sunday bonnets ! I am sure, if I pitied Isabella and Charlotte once, I pitied them a hundred times for those frightful bonnets.'

'And when did you first understand that their mother must always walk out of the room before ours ?'

'Why Miles ! She never did, poor thing. I never saw her with my mother but they were walking arm in arm.'

Harriet would have come to feel it, had she not married so well. She can now walk out of the room before Mrs. Ned.

There was not a single activity in which I could not count myself superior to Ned. I could out-ride him, out-shoot him, bowl him at cricket and beat him at cards. That I rode his ponies, and shot his father's coverts, did not occur to either of us. For Ned admired me almost as much as I admired myself. In acting, of which we were very fond, he often forgot his own part, in his wonder at me, as I gesticulated and ranted. In our studies with my father, I had always got my task before poor Ned had found his place in the book.

Ned is inseparable from all my memories of those early days. To recall them, to see him as he was then, is melancholy work, when I consider what he is now. I have so long thought of him as a sot, quite sunk, the surly husband of an odious wife, that I forget that he was not born so. He was a very good sort of boy, heavy and slow but sweet-natured, — better natured than I. He would never laugh at poor Bob Howes, the blacksmith's son,

who was a little clouded in his intellect, though a fast
bowler at cricket. Bob, Ned and I were all confirmed
together, along with Harry Ridding, a farmer's son.
Bob's blundering answers, when examined in the Catechism, never failed to convulse Harry and me, but
Ned pitied him and would often shield him from our
mockery.

Unlucky Bob! We hauled him through his Confir-
mation, but when we all stayed for the Sacrament, for the
first time, he disgraced himself in a most ludicrous way.
I suppose that he was so much stricken with awe as to be
robbed of what few wits he possessed. We had told him,
again and again, what he must do, but, being once got to
the altar-rail, he found it impossible to rise and go away,
and remained kneeling there long after Harry, Ned and I
had returned to our places. We should have observed it
and dragged him along with us, but we were so much
agitated ourselves that we noticed nothing. My father
continued to minister to his Easter congregation, until he
came to Bob again, whom he urged in a whisper to rise
and go away. Bob remained kneeling, his eyes tight shut.
My father, in despair, went on. But when he came to Bob
a third time he lost his temper, and bellowed loudly:
ROBERT HOWES! BEGONE! Whereat Bob, in absolute
terror, rose and fled from the church.

I am sorry to say that I, once I had recovered from the
scandalised sensations that this incident excited, was
inclined to tease Bob and cry out: BEGONE! whenever I
saw him. Ned would never suffer this in his presence.
He once knocked me down for it, and we fought awhile,
and I got the best of it, for I was the quicker with my
fists, though Ned was the heavier. He would not shake
hands and went off in a very ill humour, — a thing so
rare in him that I was quite astonished.

'Why don't he take his beating like a gentleman?'

cried I to Harry Ridding, who had been a spectator of the fight.

Harry, however, came down upon Ned's side.

'Nay,' he said. 'Young Squire is a proper gentleman and thou art none.'

For which I was obliged to fight him, and this time got the worst of it. But I knew that it was ungentlemanly to tease Bob and I never did so again.

This chapter does not exactly come up to its title. I had not expected to arrive at black eyes and bloody noses. If I wish to believe that my infancy was an Idyll, I had better not remember any more of it.

Aut Disce

AT thirteen we were, in any case, thrust from Eden and sent to school. I went to Winchester, by the good offices of the gentleman who had admired my mother at church. Ned went to a private academy in Hertfordshire where he was exceedingly miserable, caught the ringworm, and was partially bald for many months.

I was miserable too, but in a more glorious fashion. I had less than he to eat. I washed in cold water, exposed to all the elements. I was beaten constantly for the slowness with which my chilblained fingers buttoned prefectorial gaiters. But these *tundings* sounded more heroic than the occasional floggings endured by Ned; *bevers* was a manlier drink than beer; *conduit* more romantic than a bath. Poor Ned was very ready to believe that I was better off and he often wished that we might change places.

To hear him say so raised my spirits, for I had begun to understand some very disquieting truths concerning the importance of property. The young gentlemen with whom I now associated were not all of them as oblivious of their own consequence as was Ned. They were beaten, as I was. They lived hard, as I did. But, if their fathers were men of property, they thought better of themselves than they did of me. My prowess at games and *up to books* might advance me in College, but, in the world to which they returned in the holidays, I was nobody, because I was heir to nothing.

I can recollect the first occasion upon which this fact became apparent to me. It was towards the end of my first Long Half that a boy lamented, in my hearing, the isolated situation of his father's estate, — not another gentleman's house within fifteen miles! I asked, very innocently, if there was no parsonage.

'Oh ay! But parsons don't count.'

I said hotly that parsons are gentlemen, but he would not have it. Some gentlemen were parsons, he allowed that, since his younger brother was to be one. But not all parsons were men of family.

Any other boy, I suppose, would have discovered all this long before. But I had grown up in Eden. I had gone to school, expecting trials, but determined to excel. It had never occurred to me that the world might have fixed my consequence in advance, without waiting to ascertain my merits. I had daily before my eyes the board in our schoolroom, which promised rewards to those who would exert themselves and a whip for those who would not.

Aut Disce . . . If I minded my book I believed that I should wear a mitre, and sit among the Lords Spiritual.

Aut Discede . . . If I chose an active life, rather than that of a scholar, it should win for me a place among the Lords Temporal.

Manet Sors Tertia Cædi . . . of the whipping,

reserved for those who cannot choose, I had no fear whatever.

I discussed the question with another junior, Newsome, the son of a poor curate in Yorkshire. He had entered as a quirister, but had got a place in College through the interest of a gentleman who took a benevolent pleasure in advancing boys of that sort.

Newsome laughed and told me that his father was happy to consider himself out of debt. When summoned to dine with the squire of their parish he invariably ate in the housekeeper's room. The incumbent, who held several livings, and never came into Yorkshire, might be regarded as a gentleman. The curate, who did the duties, was not.

'You know,' said Newsome, 'there is, there must be, a vast difference between a man of property and one who must work.'

'I cannot see it,' cried I. 'The superior must be he who possesses the greater genius.'

'The world won't think so, unless the genius makes a fortune.'

I was quite certain, at that time, that I should make a fortune, but I was uneasy at the idea that these louts might not consider my father a gentleman. During the holidays I put the matter to my mother and asked her if she did not think it shocking that Mr. Newsome should dine with the housekeeper.

'Why, as to that,' said my mother, 'the housekeeper may be better company for a clergyman than her mistress. She is also his parishioner, and she may be a better Christian.'

'But should you not resent it, Ma'am, if my father were to be treated so ?'

'I should scold myself for any resentment that I might feel. A clergyman is not to be setting himself above other people, — thinking that he is too good to dine with one, and resenting a slight from another.'

My mother took an exalted view of a clergyman's calling. She was deeply and unaffectedly religious. We were all aware of it, in spite of her reserve in such matters. We had her example before our eyes, — the regularity of her devotions, her stillness and attention at church, the Christian charity which inspired the whole of her conduct.

My father was made of other metal, though association with her had somewhat elevated his ideas. When I took my tale to him, his comment was :

'Does he indeed ? But that is up in the North, you know, and they are all fifty years at least behind the times. Their manners would make you stare, if all I hear be true. 'Tis all the fault of their roads. When I was a lad one could not get to Scotland save by pack horse, and even now they have no roads to speak of.'

'But why should that make the squire uncivil to the curate ?'

'Civility depends upon some knowledge of the world. A fellow who never gets about, but crows on his own dunghill, will contract a boorish suspicion of anyone who knows more than he does. He will conceal his sense of inferiority by an insolent manner. He will flinch and jeer at words or customs which may be unfamiliar to him. Your northerners have always been so. You have the portrait of one in Harry Hotspur, with his thick speech and his scorn for the southern lord with the "pooncet ba-ax." '

After that there was no getting him away from Shakespeare.

These replies should have answered my question. Both my parents, without asserting superiority, had displayed a considerable degree of it. They were quite free from any uneasiness about their station. But it was not enough to me to know that they were superior. I desired that others should be sensible of the fact.

An excessive ambition was the outcome of all this, — an anxiety to become a person of consequence, not so much to satisfy my own vanity as to furnish proof of my parents' worth. I could not wait for the mitre which was one day to be mine ; I wished to be *first* among these boys who asserted, so insolently, that parsons did not count.

Believing my motives to be pure and commendable, I daily and nightly implored the Supreme Being to make me, some day, Prefect of Hall. This was the goal of all my prayers and vows, as I toasted bread and polished the shoes of my seniors.

Success depended largely, but not entirely, upon my progress in scholarship. Absolute seniority turned, as I soon perceived, upon favour of a tricky sort. Those were turbulent days. College was still rent by the vendetta between the Warden and the boys which, just before my time, had broken out into the Great Rebellion. Feeling was very bitter. Our treatment by Warden Huntingford was such that fresh revolts were ever near the surface. We had little government save that which we provided for ourselves. It was clear to me that, where the laurels of Senior Scholar were in question, Huntingford had a finger in the pie. To be thought a *safe man* by him was of first consequence. Yet his favour might have disadvantages ; nobody who openly enjoyed it could hope for respect among the boys.

With these diverse considerations in mind I worked and played, cultivated popularity, studied the foibles of the masters, and strove to recommend myself in that quarter whence the most powerful influence was likely to be felt.

My appearance has always been of advantage to me. I was just such a fine young man as a noble visitor, received

ad portas, might wish to see as Senior Scholar. The sight
of me was enough to contradict all those rumours afloat,
of which Huntingford was not unaware, concerning the
true state of morals and discipline within our gates. My
carriage was easy, my countenance open, — frank enough
to please those who like to believe that boys are candid
animals, yet with sufficient sensibility to satisfy a more
discerning eye. The manly address with which Pronto
makes so good an impression, his simplicity, his apparent
modesty, were all well in train before I was sixteen years
old. I *looked* like a good Prefect of Hall.

The pursuit of my ambition obliged me early to make
those sacrifices which are necessary for one who wishes to
go up in the world. Policy forced me to forgo certain
friendships which I would otherwise have wished to culti-
vate. With quiet Newsome I was always intimate. But
there were others, congenial to me in temper, with whom
I could not afford to be too friendly, for they were always
so near rebellion as to be dangerous companions. They
might at any time break out, and get me into trouble ; so
I kept clear of them, though I liked and respected some
of them very much, and felt, with a little regret, that *they*
were my natural friends.

There is no doubt that we were monstrously neglected,
that the masters could not keep order, and that every
promise of reform was consistently broken. But we had
before our eyes the fate of those who had been expelled
in consequence of an effort to secure improvement. We
could not know that the courage and energy which locked
out the masters, and set up the Cap of Liberty upon
Middle Gate, would, in some cases, win the world's
applause upon greater battle-fields. Dalbiac, for instance,
was at that time a naughty boy ; the hero of Salamanca
was as yet undiscerned. But something of his spirit was
left in College, and several were for taking measures

against the unwarranted extortions laid upon us, the unjust taxes whereby the masters enriched themselves. My sympathy was with these young Hampdens, but I made it my business to restrain them as well as I could, without entirely forfeiting their respect. I think that Huntingford, perpetually in fear lest he might again be obliged to summon the magistrates, and call out the military, regarded me as a useful ally.

How far I might have gone in abetting him it is not easy to say. I was never upon explicit terms with him. He kept spies among us and we knew it, but I was not one of them. I don't think that I got anybody into trouble; on the contrary, I kept hot heads out of trouble. I maintained a sort of order, in the absence of anyone else able to do so. In fact, I think that I *was* a good Prefect of Hall.

Ned, meanwhile, had come to love his school no better, although he had grown his hair again. While I drank the cup of success, and felt myself greater than I have ever since contrived to feel, poor Ned was always the same, — big-nosed, disconsolate and friendly, scuffling at my heels every day of the holidays, ready to do anything I chose, but expecting that we should do everything together. I began to grow weary of him. I no longer needed him as a boasting target. During the last summer holidays I sent him about his business once or twice. Newsome was staying with me and Ned made an unwelcome third.

At Christmas the tables were turned. Ned had a friend at the Park, a boy called Ponsonby, who struck me as singularly dull, though my sisters voted him a capital dancer. And Ponsonby rode the mare which I had hitherto regarded as my especial property, though in fact she belonged to Ned.

It had never occurred to me that I could not hunt because I had no horse. At the Parsonage we had three beasts : my father's horse, a pony which drew my mother's little carriage, and another pony used by anybody for errands. My father seldom hunted, but Eustace was with us, he was at home on leave, and we all planned to go out together. Eustace, who is a typical sailor and never cares how he looks, said that he would ride the errand pony. The meet was at Ribstone. After an early breakfast I set off to the Park stables to get 'my' mare. To my astonishment she had been taken out, 'for young Squire Ponsonby,' so a grinning stable-boy informed me, nor was any mount left for me. A large party from the Park was out, and all available animals taken, unless I chose to ride a broken-winded, wall-eyed beast kept for the use of Charlotte's governess.

I returned home in a very ill humour. Ned, of course, had a perfect right to do as he chose with his own horses, but I thought that he should have sent me some message. I said so to him, at the first opportunity, without getting much in the way of an apology. Ned said he thought I should have known that he must mount his guest, and how else could he, save on the mare ?

'I wonder Ponsonby don't bring his own horses,' said I.

''Tis too far. His father is very indulgent, but the expense of sending horses down into Gloucestershire would not occur to him.'

To hear that Ponsonby had got horses, even though they could not be sent into Gloucestershire, by no means mollified me. I did not hunt during the whole of those holidays, even after Ponsonby had gone and the offer of the mare reverted to me. I did not choose to be obliged to Ned, after the way that I had thrown him off in the summer, and I did not choose to ride the errand pony. I would have tried to persuade my father to buy another animal, had I not feared my mother's silence. When displeased, it was her custom to say less than usual. I had a notion that she thought all this pother about the mare very foolish and could not see why I should not ride the errand pony, as Eustace did.

I returned to College, for my last Long Half, in a sulky mood. The period of my greatness would soon be at an end, and I began to see that it would go for nothing, once I had quitted Winchester. Even Ned, in the world's view, was of more consequence than I, and many pleasures at Bramfield, which I had hitherto taken for granted, were, as I now saw, only mine through Ned's good nature. This did not suit me, since I reckoned myself superior to Ned.

Ludovic

HAVING read over my memoir thus far, I ask myself how nearly these reported conversations resemble those which took place so long ago. Very little, I daresay, though certain words and phrases are firmly lodged in my memory. I recollect, as though I had seen it this morning, the little frowning pause with which my mother considered whether she would resent any slight upon my father. And I can hear most clearly the decisive tones in which she said that she should scold herself for any resentment that she might feel. I can see Ned's look too, when I upbraided him about the mare. We were standing by the gate into the stable paddock. He had a switch in his hand and he kept switching the top rail of the gate as we talked.

I think that I have translated the sense of these conversations very well, although the chief part must now of course, be invention; and I daresay that which I recall as a single interchange may be the essence of several upon the same point. But I believe that I shall continue in this manner, for it brings back looks and accents which were often more important than words. How else can I fully recall my mother, and others now lost to me ? It will not serve that I should merely epitomise their opinions ; I must depict their style, as far as I can, if I am to fetch them whole out of the past.

I quitted Winchester and went to Oxford, where disparities of fortune were even more significant. It became clear to me that my first object must be to provide myself with the necessaries of life, and I applied myself diligently to my studies. I was destined for Orders and would probably have taken them, and now might be heading for that mitre, had I not made the acquaintance of Ludovic, a circumstance which profoundly affected the course of my life.

It was by the merest chance that I came to know him, for he was not in my college and sought nobody's acquaintance. He had come to Christ Church from Eton where he had been, I suspect, as comfortable as a felon in a convict ship. He never speaks of his school days, but I know that their memory fills him with terror. Even now he will not willingly walk along Piccadilly or St. James's, for fear of meeting a former school fellow ; and when Prinney succeeds I fancy Ludovic will take to his bed rather than face the peerage, in an Abbey full of Etonians.

Strangely enough it was Ponsonby brought us together, — that same Ponsonby who rode my mare at Bramfield. He came up when I did and, meeting me during the first week, in Turl Street, he greeted me as heartily as though he had been my oldest friend. Indeed, I think that he was very glad to see me, for he had, as yet, made no acquaintance. He had never been at a public school, whereas I, at New College, was surrounded by former Wykehamists. I was able to patronise him a little and recommended a barber as coolly as though I had lived in Oxford all my life. We proceeded to take a look at those famous horses of his, which could not be brought to Bramfield, but which had come to Oxford and were stabled near the Castle Inn. The poor fellow had had nothing to do save look at them, two or three times a day, since he came up. I, very obligingly, rode one of them for him, for about a fortnight, during which time that magnetism began to operate which enables the Ponsonbys of this world to discover their rightful friends. Our intimacy gradually dissolved and he took to riding with men who also kept horses.

I meet him occasionally nowadays, and got a place for his younger brother a couple of years ago. He was infinitely obliged to me and remembered that we used to ride together at Oxford. But he has managed to forget our first encounter with Lord Chalfont.

It was towards the end of that first fortnight that we returned, after riding, to Ponsonby's chambers in Brasenose. We crossed the quadrangle to the music of a flute which somebody was playing in the vicinity. I recognised the air, — my sister Caroline sang it — and I hummed the words as we mounted the staircase.

> What though I trace each herb and flower
> That drinks the morning dew?
> Did I not own Jehovah's power
> How vain were all I knew!

By now we had reached Ponsonby's door, from behind which these strains seemed to issue. Ponsonby changed colour a trifle and hesitated. In every college there are wags who divert themselves at the expense of freshmen,

and I daresay he had already suffered at their hands.
Those who have survived a public school are more likely
to be spared. At length he plucked up his spirits and
strode in. I tactfully hung back.

'And who the devil may you be, sir?' I heard him
demand.

Handel ceased and a shrill voice pronounced the name
of Ponsonby.

'That is my name. But who are you and why do you
play the flute in my chamber?'

'I am here, Mr. Ponsonby, because your scout brought
me here, assuring me that you would return very shortly.
I play the flute because I have nothing else to do, you
know.'

'And where might you get a flute?' asks Ponsonby,
very suspiciously.

'I brought it with me. But I should tell you my name,
which is Chalfont. My father desired me to call upon
you, since he is a friend of your father.'

'Oh!' says Ponsonby.

I can tell by his tone that he does not believe a word
of it. Neither do I. I take a peep through the crack of
the door. Our visitor is a wizened little creature, standing
perhaps at five foot four, and of no calculable age; he
might be an elderly fifteen, he might be a juvenile fifty.
He wears his hair long and cut straight across the brow,
in imitation of Buonaparte, whom he does not otherwise
resemble. His finger-nails are very black, his cravat
under his ear, and a button is missing from his coat.

'Did your father say nothing about me?' he enquires.

Ponsonby had already told me that he expected the
acquaintance of Lord Chalfont and the reason for it. I
daresay he had informed a good many people of his
expectations. This visitor had a spurious appearance,
but poor Ponsonby, unused to being *foxed*, knew not how

to act. Straightening my face as well as I could, I went to his aid, for I had, after all, spent the morning upon his horse.

'Lord Chalfont?' said I hastily, joining them. 'How do you do? How charmingly your lordship plays the flute! Pray continue! We love the flute, don't we, Ponsonby?'

'Do you indeed?' cried the little fellow.

'Oh, beyond all things. We have been pining for a little music. We must beg, we must insist, that you continue!'

He did so, nothing loath, which was as well for him, for, if he had refused, I should have dropped him out of the window. I meant to turn the tables by forcing him to play until he was completely blown. But the air which he gave us was so charming that I felt inclined to let him off short of that. I am very fond of music and he played exceedingly well.

Ponsonby meanwhile, too stupid to understand my tactics, stood gaping at us both.

'What's this?' I cried, when the air was over. 'I never heard it before. Who is the composer?'

Our visitor explained that it was from *Idomeneo*. I asked where it might be procured, for I had it in mind to send a copy home. My mother and sisters were always very glad to get hold of new songs.

My question brought down upon me a torrent of information. I had never heard of Mozart, but I heard of nothing else for the rest of the day. Ludovic's dotes are like a hurricane. This one swept us all out of Brasenose and into his chambers in Peckwater, where he undertook to play us all the works of Mozart upon his pianoforte. As we walked he chattered incessantly, occasionally breaking into song and beating time with his flute. The bewildered Ponsonby trotted at our heels. I had ceased to care whom the queer little fellow might be; I was charmed by his talk and eager to hear him play again. But Ponsonby, finding himself actually in Christ Church, reading the name of *Chalfont* upon the staircase, and perceiving the luxury of the quarters into which we were got, comes out with a bellow:

'Then you ARE Chalfont!'

'*Batti! Batti!*' carols our host, at the instrument.

He passes from one air to another and after a while I observe that Ponsonby has disappeared. I ask what has become of him. My host is puzzled, since he has now got it into his head that I am Ponsonby. We have got through a good deal of port wine, between songs. If I am not Ponsonby, says he, then the fellow was lying who said I would return very shortly. When I try to set him right he exclaims:

''Tis of no consequence since that other man is not here.'

Within a very short time we are 'Miles' and 'Ludovic' to one another, but it is months before he is certain of my surname. He is liable to introduce me everywhere as Ponsonby.

I am exceedingly fond of Ludovic. I cannot follow him in all his dotes, but he has introduced me to so many pleasures, since that first evening of Mozart, that I am deeply grateful to him. His enthusiasm for all the arts is prodigious but I am not sure that his judgment is entirely to be trusted. I have yet to be persuaded, for instance, that *La clemenza di Tito* is Mozart's finest work.

In the realms of poetry he is equally eccentric. Neither Scott nor Southey will do, and he has not very much to say for Byron. He insists that Wordsworth and Coleridge are superior in genius and execution, yet is hard put to it to say why. He cannot criticise; he can only dote, chirrup his favourite airs, and declaim his favourite verses, with so much absurdity of expression and gesture that the most elegant lines could scarcely come off well. I shall never forget one summer at Brailsford when he was in perpetual lamentation for a young woman called *Lucy*, bewailing her untimely death in verses which struck me, at that time, as sad doggerel, though I have since come to understand and share his enthusiasm. He would mutter them to himself, as he went up and down stairs, with so much woe in his countenance that I could not forbear laughing. I can see him now, pausing suddenly during a ramble across the meadows, and addressing one of his father's pedigree cows in these terms :

> She lived unknown, and few could know
> When Lucy ceased to be.
> But she is in her grave and OH !
> The difference to ME !

It was the more ridiculous in that a genuine Lucy, in a material grave, would not have made a tittle of difference to him. The whole human race, with the exception of his valet, might have perished without his taking much notice of it. He would, I think, have thought that something must be amiss if nobody brought him his morning chocolate.

Immense wealth and noble birth may enable a man to patronise the arts, but I suspect that they impede his capacity as a critic. Nobody restrains his extravagance and nobody bids him hold his tongue. Your aristocrat is a fish out of water among the artists : they don't talk to him as they talk to one another. And among his own kind he finds few companions, for these people, though they learn early the jargon of taste, and can cry up the masterpieces of the day, do not really take the matter seriously, nor are they taken seriously by the fellows whom

they patronise.   Ludovic has actually spoken to Mozart.
Lord Amersham was our minister at Vienna before the
wars broke out, and Ludovic, in infancy, was often taken
to the Opera.   During some performance the composer
was brought to Lord Amersham's box to receive the
compliments of the Quality.   His little lordship was, I am
sure, very gracious.

'He made me,' said Ludovic, 'a low bow, but said
nothing.'

In appearance Ludovic continues to be eccentric.   No
valet can keep him fit to be seen for any length of time.
He never knows what he eats and spills food upon his
clothes.   I had some conversation about him once with
his sister, Lady Sophia Harnish, and she asked me to tell
her frankly if I thought him deranged.

'We fear so,' she said, 'but there is nothing to be done.
It is my father's fault.   His severity caused a brain fever
from which I think poor Ludovic has never fully recovered.'

She told me that the family had spent a winter in
Naples when Ludovic was eight years old.   While they
were there a servant, a young lad to whom he was extra-
vagantly attached, had been discovered in the act of theft.
It transpired that his thievery had been carrying on for
some time and had been known to Ludovic, who held his
tongue out of loyalty to his friend.   Lord Amersham was
very angry and thought it right that the child should
witness the punishment of the criminal ; in this case, to
be broken upon the wheel.   Ludovic was brought home
insensible and lay for many weeks between life and death.
Ever since that time he has been subject to fits and seizures.

'He never speaks of it,' said Lady Sophia.   'But I
believe he is still very unhappy about it.   Have you ever
heard him laugh ?'

I realised, in some astonishment, that I had not.
Ludovic will go off into a transport. Pictures, poetry and
music will move him to ecstasy. But he is never merry.

At the end of our first year at Oxford, our intimacy
had become so close that he invited me to stay at Brailsford. It is but a long day's ride from Bramfield, and I
have been staying there a good deal ever since. I was
received with the greatest kindness by his family, who
were delighted that he should, for once, bring home a
friend who looked and behaved like a gentleman. He had
made no friends at school and his former *dotes*, in the way
of human affection, had been of a kind to disturb his
friends ; such attachments as he formed were all for lads
much inferior to himself in station, — for grooms and
ploughboys whom he admired, I suppose, because they
were his opposites in everything.

My *ad portas* manner was of great reassurance to the
Amershams. I think I really did a good deal for Ludovic.
I got him to cut his hair and pare his nails. His confidence
in me was so great that he would, when with me, occasionally venture into company. I could never induce him to
shoot ; the loud reports of the guns startled him too much.
But he took to riding with me and would even hunt, so
long as he was not expected to be present at the kill. I
cannot think that he is fond of me ; he is fond of nobody.
But he has feeling for me of a sort. He admires my looks ;
that has always great power with him. We have many
ideas and tastes in common. And my manners are
gentler than those to which he has been accustomed
among men of his own station, or women either.

The Amershams were grateful for this improvement
and would have had me live at Brailsford, if I would have
stayed. My position there has always been more comfortable than it has been in any other great house. I came
there first as a benefactor, which put me upon a footing

with them which Pronto has never been able to command elsewhere, among people of rank.

Ludovic came to stay with me, and, though my sisters and cousins thought him a quiz, my parents liked him. He supported my father in a notion that there might be Roman remains in Farmer Roundhay's meadow. They grew so positive that they began to dig, or rather cause a number of little scare-the-crow boys to dig, and did indeed uncover part of a mosaic pavement. They might, I believe, have dug up a whole villa, had Roundhay not rebelled.

As for my mother, he came as near to loving her as he did anyone. While she lived he talked of her continually, though I have never heard her name upon his lips since she died. From the Sex in general he has a decided aversion, though he admires my sisters for their beauty and good humour. He is, in a way, attached to Lady Sophia, I think, nor was he indifferent to his mother, to whom he paid more attention than to anyone else. He would generally try to do what she wished, as far as it was in his power. But I don't think that he loved her. His strongest feeling, in her case, appeared to be compassion, which puzzled me a little at first, for no woman asked for pity less than did Lady Amersham. She always seemed to be perfectly satisfied with herself and her lot. But I suspect that she interceded for him, and interceded in vain, upon that dreadful occasion in Naples and that this failure, in a singularly powerful woman, had made a deep impression upon him. He hated his father.

He once told me that no man upon earth had ever been more fortunate than I, in the possession of such parents. In fact, he grew so rhapsodical about the pleasures of life in a country parsonage that I advised him to take Orders himself and settle down in one of the many good livings of which his family had the disposal. He took my suggestion very seriously and told me that it would not do. He had been converted to atheism at an early age.

I, for my part, had begun to doubt whether a parson's life would suit me. Life at Brailsford had brought me into company more elegant than what I had previously known. I made new acquaintance, received other invitations, and stayed in other great houses. I had the reputation for being agreeable. I could sing, dance, talk, read aloud and play charades. A young man so gifted may hold his own very well even though he is poor and of no family. He has his value. He is dependable, he can be trusted to keep his engagements and can be invited to make up a party at short notice.

I liked to stay with people who had nothing to do save amuse themselves. I liked that kind of life very well. I had no wish to be rich; I only wanted enough money to dress well, travel post, and purchase civility from the servants. Had I possessed an income of a thousand pounds per annum I don't believe that I should have sought any profession. But I had not a hundred pounds, and it was clear that I must do something.

My new friends were all against my taking Orders. Lady Amersham talked to me seriously upon the subject. She told me that I could do very much better if I went to the Bar and afterwards into politics. A seat in Parliament could certainly be found for me, and a place would follow.

So said all my fair friends. They were determined to get me on and were able to be unaffectedly tender towards me because I could never figure as a husband, or a lover, for any of them. I might flirt with them as much as I pleased, secure that I had raised no expectations. I could read poetry to Lady Georgiana under an oak tree and later refer to it, with a conscious glance, as '*our tree*,' without reproof. This kind of gallantry is very pleasant.

'I quite dote upon Miles Lufton,' these ladies would cry, 'and it is a great shame that he should be so poor, for he is a delightful creature. We must get him a seat, we must get him a place, and help him to grow rich.'

They liked me for my interesting poverty, my sensibility, my freshness and my innocence. They were therefore in great haste to destroy in me every quality which they had praised and found delightful, to corrupt Miles and to conjure up Pronto in his stead.

I have ever demanded the impossible. I wish that elegance should not depend upon wealth. I wish that pretty women should flirt with me and flatter me, — and yet would like them to read great books all through, understand the poetry which they quote so readily, and feel a genuine pang whenever they choose to sigh.

Edmée

I BECAME, in due course, a fellow of my College, but I delayed for some months in the choice of a profession. During that period I fell seriously in love, a circumstance which, at one time, seemed likely to settle the question for me.

Her name was Edmée de Cavignac and we had been hearing of her for many years before we saw her, since her mother was English and a distant cousin of the Chadwicks. Cousinly feeling is, or was, strong at Bramfield. When the revolution broke out in France the safety of the Cavignacs was our principal interest. Much anxiety was felt by us during the disturbances which followed, and when, at last, news reached us we were horrified. The whole family had perished, — the father by guillotine and the rest in the *noyades* at Nantes. We were far more impressed by this atrocity than by anything else that the French had done ; that they should decapitate and drown each other was but natural, but that Chadwick blood should be shed was another matter.

A few months later the rumour reached us that one child had escaped. As the dreadful procession moved towards the bridge there had been some pause, some halt, which brought Mdme de Cavignac and her children to a standstill close beside a spectator — a man in a very long cloak. He whispered that he might save *one*. Immediately, by tacit consent, the other children pushed the youngest under that long cloak. The procession moved on. The other Cavignacs, tied back to back, were flung from the bridge into the river.

This story was brought to us by later émigrés, who assured us that the young lady was safe in the care of her preserver and that he would send her to her friends in England when opportunity offered. And at length she came, during the short cessation of hostilities, after the Treaty of Amiens. She brought with her sufficient proof of her identity. Her preserver had been an artist and she had grown up in his family, somewhere in Provence. To our surprise she was reported to be a very pretty, genteel girl. We had often wondered about *the child under the cloak*, as we called her, and pictured her living in a cave, perhaps, and eating wild berries. We had supposed everybody in France to exist amidst riots, tumults, caps of liberty and guillotines, but, in many parts of the country, life seems to have gone on much as usual.

I suppose that I may have been a little in love with her before I ever saw her. I had thought of her often and her story had made a deep impression upon me. As a boy I had imagined our own family in such a situation. I hoped, I believed, that I should have had the courage immediately to push one of my sisters under the cloak.

I was sure that an instant's reflection would have enabled me to proceed and die with my mother; I could not have wished to survive her. But might not that instant's indecision have ruined all? Nor was I certain that I should have chosen Sukey for preservation, although she was the youngest. I wondered what marked quality in Edmée, beyond that of simple minority, had impelled the Cavignacs to so immediate an agreement. I imagined her a very lovely child, an angel whom everybody cherished. And I wondered what this angel must have felt, when bidden preserve herself while the rest went on to die. Had she understood that she would never see them again? Had she tried to resist the little loving hands which pushed her into safety? Had she been too young to understand? When she came to understand, could she ever smile again?

She spent some time with a relative of her father in Essex. Upon his death she came to pay a long visit at Bramfield. She had been there for several days when I returned for the summer vacation and I lost no time in asking for an account of her. A chorus of voices broke out, in a variety of assertions.

She played the harp. She spoke English very well. She wore no cap. She was a Protestant. She could not ride. She had very good teeth. Nobody had liked to mention Nantes, and she had said nothing upon that subject. She was afraid of dogs and of cows. Her dress was very queer, but doubtless in the latest fashion. Ned had offered to teach her to ride, but she had refused. She was very good-natured and had offered to teach everyone the harp. She was of middle height, taller than Kitty but not so tall as Caroline. Her gowns were of muslin, almost untrimmed, exposing the ankles and so scanty as to be barely decent, nor did she appear to wear many petticoats. But in conduct she was prudish; she had refused Ned's offer because she thought it improper. Isabella might be a little jealous of her. She must be very clever; it was a wonder to hear her speak French so fast.

The chief of this information came from Harriet, Kitty and Sukey, though my father contributed the items concerning her religion and her teeth. My mother said nothing until George had, for the third time, exclaimed upon our cousin's cleverness in speaking French so fast. She then observed that, in a Frenchwoman, this was not very astonishing, nor would she allow that the accent was good; it was not Parisian, but Provençal. I got the impression that my mother did not much care for Mlle de Cavignac. Caroline, upon whose opinion I should most have depended, was no longer with us. She had married a naval lieutenant the year before, and was living in Portsmouth. If I wished to know how *the child under the cloak* had really turned out, I must judge for myself.

During the following morning I walked up to call at the Park. Nobody was within, but I was told that the ladies, who had gone to visit a cottage, would be at home within half an hour. So I turned into the morning room to wait for them, and there encountered the most beautiful creature in the world.

I really think that she was, at that time, very lovely. It was a matter of colour, complexion, youth (she was but seventeen), grace — I know not what. The features, apart from that April freshness, were not good; they were sharp, — the lips too thin and the brow too low. But nobody, seeing her then, could have been so nice as to complain of such blemishes. In beauty we prize most highly that which has least permanence. If a rainbow were to be always in the sky we should seldom observe it; we pause and exclaim because we know that it is there but for an instant. And, in a woman, it is the transience of youth which heightens every charm. I have admired many beautiful women, yet am still sensible of a particular pang, half ecstasy, half anguish, when I catch a glimpse of Edmée in some young creature, — that transparent skin, the changing colour, the glancing grace and sparkle of a dewy morning.

I saw, in Paris, a painting by David which recalled her to me ; a young girl drawing by a window, who turns to look at the new-comer just as *she* turned from her embroidery frame. By what genius is that evanescent magic caught by the painter ! Long after we are all dead she will glance up from her drawing-board with a look that shall recall, to men unborn, the loved and the lost, — the transport of an hour, the regret of a lifetime.

I was better acquainted than were my sisters with the newest fashions. I was accustomed to the simple classical dress of the Consulate, but I had never seen it worn to better advantage. Her hair, a rich chestnut, was arranged with an artful negligence which would seem to owe nothing to the curling-tongs. Part of it was knotted up and part fell upon her neck in careless, childish ringlets. Her form was exquisitely rounded, — too much so for her age. Perfect symmetry at seventeen is often the precursor of excessive *embonpoint* at seven and twenty. But I did not know that, nor did I perceive any vacancy in her eye, for there is a certain lustre which vanishes from eyes as soon as they have anything to express. I thought her perfect, — the ideal embodiment of *the child under the cloak*. No wonder they should think that she, among them all, must live !

The memory of that episode was so strong upon me that I could scarcely speak or explain myself. She had started up, curtsied, and was about to quit the room before I found my voice. I detained her, however, introduced myself, and claimed kinship. Her extreme delicacy, which my sisters had called prudery, kept her hovering for awhile before she would consent to stay and talk to me. She was evidently uncertain of the propriety of sitting alone with a young man. French rules of chaperonage are, I believe, much stricter than ours, and the effect is provocative, for to suggest that a man cannot safely be left alone with a woman is to turn his mind inevitably to thoughts of what might ensue if he were; it supposes a natural licentiousness to be so near the surface that neither his honour nor her virtue should be exposed to the ordeal of propinquity. Edmée's flutterings had something of this effect upon me, — they certainly reminded me that I was a man and she a woman, and, when I prevailed upon her to stay, I had a feeling, which was far from unpleasant, that I had triumphed over her discretion rather than her reason, — that she did not think it quite proper but had been charmed into staying.

She reseated herself at her work and was soon speaking, in her pretty English, of the kindness which she had received from my family, of my mother, and of the pleasure that it had been to her to find a friend at Bramfield who could talk French so well, and who had been in Provence.

As she talked, that picture of the bridge at Nantes again flashed upon me. I thought of *her* mother, parting from her for ever, without a word, without a gesture. Tears rose to my eyes and I was obliged to turn away. I believe that a strong degree of compassion is implicit in all love. We never apprehend the woes, the anguish, of the human lot more clearly than when we love, — when we know that the beloved object has suffered, will suffer, must die.

For the first time in my life I felt displeased with my mother. She had criticised Edmée's accent. I could not understand how she had found anything to criticise in such a creature.

My cousins joined us far sooner than I could have wished, whereat my charmer became intent upon her embroidery. I must make an effort to talk connectedly, to answer questions, to listen to the local news. I wondered to see them sit there, chatting so composedly, as though no miracle had been present in the room with them. I took my leave as soon as I could, got one more glance from her, and departed, to roam the park in a kind of solemn ecstasy. I believe that I wept. It was some hours before I could calm myself sufficiently to face my fellow creatures.

My state needs no further description for it is a pretty common one. I was violently in love. Subsequent meetings did but increase my passion. I believed Edmée to be as intelligent as she was beautiful, and I don't blame myself over much for that illusion. Her accomplishments were all novelties to us; she played the harp, she had a pleasing voice, and, though she sang but a dozen songs, they were songs which we had never heard before. Her conversation had freshness. A translated phrase would seem to be more apt and witty than its English equivalent. A comment which had been inspired merely by contact with the unfamiliar was, to me, evidence of penetrating observation.

Some weeks of that delightful summer drifted by, during which I formed no project. I was simply content to be in her company as often as possible. If she had not continually, by her manner, assured me of her preference, I might have been more uneasy.

It was my mother who put an end to this happy dream. I had always been half aware that she did not like me to spend so much time with Edmée. She had made efforts to prevent it, — had suggested that I might like to visit

Ludovic, and finally tried to take me with her to Portsmouth, where Caroline was expecting her first confinement. But, as I pointed out, it was a most unseasonable time for me to be visiting my sister ; how would I pass my time while she lay in and my mother attended her ? I had no acquaintance in Portsmouth and my brother-in-law, Lieutenant Dawson, was at sea. I would escort my mother on her journey with all the pleasure in the world, but I would not stay there. She gave up the point, refused my escort, and, before she left, spoke to me very seriously about Edmée. She said that I ought not to pay such marked attentions to any girl unless I meant to marry her. I was startled. I did not above half like to hear my behaviour thus described.

'I pay her no more attention than all the world does,' I protested. 'At the Stokehampton Ball there was a positive stampede to stand up with her. And Ned is never out of the way when I am at the Park.'

'I have perceived as much,' said my mother. 'She receives a great deal of admiration. But not every young man who stampedes to dance with her is in a position to marry her. Such attentions from *you* may raise an expectation of more than you have intended.'

'I'm not near so well in a position to marry as Ned or Charles Pinney, Ma'am. They are eldest sons. I have no income save my fellowship, which I must resign if I marry.'

'It is generally supposed that you will soon take Orders and that the Amershams will give you a living.'

'I cannot help my neighbours' suppositions.'

'No, Miles. But you should be a little careful. Vulgar people might call you a good catch for such a girl, for any young woman in this neighbourhood. I think you are aware of that ; I notice that you are always very much upon your guard with Maria Cotman.'

I blushed, for I thought nobody had noticed that affair. I had, at Christmas, begun an idle flirtation with Maria, the prettiest of the Cotman girls ; then, perceiving that I should be caught if I did not look sharp, I kept out of her way.

'I do not see why I am to be raising more expectations than Ned or Charles Pinney,' I repeated, a little sulkily.

'You all behave,' said my mother, 'in a way to turn the poor girl's head. But their conduct is no business of ours. I want you to consider your own. Edmée has no fortune and she is alone in the world. The Chadwicks do not mean to keep her here for ever. She must go out as a governess or companion, I suppose, unless she can settle. If she supposes you serious, and you are not, it may make her very unhappy, — it might lead her to reject other offers. You should not raise her hopes, simply because you enjoy her company. That is very selfish.'

This was too much. I assured my mother that I had never been more serious in my life and that I fully intended to marry Edmée some time or other.

'Then,' said my mother, after she had agreed with me, several times over, that Edmée was a most beautiful girl, 'you should make up your mind what you mean to do.'

'I cannot afford to marry yet.'

'Then don't pay court to her so openly. If you go on so, with no engagement, you will put her into an awkward position and might be censured yourself as a trifler.'

'Then we had better be engaged, Ma'am. There is nothing for it. I will ask her, and tell her that we must wait.'

'Are you sure of *her* feelings ?'

I confessed that I was pretty sure of them. Edmée had given me very little uneasiness upon that score. Many admired her, but she had given me evidence of a decided preference.

My mother listened to my raptures rather sadly. I know now that she wished me not to commit myself; she was positive that Edmée could never make me happy. But happiness was, to her, inseparable from strict honour and the most scrupulous attention to the rights and feelings of others. What I said convinced her, to her great regret, that I *was* committed. She feared that Edmée might be in love with me, and she forced herself to remember that the girl had no mother to protect her. That dead mother was as much in her mind as in mine. She resolved to accept Edmée as a daughter and to love her, not only for my sake, but for the sake of that poor woman at Nantes.

'I scarcely think,' she said at last, 'that it would be fair to bind her to a long engagement. You can assure her of your regard, so that her feelings may not suffer if you behave with more caution. She may get other offers, you know. If she does not love you, she should be free to accept them. If she does, she will wait for you. But you should not go on as you do, for you are exposing her to comment.'

What she said was so kind and rational, it expressed so much genuine concern for Edmée's welfare, that I could scarcely disagree with it. But I was by no means pleased at having the alternatives before me so plainly stated. I wished to marry Edmée, but I was not sure that I wished to take Orders. An engagement would force me into choosing a profession and I had not yet made up my mind.

My mother set off for Portsmouth upon the following day, and very disconsolate were we without her. I tried to keep out of Edmée's way, for I could not trust myself to act with caution when actually in her company. Some kind of explanation I must have with her, and I had settled upon nothing. But life without her was intolerable.

I endured three days of it and then thought that she looked at me reproachfully when we were obliged to meet at church. That was intolerable. I spent the whole of Sunday afternoon in miserable indecision, trying to determine what I meant to say to her. In the evening, unable to endure the rack any longer, I set off to see her, having come to no conclusion.

I half hoped that I might not see her alone; that the decisive interview might be postponed and that I might be rewarded by an hour spent in the same room with her. But I met her strolling in the moonlight down the avenue. I instantly asked her to marry me, promising to take Orders and to provide a home for her as soon as possible.

She accepted me. What her words were I cannot remember; even a week later I could not be sure of them. But I am positive that I was accepted, else I would not have ventured upon caresses which were received and returned with a warmth equal to my own. I went much further, in that way, than I could have believed possible an hour earlier, further than I had ever permitted myself to imagine in my most rapturous dreams. No word or gesture of protest came from her; my own respect for her youth and innocence restrained me a little, and besides, Ned interrupted us. He came whistling down the avenue and we were forced to part. Edmée ran off and I returned home in a state of remorseful exaltation. I was ashamed of the precipitate liberties which I had taken, but uplifted by the proof they gave me that my passion was returned.

A long engagement was not to be tolerated. She must be all mine as soon as possible. I became certain that I had always meant to be a parson, and decided that I had better see Ludovic at once about a living in Devonshire which was in his father's gift, and for which I had put in a word on behalf of my friend Newsome. I now required that favour for myself and I set off very early next morning for Brailsford, fearing that a letter might be sent to Newsome if I delayed.

I knew that Ludovic was alone at Brailsford and I was by no means sure that he would receive my news very kindly, for he was no friend to matrimony. He was, however, unexpectedly sympathetic. I told him the whole of Edmée's history, which was of a kind to capture his interest. He was ready to believe her everything that she should be in the way of poetry and romance; if I must marry he was more content with *the child under the cloak* than with any other choice I might have made. No letter to Newsome had been sent, and he promised to speak to his father about the Ullacombe living.

'I am sure,' said he, as we sat over our wine, 'that Mlle de Cavignac must resemble your mother a little.'

I declared that she did, although I could not imagine my parents in any such scene as had taken place in the avenue twenty-four hours earlier. But to suppose passion in one's parents is very indecorous.

'What a good thing,' said Ludovic, 'that we have not yet started upon the great picture that I plan, for now we must include your Edmée in the garland.'

This was to be a portrait group of my mother and sisters which he was always proposing, though he never could decide upon the artist who should paint it. His idea was to illustrate some verses which my father had written to my mother upon their wedding anniversary, in which he said that, in that fair garland, she shone forth herself the crown : *Eklampei tou stephanou stephanos.*

'If Ullacombe is to be another Bramfield,' said he, 'I shall forgive you for marrying.'

'Ah ! Bramfield is one of your dotes.'

'It is indeed. Everyone is happy there. Some deity protects it. And seriously, Miles, I believe that it is your destiny to be happy. I know no one else of whom I should venture to say that. Of others I should merely enquire how well they might support misery. But you will listen an hour contentedly to a nightingale; in that you are unique among my acquaintance. My mother, I know, has other ideas, but I am glad that you will not listen to her. She means to turn you into Somebody. That would never satisfy you, for you would be for ever regretting the nightingale.

We spent the evening making plans to improve the parsonage house at Ullacombe. Ludovic had never seen it, but he insisted that it must face south, with a slope upon which we could make a flower garden for Edmée.

We went to bed pretty sober and very happy. I was never, before or after, so happy as I was upon that night.

> The future cheats us from afar.
> Nor can we be what we recall
> Nor dare to think on what we are.

I had no human fears

I was awakened in the dawn by a rattling of my bed curtains and the agitated voice of a servant. A letter had come from Bramfield by express, — a few hurried lines from Kitty. Caroline was dead. News of her death in childbirth had reached them soon after I left home. My father was gone to Portsmouth and Kitty wrote begging me to return.

I rose and dressed myself, so stunned that I was almost calm. Ludovic was fast asleep when I went to his room. I woke him. A kind of frost settled upon his thin face as he heard me. He could not speak save to urge food upon me before I set out; he cried to his man to see that I breakfasted well. No word of condolence came from him, but, as I turned from his bed, I heard him mutter: *A slumber did my spirit seal.* He vanished under the bed-clothes, leaving only the tassel of his nightcap visible as a hint that he had nothing else to say. But I understood him. It was a line from one of his odd *Lucy* poems. It haunted me, the whole piece haunted me strangely, all through that long and lovely day as I rode homewards, past busy market towns and fields where the corn was carrying.

We had supposed that nothing could touch Bramfield, — that it was exempt from the toll of human woe. My consternation was still so great that I did not wholly believe in Kitty's note. Childish hopes were mingled with premonitions of the truth; some mistake might have been made, — the first news might have been a false report. At times I thought of my mother and her anguish. Then I would see Caroline, radiant, a bride, as I handed her into the carriage at the church door and she drove away from us all: *A thing that could not feel the touch of earthly years.* I remembered her, always waiting for me at the turn of the lane when I came home for the holidays. Now she lay, stiff, white and shrouded, upon some bed in Portsmouth. *No motion has she now, no force; she neither hears nor sees.* It could not be true. It was impossible. When I reached home other news might have come.

My father too! What a journey for him! And her young husband, at sea, already cheated by the future, believing himself a happy man. It might be months before he knew. Her grave might be growing green and she at one with these busy harvest fields: *rolled round in earth's diurnal course.* . . . Ah Caroline! Ah my sister, my beloved sister!

They were still harvesting in the twilight as I rode

into Bramfield. But here the cottagers did not turn to shout after me as my tired horse clattered past; they knew why I came and watched me in silence. Every window at the Parsonage was alight. Kitty came running from the house as I dismounted and threw herself upon my neck, and wept with relief to see me, and wept again because it made no difference. Grief, to our young hearts, was as yet an unstudied book.

Mrs. Cotman and Maria were in the house. They had been there all day and, though my sisters found them very tiresome, nobody knew how to send them away. They sat in the parlour, consuming cake and wine, while my sisters sobbed above stairs and the maids sobbed in the kitchen.. Kitty did not warn me that they were there. She ran up to tell Harriet and Sukey that I was come, and I blundered into the parlour.

'Old heads are better than young ones,' said Mrs. Cotman, in answer, I suppose, to some look of astonishment from me. 'Your sisters should have some older person about them.'

Maria, who had risen and curtsied slightly, said nothing. She gazed upon me with a kind of frightful curiosity. Perhaps she had never seen a man weep before.

'The Lord giveth,' continued Mrs. Cotman with unction, 'and the Lord taketh away. Blessed be the name of the Lord. Maria, my love, step into the kitchen and tell Betty to bring the ham, for I daresay Mr. Miles is hungry.'

I said that I wanted no ham, and was beating a retreat when Maria spoke. Casting down her eyes for a moment she murmured:

'Had any of the Chadwicks been able to come, we should not have intruded. But since they are in such trouble themselves——'

'Troubles never come singly!' sighed Mrs. Cotman.

'What?' cried I, turning at the door. 'Is there trouble too at the Park?'

'Did Kitty not tell you?' exclaimed Maria. 'I made sure she would have told you immediately.'

Both were fixing me now with this avid glare. The thought that *Edmée* must be dead burst upon me and turned me to ice. I could not speak. I could only wait for them to say it.

Their merciless eyes were before me and their intolerable whining voices rang in my ears. But it seems as though they must have talked for a long time before I was quite able to comprehend what they said.

Edmée was gone, and Ned with her. They had disappeared upon the preceding night, when I was sitting with Ludovic and planning a flower garden for Ullacombe. It was thought that they had gone to Scotland. Ned's father had had some kind of seizure at the news and all was in confusion at the Park.

Mrs. Ned

I WILL begin this chapter by mentioning an agreeable circumstance, for I have little else that is cheerful to relate. The Ullacombe living went to Newsome, who was a thousand times more deserving of it than I. He subsequently married Kitty, upon whom his heart had long been set. He sticks to it that he made up his mind when she was but fourteen and was suffered, as a great favour, to field for us at cricket. But he did not immediately make her an offer, when he got his preferment. He thought her too young. He knew that he was a favourite with her, upon my account, and feared lest inexperience might lead her to suppose her preference greater than it was.

'I wished her to get about a little,' he told me once, 'and see the world, and compare me with others, before choosing. If, after meeting livelier fellows, she still preferred me, I might be sure that she knew her own heart.'

Kitty, when applied to, accepted at once and laughed at him for all this caution. She declared that she had never meant to marry anyone else, and had been sure that he would offer as soon as he could, supposing some good reason for the delay. She knew that his first care, upon getting Ullacombe, must be to assist his own family in the education of his younger brothers and sisters. It was, indeed, three years before he could afford to marry.

I like to think of Newsome and Kitty. I still call him so, although he is now my brother, because his baptismal name is Augustus, which suits him so ill that I refuse to pronounce it. I like to think of people who knew their own minds so well and who managed their affairs so rationally. They are as happy at Ullacombe as ever I intended to be, though neither of them attends much to the nightingale. And they never change. Time's foot spares Ullacombe and will do so, I hope, for many years. Newsome is still the same tall, thin, black-haired creature with whom I climbed Hills at Winchester. Not all the cream in Devonshire will put an ounce of flesh upon him. The wig which he wears in church so transforms him that I always feel as though a stranger were preaching his sermons. He talks of discarding it; many parsons have begun to do so, I believe. I hope that I shall be present when he does, for the first sight of that black poll in the Ullacombe pulpit will, I am sure, cause an immense sensation among his flock.

I write of Newsome because I shrink from getting back to Edmée and the days which followed her disappearance from Bramfield. She gave me so much pain that my mind still falls into a kind of confusion when I remember it, although it is so long ago. I could not think. I could only suffer.

Her conduct was, for some time, a complete mystery to me. Only when I came to understand her character better, as I have since had every opportunity to do, did I begin to piece it out. She was determined to secure a husband. She would have preferred Ned or Pinney, as better matches, but had despaired of her power with either when she accepted me. To marry a parson was better than nothing.

It appears that there had been some trouble at the Park during those three days when I kept away. Ned's admiration became more apparent to his family when I was not by to cut him out. His mother felt some alarm. They had all thought of *me* as her suitor and had flattered themselves that she would settle well. To welcome her as a wife for Ned was another matter. They were too kind to put her out of doors forthwith, but plans were making to despatch her to Lincolnshire as companion to an elderly lady, a distant connection. Edmée got wind of this, no doubt, and made haste to provide for herself.

Some love passages must have already taken place with Ned, and I expect her trouble lay in getting him to run off. He was a good and affectionate son ; he must have balked at so open an offence to his parents. For her, nothing short of an elopement would do. She would not trust to his constancy, once she had been sent to Lincolnshire. Knowing nothing of honour herself she would not, naturally, depend upon it in other people. I think that Ned would have been true to her, for he was very much in love. He would have wished to wait until his parents came round. But she bore him down, at some time during the twenty-four hours after she had accepted me. Perhaps he caught sight of me, parting from her in the avenue; perhaps there was some jealous scene and her hopes of him revived. I know what her power is, for I have had a taste of it. She can put a man beside himself; she can excite him to any act of folly. I am sure now that she meant me to compromise myself beyond retreat. She suspected that my mother was against her, and meant to put me into such a position that the Chadwicks could insist upon my marrying her. I daresay that she had tried the same tactics with Ned, and our gentlemanly scruples must have annoyed her very much. Pinney, who had fewer, got off better than we did. He had quitted Gloucestershire suddenly, just before all this, and gone on a visit to friends in Scotland. Long afterwards, when in his cups, he once let fall something which explained this prudent flight. Somebody had spoken contemptuously of Ned, and Pinney said:

'He should have run away, as I did.'

Of one thing I am certain. Ned never suspected that he had done me any injury. He was jealous. He knew that we were rivals. But he thought that he had cut me out quite fairly.

I had, fortunately, told nobody at Bramfield of my engagement. Ludovic had been my only confidant. I sent him a line telling him that I no longer wanted Ullacombe and begging him to renew his efforts on Newsome's behalf. I did not tell him why, and he never asked. We did not refer to the episode again.

Nobody else knew. I had meant to tell the whole to my mother, but I never did. During the first weeks we were all in such grief that I felt unable to obtrude my private sorrow upon anyone. I felt indeed a little ashamed of myself for having a private sorrow. Caroline's remains were brought back to Bramfield for burial. Her poor little infant had survived her, and he provided a certain degree of consolation for the women of the family. Our old nurseries were set up again. My mother had a child in her arms once more, — a child who pretty well monopolised her attention for a long period. When she was at leisure to listen to me, I no longer cared to speak, or to reopen a wound which had healed after a fashion.

Ned's father suffered no lasting damage from his fit, if he ever had one. (I daresay that particular had been invented by the Cotmans.) He did not disown or disinherit his son. I have heard of parents who do such things, but I never met any. Some talk there was of never receiving Edmée at the Park, but I doubt if anyone took it seriously. Ned had a little money of his own, inherited from a great-aunt. The young couple were next heard of at Tunbridge Wells, where they took lodgings and waited for the Chadwicks to come round. By Christmas they were back at Bramfield, not forgiven perhaps, but accepted.

I dreaded the idea of meeting her again and would have avoided it if I could, but I shrank from the comment which my absence at Christmas would provoke. I feared my own feelings, lest her beauty might still have power with me, in spite of her conduct. Those feelings were not now restrained by any illusions as to her character. There were moments when I was visited by the notion of serving Ned as he had served me, though I fought against it, for I knew that he was blameless. Had I confided in my mother I should not, perhaps, have been plagued by such base thoughts. Nor need I have apprehended a temptation which was not in the least likely to arise. I must have been very green if I really entertained the idea of seducing her. I believed her, by this time, to be all that was bad, and was innocent enough to suppose that bad women are easily seduced. I still could not quite believe that her ardour had all been calculated, and that I was nothing to her; I was half persuaded that she had wanted me and only took Ned for his money.

All this agitation I might have spared myself. I saw her first at church upon Christmas day, and for some seconds could scarcely recognise her. The beauty I had so much feared was completely gone. She was pregnant, though nobody knew of it then and her shape was not altered; her complexion had suffered, — she looked pinched and sallow. She wore an ugly snuff-coloured bonnet and pelisse. My imagination must have been greatly disordered, for I had expected to see her, at Christmas, in the airy muslins of high summer. I realised, with mingled anguish and relief, that Edmée was gone for ever and that Mrs. Ned could be nothing to me.

Nothing did I say?

What she was to be, as Mrs. Ned, was then unknown to us. We did not think well of her but we little guessed how much worse we were destined to think. For it is she who has put an end to all the happy, easy affection which used to subsist between the Parsonage and the Park, and which once made Bramfield such a pleasant place. She has done it slowly but very thoroughly. With my mother's death vanished the chief of our happiness, but something of the past might have remained had Ned married a more amiable woman. Sukey's life would have been far more tolerable. There would have been company, small parties, picnics and dancing, in which poor Sukey would have had her share. My father would have continued to receive all those little attentions to which he had become accustomed.

That woman understands nothing of the duties of a country gentleman. Her foreign education may in part account for this, but the chief cause is in a grasping cupidity, a determination to get, in every transaction, two pennyworth for a penny. This had begun to appear before she married Ned; her 'good nature' in offering to teach my sisters the harp had turned out to be expensive for them, since they found themselves paying for their lessons with ribbons, feathers and shoe roses, demanded with such assurance that they knew not how to refuse.

She began to make mischief at once, but her full power was not felt until the death of Ned's father, a couple of years later. I shall not here enter into the details of her contemptible conduct towards his family. His mother and sisters removed, as soon as possible, to Clifton, to be out of her way. Tom is in the Army and Sam in the East India Company; neither of them ever comes near Bramfield. Mrs. Ned has got the Park all to herself. They entertain but little, for it is agony to her to put a dinner before a guest unless she is immediately to get something by it. Ned still hunts occasionally. To be sure they have heavy expenses, for they have now at least ten children, or it may be twelve. I forget. They have been about it for fifteen years without any noticeable intermission.

But their neglect of their neighbours is as nothing in comparison with their inhumanity to those whose comfort *must* depend on them, — I mean their people and their tenants. Ned is such a bad landlord that he is losing the better class of tenant. Many farms have changed hands; when a farmer dies his son prefers to move and start afresh elsewhere, if he has any enterprise. Only poor, thriftless farmers will put up with it and the land is being ruined among them.

As for the cottagers it is abominable. People of that sort get such a small wage that they must receive some kind of assistance if they are not to starve. They cannot provide for themselves in old age, or lay by in case of sickness. It is the squire's duty to see to that; it is a matter of plain justice, for he owes it to them over and above the money that he pays them. Ned's father, though something of an autocrat, understood that principle perfectly. He never turned old people out because they were past work. If a family were in want through sickness he relieved them. He repaired their cottages and their wells. He exerted, on their behalf, his own advantages of position and education. If a widow's son were taken for the militia he set the matter right. Our people never felt that they had no friend to protect them. He believed, in fact, that the rich have a duty to the poor. It is a principle which is, I think, generally *recognised* in this country, though it may not be universally *practised*. I know men of property who neglect their people ; I have never met one who would have maintained that he was right to do so. I never met a rake so abandoned that he did not know how a good squire *ought* to behave.

But for Mrs. Ned this principle does not exist. If there is an *ought* for her, it is that she ought to drive the hardest bargain that she can. To give anything is impossible to her. She feels no duty whatever towards the poor people here, will not allow that they have any rights, and the result is that they starve. We see no rosy children nor tidy old women in our village ; hungry sullen faces scowl at us, and curses are muttered behind our backs. They drink, thieve and poach, and I don't blame them. I often wonder if all the Cavignacs were as bad as she ; if they were, then the man in the cloak was a blockhead. But I don't believe that anybody pushed her under it. I am certain that she secured that advantageous position for herself before the rest knew what she was about.

It is curious to reflect that much misery might have been spared had she married *me*. I should have been very wretched, no doubt, and perhaps a child or two might have had the misfortune to call her mother. (*But not ten or twelve.*) Her marriage with Ned has wasted a

prosperous countryside. He is clay in her hands and
grown so sottish that he is, now, hardly up to managing
any business for himself. I think that he drinks in order
to escape from his thoughts, for he must know how low
he is sunk, — despised by all his neighbours and hated by
his people. Poor good-natured old Ned ! He meets one
now with a surly, suspicious stare, as if he expected some
insult. Yet he fought me once, for laughing at Bob
Howes, and Harry Ridding once called him a 'proper
gentleman.'

I am the least pitiable of Edmée's victims. I daresay
that I might have taken no lasting harm from her betrayal
had I confided in my mother. Then the wound would
not have healed with poison in it. She would have told
me not to despise myself for loving, even though my first
choice had been unlucky. She might have given me
courage to love again. But *that*, hardening my heart in
bitter silence, I was determined never to do. This
decision was greatly to Pronto's advantage. So far as
the Sex is concerned, he henceforth took charge of our
affairs, and he is very much the ladies' man.

Of Pronto's career I don't mean to write more than I
need. I will, however, mention one circumstance which
will not, I trust, appear in any of his biographies, since
he is a monument of discretion. Nobody supposes him
an anchorite and he is as much at his ease among the
poplollies, when taken into their company, as he is everywhere else ; but nobody knows what provision he has
made for himself in that way. Has he got a poplolly of
his own, and where does he keep her ? None of his
particular friends are able to answer that question.

Since I know that he will one day destroy this manuscript I will here record that he did, at one time, pay the
rent of a small villa in St. John's Wood, but, finding
it confoundedly expensive, gave it up. Pronto is ever

careful of his money. He had been so discreet that his charmer got no chance of reverting to any of his friends and was obliged to marry a haberdasher at Edgware. But Pronto gave her all the furniture which, when sold, fetched five hundred pounds. He is not a bad fellow in his way.

Aut Discede

THE loss of Edmée turned me against all thoughts of the Church as a profession. I had only half liked it before ; to make a home for her had been my principal object. I now determined upon the Bar as the gate to a political career. Politics had no great attraction for me, — no course, during those despondent months, had much allurement. But I felt some satisfaction in the prospect of becoming, some day, a greater man than Ned. If I had any positive ambition, it was to come rattling in my carriage through Bramfield, a member of the Government, to dazzle everybody with my wealth and consequence, to receive obsequious invitations to dine at the Park, to patronise Ned, and to catch a sparkle of regret in Edmée's eyes.

My father was frankly disappointed at my decision, but I knew that my mother was relieved. She did not, I daresay, think me fit to be a clergyman. Her power with me, during the years that followed, declined considerably, though I loved her as much as ever. She could give me no advice in the life that I had chosen, and I suppose that I might, though I did not then know it, have harboured a little resentment against her for her preoccupation with her grandson at a time when her son was so much in need of consolation. Her place, as guide and mentor, was largely taken by Lady Amersham of whom I think I should here give a short account, since she might almost be called Pronto's mother.

She was a remarkable woman. I was always a little afraid of her, — why, I cannot tell, for she was uniformly kind to me. She was kind to everybody, yet I think all were afraid of her. She had no foibles, no human frailties, no tender spots. Nothing appeared to hurt or discompose her, which was as well, for her life, between such a husband and such a son, cannot have been very agreeable. I sometimes wondered whether she had not, in her youth, suffered extremely. If she had, no trace of it was visible. But she may not. She may have been born without the power to feel. Recent experience has taught me to wonder if there is much difference between a broken heart and no heart at all. In any case, she could make one feel that emotion is a trifle vulgar.

She can never have been a beauty, but had the knack of making beauty look cheap. She had a fresh healthy complexion which survived the loss of youth ; in spite of corpulence and lameness she always moved with great dignity. Her nose was prominent and her mouth small. She had sharp grey eyes which observed everything, but I am not quite sure how much they saw. Everything, to her, was quite definite ; she had no doubts, no hesitations, no confused ideas. That which she could not understand did not exist, so far as she was concerned, — in certain matters she was oblivious rather than ignorant.

A faint, ironic smile was her most striking trait, the smile of one who is amused rather than pleased. (It is strange that the same word must serve for her and for my mother, — they were both smiling women. But with what a difference !) She was proficient in German, French and Italian, had been everywhere, met everybody, and could talk as though she had read everything. I cannot exactly say that she had taste, or particularly praise her manners. They were adequate, — they could not be criticised, but she had a kind of grand carelessness, as though taste and polish were all very well for lesser people.

Her influence in politics was enormous. Amersham was but a cypher in her hands. She knew everything that went on and, what is more, foresaw much of what would shortly be going on. I have seldom known her to be out in her judgments unless some totally unexpected circumstance capsized the board. She could predict exactly what everybody would do for the next half-dozen moves. She was the best player at human chess that ever I saw.

This chess-board was the entire world to her. I doubt if anything else had any significance at all. With that faint smile she would watch and applaud Siddons at the play, ask what one thought of *Marmion*, report that Buonaparte had returned from Elba, repeat the General Confession, or deplore the frost which had ruined her tulips. She was like a person who lives at the summit of an unscaleable mountain, who sees the world with a clarity impossible to the dwellers below, — sees how all rivers must run and whither all roads go, — but sees it in a lack of detail which destroys proportion and reduces all to equal insignificance.

Of greatness I suspect that she knew nothing. Her few mistakes sprang from her complete ignorance of those qualities which inspire greatness in a man. She knew to a hair's breadth what lesser men will do, and for this reason her acumen was at its height in the years immediately succeeding the deaths of Pitt and Fox. Two powerful and, to her, slightly incalculable pieces had been removed from the board. The survivors were well within the scope of her comprehension. She knew how both parties would flounder and scramble, when thus deprived of their leaders. Castlereagh was the only man left concerning whom she hesitated to prophesy, and even there she was generally right in anything that she ventured to say.

It was by her advice that I chose the Chancery Bar where the Amersham interest could procure me such connections as might help me forward as a conveyancer. Since I must resign my fellowship she got Arisaig to secure me the post of Warden of Slane Forest, a small sinecure upon which I was to live until I had found my feet. But her plan turned out to be much more costly than I had expected. She knew nothing of poverty, and never thought of money save in large quantities. I dined out a good deal, in the best circles, but there were days when I had nothing for breakfast. As 'poor delightful Miles Lufton,' a guest in some great house, I had not been put to any great expense. It was not expected or desired that I should appear as a man of fashion, bring a servant with me, or pay much attention to the cut of my coats. As Pronto I must make a greater show ; I must not seem to be too poor, — I must not seem to consider money at all.

Frank poverty is hard enough, but it is not near so disgusting as covert poverty. Pronto is as little inclined as I am to remember all the shifts to which we were put, especially in the matter of clean linen and paying the laundress.

Our most painful memory is of Richmond Hill. Arisaig, Crockett, Dysart and I drove four smart girls down to the Star and Garter. I had not wished to be of the party, I had never cared for that sort of scheme, but Arisaig was insistent and I could not very well disoblige him, after what he had done for me. By some mischance I was left to pay for the whole frolic, including boats upon the river, supper and wine. That was bad enough, but, to my great mortification, I had not the necessary sum upon me to meet the bill when it was brought. Had I been a rich man I should doubtless have bellowed this news from the top of Richmond Hill. Being what I was, my first object must be to conceal my predicament. I sat in silent consternation, racking my brains for some way out of the scrape, and strongly averse from applying to my companions. Any reputation for meanness would have sat ill upon Pronto.

At this point my fair neighbour dropped her handkerchief. As we both dived to retrieve it I found a banknote pressed into my hand and heard a whisper :

'Don't mind them ! I know you will pay me back.'

I settled the bill with the greatest unconcern and called upon her next day, to pay my debt, with a dozen pairs of gloves by way of interest. She was Dysart's mistress at that time, and a world too good for him, — a most beautiful girl with great sweetness of disposition. Her action in saving me from humiliation was just like her. It was a trick put upon me by Dysart and Crockett. I doubt if Arisaig was party to it ; he is so rich that he never pays for his supper. But Crockett is a very malicious fellow. Poor Fanny had known how it would be and had brought this bank-note with her and seated herself beside me, meaning to help me out of the scrape if she could. She scolded me a little, very kindly, for keeping such company.

Sweet Fanny Osborne ! Shall I ever forget you ? Mine was not the only sad heart when you died. I remember Harrington coming into White's, — it was just before we had the Corunna despatches, and we asked him if there was any news.

'Nothing from the Peninsula,' he said, 'but I hear that Fanny Osborne is dead.'

I remembered Richmond Hill and walked off, unwilling to hear any discussion of her. I had not gone far when little Bowman caught me up; he was almost in tears and told me that he had been to see poor Fanny a few days before. He had heard that she was very ill and wished to know if he could do anything for her. She told him that she was dying and wanted for nothing.

'We know that God is an indulgent parent,' she whispered, 'and I am sure that He will receive me kindly.'

The worst of the Richmond frolic was that I could not give the handsome wedding present of plate which I had intended for Newsome and Kitty. Repayment to Fanny took up most of the little hoard that I had laid by for it. I was forced to give Kitty a paltry locket of which I was ashamed, and the more ashamed when I reflected how the money had been spent, upon what company, with what total lack of satisfaction. Pronto, so soon as he was assured that nobody would know he had borrowed from a poplolly, was perfectly comfortable. Yet it was Miles who got the money for him, — that frank, ingenuous creature behind whom Pronto masquerades. Fanny had been distressed, as she said herself, to see an honest, pleasant young man in such difficulties.

Upon the whole we kept out of scrapes pretty well. We avoided play, abhorred the Jews, and drank very little. Though taking pains to be liked by the men, we knew that our future must depend upon the good graces of the women, with whom we preserved our reputation for interesting sensibility. We read to them, sang with them, danced, flirted and sauntered, ran errands for them, took notice of their bracelets, listened to their advice and escorted them to church. If our manner was less candid, our sentiment less unaffected, our flattery a little grosser, than it had been a year or so ago, these well-bred women did not observe the fact. Only one woman in ten million has genuine taste.

In due time we reaped our reward. We began to make

money at conveyancing. We got a seat in Parliament; Amersham gave us West Malling as soon as it was available. We grew easy, were sure of clean linen, and breakfasted as often as we dined.

Nor did we fall out. Though accomplices, we were never friends enough to quarrel. Each meant, at some time, to be rid of the other. Miles was content to let Pronto take the lead to a certain point : he did not mean to put up with fellows like Crockett for ever, but he was anxious to secure an income of £3000 a year. Having got that, Pronto was to be dismissed ; a pretty little property in the country was to be rented where Miles could retire and listen, in elegant surroundings, to the nightingale.

Pronto is an active, Miles a passive creature. Pronto never expects, never prepares for, those sudden bursts of feeling on the part of Miles which threaten, from time to time, a revolution. They always take him by surprise, and he is powerless before them. He takes cover when the gale blows up and only ventures forth when it is over. So far they have done him little damage. Since they invariably blow themselves out he very properly ignores them.

Gulley's Cove

OUR country, meanwhile, had been 'saving herself by her exertions and Europe by her example.' Very proud of themselves were Miles and Pronto, whose exertions, described above, had been of the most heroic order. We daily defied the Corsican on *terra firma*, drinking many loyal toasts, while our brother Eustace defied him less comfortably upon the seas. And it was in this connection that one of those sudden divergences took place between us which are to supply the subject matter for this memoir.

Were it not for these upheavals, these Declarations of Independence, upon the part of Miles, his story must have ended when Pronto's began.

When not in town I spent a good deal of time at Ullacombe, both before and after Newsome's marriage. It is by the sea and there is good fishing. I kept a small sailing-boat in which I roamed up and down the coast, sometimes with Newsome, sometimes alone. In the course of these explorations I made some new friends of the class which is generally called *humble*, though no man was ever less humble than William Hawker.

I had gone out one day alone in my boat and was caught in a sudden squall of great violence, which blew me on to some rocks near a sequestered cove some twelve miles from Ullacombe. There was no great danger, but I was obliged to swim for it. When I reached the cove I got such a pounding from the surf on the beach that I was pretty well exhausted. A man came running down from a solitary cottage above the cove. He brought me up to his house, gave me dry clothes and hot rum, and set me by his fire.

When I had a little recovered my senses, and begun to look about me, I had a curious sense of ease and pleasure for which I could not exactly account. I might still have been a little dazed by my buffeting. I was almost positive that I had seen this place before, or had known of it in some way. And then it would seem to me as though it might be some old picture into which I was got. It was a common enough room, — a clean sanded kitchen and a bright fire, the points of light winking in the pewter plates ranged along the dresser. The cottager's wife rocked a heavy cradle with her foot as she sat gazing pensively into the fire. In her blue gown, checked handkerchief and round-eared cap, she was very neat and pretty; she reminded me of some old Flemish pictures that Ludovic has.

Every article in the room had a charm for me. I liked the side of bacon and the herbs that hung from the rafters, a heap of nets and lobster-pots in a dark corner, and an old dog snoring upon the hearth.

The storm without increased in violence. Presently my host returned. He had been seeing to his stock.

'I think,' he said, 'that you should not attempt the walk to Ullacombe by night in this wind. The path goes by the cliffs and is dangerous unless you know it well. You had best remain with us till daylight, for there is not a house nearer than Gulley's Cross, and none where you might get a bed.'

I assented readily enough, for I was in no hurry to change my quarters. I wondered, though, where my bed might be ; the cottage had but one room and I could see no bed in it. The young woman rose to prepare supper and I was quite sorry that she did so. I would have liked to sit on for ever in this dreamy repose, contemplating my old picture. But I continued to watch all that they did with great satisfaction, — as though I had arrived at some long-desired bourn, and had come to stay there for ever, after a desperate and perilous voyage.

The man lighted a tallow dip and placed it upon a shelf in the corner by the fish-nets. Seating himself there he began some task of mending or fitting. The faint light falling on his face, the strong shadows, made a picture of another sort. I thought of Rembrandt, and wished Ludovic there to agree with me. He was a fine fellow ; I judged him to be between thirty and forty years old. His features were strongly marked and of a thoughtful cast, though glowing with health. His eye was bright and his manner decisive. He was very much his own master. I had been aware of that from the first ; even in the few sentences that had passed between us, I had been struck by something unusual in his air.

There is about most labouring people a kind of blank-ness of countenance, when addressing their betters, which is not natural. It is assumed in order to keep us at a distance. They will seldom volunteer an opinion and, if questioned, will give as indirect an answer as they can. They don't wish us to know what they think.

I once rambled beside a lake with my father, and we watched some people in a boat a little distance away across the water. We could not imagine what they were about, for they rowed continually up and down over the same spot and a great discussion was carrying on amongst them. Only a word or two occasionally reached us. Presently my father remarked that the man in the stern must be a gentleman because he had just begun a sentence with the words : *I think*.

'Your labourer,' said my father, 'would never do so. He may state a fact, but he will never express an opinion without some preface such as : "They do say . . ." or "I've heard tell . . ." This is not, I believe, because he does not and cannot think ; it is because nobody ever asks him what he thinks. Since Adam was driven from Para-dise, to earn his living in the sweat of his brow, nobody has enquired what he thinks.'

I remembered this as I contemplated my Rembrandt, and it occurred to me that he had told me what he thought as coolly as though he owned half a county.

The woman meanwhile had put plates, knives and mugs upon the table. She brought ale, bread and cheese, and took a mess of beans and bacon from the pot over the fire. A little shyly she asked if I would be pleased to take supper with them.

We talked of the crops and of the weather. I learnt that he was both farmer and fisherman in a small way. He had a little plot of land above the cove, — a field or so in plough and some pasture ; he kept cows, fowls, pigs and bees, and in addition caught lobsters. These last he kept alive in a salt-water tank that he had made, until he could take them, with his wife's butter, cheeses, eggs and so forth, to Torhaven, a sizeable market town some way farther up the coast. He made this trip once a week, taking his boat in fine weather, and his pack-horse when it was stormy.

'I wish,' I said, 'that you would go to Ullacombe, for we cannot get good lobsters there.'

He said briefly that he never did, which astonished me, because it was so much nearer than Torhaven. But a faint sigh from his wife restrained me from further questions ; it struck me that he might have some particular reason for avoiding the place. I could not quite make him out. His accent, though pleasant, was unfamiliar to me. He pronounced his words very clearly ; he did not slur them as country people usually do. I understood him to say that he came from Lincolnshire, but this was not so. I was a little tired and sleepy and I could not have been fully attending to what he said. I had taken notice of a pewter spoon that was set for me ; it was of a very graceful design, — much less clumsy than cottage spoons usually are. He said that it had been his mother's spoon and that it was made in Boston, where the pewter smiths are the finest in the world. I asked if he came from Boston and he replied that he was born not far from it, in Marblehead, a little town upon the coast, some way to the north of it. I had never heard of it, and never surmised that such a town is nowhere to be found in this island.

From my place at the table I could see rather more of the room, and my eye was now struck by some forty or fifty books, arranged upon deal shelves behind the settle where I had been sitting beside the fire. This was so unusual a sight, in a house of that kind, that my surprise burst out at the expense of my manners.

'I see,' said I, 'that you have a very pretty little library! I suppose that you are fond of reading?'

His smiling assent left me with the impression that he thought my remark too foolish for any lengthy reply. And I felt it so myself, but knew not how to talk to him. But these books filled me with curiosity and when the meal was over I took a rush-light to that corner, in order to examine them. They were old and shabby but their titles startled me. He had a good collection of poetry and essays, some novels, and Shakespeare's plays. The chief of his library, however, was of a philosophical or political nature. He had, among others, Hume, Locke, Berkeley, More's *Utopia*, Smith's *Theory of the Moral Sentiments* and *The Wealth of Nations*, Rousseau's *Social Contract*, Hobbes' *Leviathan*, all the works of Thomas Paine, and a small pamphlet, — *A Summary View of the Rights of America*, edited by Burke and written, I believe, by Jefferson.

I regarded them silently, not venturing upon any comment. Presently he joined me and asked if I was fond of reading aloud. I said that I was. He then asked if I would be so good as to read to them a little.

'Mary,' he said, 'cannot read, though I am teaching her. I generally read aloud to her in the evenings.'

'What?' cried I. '*The Age of Reason?*'

He laughed and said that he had not, as yet, tried her with that.

'She likes a feeling story and we are half through *Pamela*. But we will leave that this evening, since we have you with us. It was in my mind to ask you to read us some poetry, for that is work at which I make but a poor hand. I should like Mary to hear a gentleman read poetry.'

'With all the pleasure in the world,' said I, 'if you will tell me what poetry you prefer.'

'No, sir. If you please, you will read what you prefer yourself, for you will read that best.'

I accordingly found a volume of Milton and read *Comus* to them. This poem has always been a favourite with me, but Milton is quite out, just now, and Pronto is seldom invited to read him. I think that I acquitted myself well. My hosts listened with close attention and he seemed to take great pleasure in the entertainment. As for Mary, half the words must have been unintelligible to her, but she liked it in her way, for her greatest pleasure was ever to see her husband happy. When I had done she thanked me very prettily, declaring that it was a sweet piece and that she was 'sure the poor Lady would get off at the last.'

'I told you,' said he, with a laugh, 'that she is all for a pathetic story.'

The hour was now advanced, for people of their habits. He asked me if I would choose to go to bed. When I assented he drew back some check curtains, revealing a box bed set in the wall. I had thought it a window.

'If you will take the place over against the wall,' said he, 'I think you will be comfortable enough, for it is a large bed.'

I now understood that I was to share it with them. Hastily following his example I stripped to my shirt and got into the bed, whilst Mary sat with her back to us, in the chimney-corner, suckling her child. A moment later he joined me, talking of poetry with an enthusiasm almost equal to anything Ludovic can do in that line. The reading of *Comus* had quite thawed any natural taciturnity in his manner.

'It is a kind of language,' said he, 'which is not the worse for being hard to understand. There is always meaning of a sort, and fancy feeds upon the sound of it.

I may not always comprehend what your poet means, but that does not extinguish my pleasure in what he says. Whereas, in all other books, there is no enjoyment save in following the argument.'

I asked him how he got his books. He explained that he bought them of a pedlar who travelled the country and to whom he had given a list of the works which he most desired to possess. This man was able to get them cheap, at sales or at houses where a removal was expected. When he came to Gulley's Cove he always brought one or two volumes in his pack. He had got the *Human Understanding* from a dairy-maid in exchange for a cap ribbon. She had been using it as a scale-weight for cheeses.

He in turn asked me if I could recommend any new works, lately out ; he said that he had little opportunity to learn of new books. I mentioned some of Ludovic's dotes, and quoted some lines from Wordsworth which struck him very much. He asked me to repeat them and had almost got them by heart when Mary clambered in beside us and blew out the rush-light. But he would not sleep until he was sure of these lines and kept mumbling : *Whose dwelling is the light of setting suns* . . . until I burst out laughing. I could not help it. Our situation, — the three of us laid there in a row, — was too much for me.

My guffaw was echoed, a moment later, by a smothered giggle from Mary.

'And at what,' asks he severely, 'might you two be laughing ?'

'At you, to be sure !' says Mary.

In a little while he began to laugh himself, though protesting that he could see nothing ridiculous in his proceedings. The bed shook with our laughter. For some time afterwards one or other of us would give a drowsy chuckle.

For my part, I half believed that I was dreaming. My heart was so light. I could not remember when it had last been as light as this. I wished that I should not have to go away in the morning. I wished that this had been in truth my bed, and that I might sleep in it for ever.

The American

I WAS up, however, in the dawn, and off to Ullacombe, for I knew that Newsome would be alarmed at my absence. My new friends bade me a kind farewell. I felt that it would be indelicate to offer payment, but I promised myself that I would return to Gulley's Cove very soon, with books for him and ribbons for Mary.

Newsome (he was still a bachelor at this time) was much relieved to see me. As I ate my breakfast I related my adventures.

'What?' cried he. 'You have been staying with the American?'

'Is *that* what he is?'

'That is the name they have for him round here. I hardly know him by sight. I believe that his name is William Hawker. He came here some ten years ago with his father, and they bought the little farm at Gulley's Cove. But the old man is dead, is not he?'

'There was no old man to be seen,' I agreed. 'Only a pretty wife, whose bed I shared last night.'

'Good God!'

'The American between us, as chaperon,' continued I, ignoring his start. 'But tell me about him, for he is a queer fellow. Why does he never come to Ullacombe?'

'It may be because he has quarrelled with Lockesley.'

This was a man who owned most of the land in that

part of the country. He was a Justice of the Peace and a notable tyrant.

'Don't tell me,' cried I, 'that my friend Hawker is afraid of Lockesley ! I should be sorry to think it.'

'He may not be, but others are. Since their quarrel, nobody in Ullacombe dare buy Hawker's lobsters for fear of offending Lockesley. If Gulley's Cove Farm were not a freehold, Lockesley would have sent him packing ; it enrages the old man to have a cottager, like Hawker, defying him with impunity.'

The fact was that Hawker had voted against Lockesley's man in an election. Lockesley had gone himself down to the hustings to see that all his people were voting as they ought, and was outraged to perceive Hawker, from whom he had bought lobsters, in the hostile enclosure. He immediately withdrew his custom from the rebel and let all his people know that they must do likewise, on pain of his severe displeasure. This was why Hawker was obliged to take his wares to Torhaven.

'And you,' said I to Newsome, 'do you tolerate this ? Do you buy lobsters as Lockesley bids you ?'

'Why no,' said Newsome. 'I am fortunately independent of Lockesley, and not, as you know, upon very good terms with him, though I do my best to avoid an absolute breach. I would buy Hawker's lobsters, if he came this way. But it is not worth his while to come for one customer.'

All this increased my liking for Hawker. I lost no time in obtaining several new books, and within ten days I took them over with me to Gulley's Cove. It was the first of many visits, during which I gradually learnt much of Hawker's history.

His father had been a Devonshire man and came from Exeter. He had gone to the American Colonies in consequence of some trouble known to the Hawker family as *the riot*. What riot it could have been William did not know. As a child he had supposed it to be some immense, historic upheaval, comparable to the Porteous Riots. But it would seem to have been one of those little commotions which history ignores. Some injustice, real or fancied, led to violence in the streets of Exeter. Some heads were broken, some ringleaders jailed, and Richard Hawker decided to get out of the country. I do not know whether this was from fear of the law or fear of his neighbours, but I should guess the latter, for he would appear to have been the kind of man who inevitably runs counter to popular sentiment.

He settled in Massachusetts, married, and did well in the trade of a cordwainer. He had several children but none, save William, survived infancy. When the American revolt broke out, this same contrary strain drove him to assert his loyalty to a German king whom he had never seen. He would not become an American citizen and removed with his family to Canada.

My friend William deplored this decision. He could remember very little of Marblehead, where he was born, but he would speak of it with such enthusiasm that I asked him once why he did not return to it.

'I should,' said he, 'if I were not happy here. I always intended to go, but could not while my father was alive. And then I married. So I said to myself that I am perfectly contented here and want for nothing. I have had enough of travelling. This is a sweet place. I don't care to leave it.'

The Hawkers remained in Canada until William was about fifteen years of age. The mother then died, and the father took to a roving life. He seems to have been the kind of man who never settles. William roved with him; some unexplained tie kept them together, for he grew very tired of it, yet would not leave the old man.

They were in the West Indies for some time. Word at length reached them of the death of a relative in Exeter and a small inheritance. They returned to England, claimed the money, and ended their wanderings by purchasing the farm at Gulley's Cove.

In William Hawker these circumstances had combined to produce a striking character. He had his father's independence of temper, but was a good deal more rational. Though a Briton there was little about him that might be described as English. He was, as near as may be, a man with no country at all, living on his little plot at Gulley's Cove like Alexander Selkirk upon his desert island. His neighbours called him *the American*, and I fancy that there was some justice in this, — that in spirit he belonged to that country rather than to any other. He should have returned to Marblehead. Had he done so he might have got the better of a certain melancholy which was not, I think, natural to him, but which sprung from too much solitude. He had seen too much of the world. Travel is a fine thing only when we can call some place *home*, and think it superior to any other.

He studied philosophy in an attempt to discover some logic in human affairs, which his wanderings had shown him to be totally disordered. He had a remarkable intellect. Upon many subjects, of course, he was very ill informed, but he was perfectly aware of that, and anxious for information.

In principle he was a Republican. He thought poorly of our British institutions, and many an argument did we have upon the subject. But, upon the other hand, he had none of the enthusiasm which generally accompanies revolutionary opinions. He expected little good to come of reform. He believed that injustice and the abuse of power are ineradicable evils in human society. We might, he said, get new masters, but we must for ever expect to live under tyranny of some sort.

He regarded himself as the equal of any man, but was quite free from that peevish, levelling strain which cries : *I am as good as you are.* True superiority, in any direction, he readily recognised and respected. I was struck by the calm impartiality with which he spoke of his foe, Mr. Lockesley, to whom he allowed some very good qualities.

'We might have a worse man to lead us,' he said, 'should Boney land upon our shores some dark night. Squire Lockesley would not run away, not he! He would never suppose that he could be beaten or that any of his people would disobey his orders to stand and fight. He is so stupid that I daresay he would give us guns and forget powder. But he would have us all there, in Boney's path, and Boney would have to account for every one of us, beginning with Squire Lockesley, before he could get on. And then he would but get five miles, and there would be another Lockesley in his path and it would be all to do over again.'

I think that it was William's innate sense of justice which most commanded my admiration.

Since his marriage he had been very happy. Mary, too, had had a hard and solitary life. An orphan, brought up by the Parish, she had been put to work at eight years old. When William first saw her she was servant to a farmer at Gulley's Cross. William was the first creature who ever spoke a kind word to her. I think his love must have begun in compassion, but, by the time that I knew them, it had become a strong and tender attachment.

For her he was the whole world. She could neither read nor write, but she was by no means a stupid girl. She turned out to be an excellent manager and she had, in her own way, a strong poetic strain. She was the sweetest singer I ever heard. I suppose that music had been her only joy, — the only release that she had ever known, in the brutish slavery of her life. She had but to hear a song or ballad once to remember it ; she knew scores. And there was, in the tones of her voice, a kind of wild pathos, and an attention to the sense of what she sang, which is unusual, even in the finest singers. William loved to hear her, and so did I, once we had overcome her natural shyness and got her to sing for me. For the most part she sang the rhymed psalms, or old country songs, — simple ditties of parted sweethearts, old battles, harvesting, sheep-shearing and the like, that you may hear in any ale-house or farm kitchen. But to many she imparted a strong degree of feeling, as though she gave a voice to those countless myriads who have worked, and loved, and died, leaving no memorial behind them save these strains of 'the unlettered Muse.'

There was one in particular, a favourite with me, for which I often asked. I wish now that I had not done so, and had not learnt to remember it so well. It was a kind of dialogue between a girl and her drowned sweetheart, whose phantom appears to her in the dead of night. He complains that he cannot rest for her endless lamentations and asks when she will have done weeping for him. She replies :

> When acorns fall from the mulberry tree,
> And the sun rises up in the West.

It is but a country jingle, but the pathetic note in her voice always brought tears to my eyes.

This friendship flourished for several years. After Newsome's marriage I once took Kitty with me to Gulley's Cove, hoping that she and Mary might become friends. But this scheme did not prosper. Kitty could not understand my regard for the Hawkers. She thought them very odd sort of people and could not quite forgive them for never coming to church. For my sake she tried to be affable. As a rule she gets on very well with cottagers and has the right manner with all, but here she was totally at a loss. She praised Mary's tidy kitchen and advised her in the management of the children, of whom the Hawkers now had two. William resented this. He was himself proud of Mary's good housekeeping, but this way of talking was new to him, — as though Mary were clean and industrious in order to win the approbation of her betters, rather than to make her husband and children comfortable. He became a little stiff. And it did, indeed, strike me as impertinent, though I had never thought so before, when I heard our ladies commending cottage women.

Kitty, for her part, did not like to see so many books in a house of that kind. She said that, for a man of Hawker's station, too much reading might be an evil and likely to unsettle his mind. The Bible should be enough for him. Both she and Newsome were puzzled at my attachment to Gulley's Cove. But they were as distressed and indignant as I was, when the blow fell which annihilated that little Eden.

Mr. Justice Hyde

IT was upon a night in July, and we were about to retire, when we heard a knocking at the Parsonage door. Newsome, supposing it a call from some sick parishioner, went out into the hall. A moment later we heard Mary's voice, raised in agonised supplication. Then she was with us, her dress disordered, her cap half off her head, and herself so distracted that she hardly knew what she did, as she flung herself upon me, grasping my arm and crying :

'Oh, Mr. Lufton ! Oh sir ! Save him ! Oh save my William ! They have taken him. They have pressed him for a sailor !'

We all exclaimed that this was impossible. A farmer could not be pressed. By whose authority had it been done ?

'Squire Lockesley——'

'But he has no power——'

'He says that William's books are wicked. They have found some wicked thing in one of William's books.'

It took a little time to get the story clear. William had been obliged to go to Ullacombe upon some business and had there, outside the ale-house, encountered a very foul-mouthed and drunken carter, one of Lockesley's men, with whom he had got into a fight. William was a peaceable man, but the carter had shouted out such intolerable insults, calling him a traitor and a rascally American, that he was obliged to knock the fellow down. Other Lockesleyites joined in and there was a brawl, and William was taken up for a breach of the peace. Lockesley, before whom he was brought, committed him to jail for assault and sent two constables to Gulley's Cove, in search of treasonable books. They removed several, including *The Rights of Man* and the Jefferson pamphlet. Lockesley, having these laid before him, declared that William was 'a malcontent and a notorious spreader of sedition,' and, as such, fit to be despatched forthwith into His Majesty's Navy, since the magistrates and sheriffs had been instructed, in every county, to make up the quota by impressing persons of that description.

We knew that any appeal to Lockesley would be useless. He had been long determined to get rid of

William. I set off next morning, at daybreak, to see the Sheriff, having rashly promised Mary that I would bring William back with me.

The Sheriff received me civilly enough and may have been impressed by the great names with which I bombarded him. I did not scruple to assert that I was intimately acquainted with half the peerage and that an uproar would ensue, in both Houses, if William were not instantly released. He was obliged to agree with me that the 'seditious' books in question might be found upon the shelves of the most respectable citizens, that the evidence against William was of a highly questionable sort, and that farmers are exempt from impressment. But he told me that he had no power to set aside the decision of a Justice of the Peace; for that I must get a writ of habeas corpus from a Judge of the High Court.

I might have known as much, and I cursed myself for the waste of time. When Miles is agitated he acts without reflection. To ride off instantly, and threaten somebody, had been my first impulse, and I had wasted the better part of the day in getting to Tipton St. John's, where the Sheriff lived.

Pronto, were he ever to exert himself upon another's behalf, which is not likely, would have managed the matter more wisely. Precipitate folly is not his weakness; he never acts without reflection, is seldom agitated, nor does he make applications in the wrong quarter. He would have foreseen the unlikelihood of getting the Sheriff to engage in a controversy with Lockesley.

I had, besides, some scruples about applying for a writ; I was far from sure of my ground. I meant to plead that farmers are exempt from forced service, but I doubted whether a judge, if he knew all, would rate William entirely as a farmer. At least half of his livelihood was earned by catching lobsters. And as for the charge of sedition, — a cottager who studies philosophy is so uncommon a creature that a stranger might not believe in my account of him. My case for False Imprisonment must depend upon a number of evasions and suppressions from which I shrank, and I had hoped that intervention by the Sheriff might save me from applying to a judge.

There is, I fear, no doubt whatever that Pronto at this juncture would have been a better friend for William, were he anybody's friend but his own. He would have gone directly to a judge, with a very good story ; he would, moreover, have known where to find a judge, for he makes it his business to know that sort of thing. But I never brought Pronto with me into Devonshire. I regarded my visits to Ullacombe as a vacation from Pronto ; I took no trouble to make acquaintance, and visited no houses where Newsome and Kitty were not received. I was perfectly unaware that Mr. Justice Hyde had a house near Dawlish, where he would certainly be found in July, since the Courts were in recess. Pronto would have known of it and would have dragged me off to call upon the old fellow, years before.

The Sheriff, however, gave me this information and told me, what I knew already, that I might come to the judge, for such a purpose, at any hour of the day or night. He told me also that I had little time to lose ; William would probably be at Exmouth, where a number of Devonshire men, recently pressed, had been collected, and they would be hurried aboard some vessel with all possible speed. They might indeed be gone already. He advised me that my quickest route to Dawlish would be to go to Exmouth and then cross the bay by boat, since I must otherwise take a wide detour inland.

The day was so far advanced that I decided to spend the night at Exmouth and to take a boat early in the morning. I asked him for a pass, enabling me to see

William, which he readily gave me. And so I set off
again, refusing his kind offer of refreshment, for I was in
a fever to be gone.

I could see that he wondered at my agitation and
thought me a very odd sort of Member of Parliament.
That I should exert myself on behalf of a friend did not
surprise him ; he seemed to be a just man and by no means
a tyrant of the Lockesley sort. But, though I tried to be
calm, I knew that my manner was that of an impulsive
youth who does not know the world. I could not help it.
Mary's tears, her anguish, were ever before my eyes.

Off I set, over some upland country which lies between
Tipton and the estuary of the Exe. The sun was setting
as I came out upon a view of the bay, with Exmouth lying
below me. Across the water lay the red cliffs of Dawlish,
and I saw how quickly the trip might be made by boat.
Exmouth has no harbour, but a good deal of small craft
lay at anchor in the bay and among them a sloop which
flew the Ensign. My heart sank when I saw this. I
feared that William might already be aboard of her.

I had meant to take some food before trying to see
him, but my agitation was so great that I hastened at once
to the guard-house where the Sheriff had said that he
might be confined. There I learnt that the pressed men
had not yet been taken off. They were waiting for a
party to come in from Dartmoor. The sloop was taking on
supplies and would not sail until the following afternoon.

The Sheriff's pass, my own credentials, and a guinea
to the guard, got me the accommodation of a small
chamber where I might talk to William undisturbed. I
waited there, and presently he was brought in to me. He
looked very pale, but calmer than I had expected. When
he saw who it was he smiled and grasped my hand.

'This is very good of you,' said he. 'How is Mary ?
Have you seen her ? How does she bear it ?'

'Please God,' I cried, 'I shall take you back to her tomorrow.'

I told him what I meant to do, but he shook his head and said that he feared I might be too late. Among his fellow captives it was believed that they would not wait beyond midnight for the Dartmoor party. They expected to be taken aboard at daybreak and to sail upon the morning tide. He thought that the sloop would go down to Plymouth, where they should be drafted to the vessels upon which they were to serve.

'In that case,' said I, 'I shall go on to Plymouth, as soon as I have got my writ. Once I have that, I can demand your release.'

'From whom could you demand it? You never saw Plymouth Roads! You might search among the vessels laying there for a week, and never find me, even supposing your writ gives you the right to board them. Nor is it to be supposed that anyone will help you. Having got their men, they will keep them if they can. No, no! Go back to Mary. You may be of the greatest service to her, but for me I am afraid that you can do nothing.'

He began to give me instructions as to the care of Mary and the children, to which I hardly attended, so resolved was I to bring him home. He seemed quite to have accepted his fate. He said that she must sell Gulley's Farm, for that there was more work there than she could well do alone. And he gave me a letter which he had written to her, hoping that he might find some means of sending it, before he was taken off. It was a great evil, he said, that she could not read, but I must read it to her and explain it, and I must assure her that he would come back, safe and sound, when the wars were over.

'And then,' said he, 'I shall take them all home to Marblehead.'

'How!' cried I. 'You mean to accept this injustice?'

'Why, what else can I do ? Mutiny, and get myself hanged ? A fine thing for Mary that would be !'

'But you are taken unjustly.'

'We are all taken unjustly, to my way of thinking.'

I burst into invective against the tyrant Lockesley, but he cut me short.

'As to that, a little tyrant sends me to fight a great one. Somebody, you know, must fight, if we are to keep Boney off. Why should I lie snug in my bed while others fight my battles for me ?'

'And why should I ?'

I thought that he gave me a queer look. He said nothing for a moment and then spoke of a cow in calf that was to be sold, or not sold, — I could not listen. I was thinking of Pronto's snug bed in Dover Street. Presently I interrupted him to ask if he did not think that the guards might be bribed to accept a substitute. I had plenty of money with me ; I had at least thought of that. Some poor creature, with nothing to lose, might well be willing to take William's place for fifty guineas : I did not suppose that the guards would be so nice as to mind whom they sent on board, provided they sent the correct tally.

'Easy enough,' said William, 'if any were willing to go. Two of my companions have tried it. But all the quota men of that kind are gone from these parts, long ago.'

'Then,' cried I, 'if all else fails, I shall go myself. No ! don't gainsay me ! I have no wife. I have no farm. Nobody would be a pin the worse if I died tomorrow. If anybody can be spared to defend our shores, I can. I am singularly useless to my friends in any other way.'

At that he became angry and desired me not to harass him by talking nonsense. What should a gentleman like myself do upon a ship of war ? I should be of very little use.

'You had best go back to your Parliament,' he said.

'For you know how to set about work of that kind. I am used to hardship and rough company. I know how to look out for myself. But you — you would be as helpless as a kitten.'

'I cannot go back to Mary without you. She was sure that I could save you, and I promised her.'

'Ah, poor thing ! She is very ignorant.'

This nettled me a little, for I knew that he thought me equally ignorant to have made such a promise. He had often accused me, in a good-natured way, of what he called 'a gentleman's ignorance.' He would have it that British justice, which I maintained to be the best in the world, had one face for the rich and powerful, another for the poor and weak. I had thought him prejudiced by his enthusiasm for the American institutions. I could see now that Lockesley's action shocked him less than it did me ; it was no more than he expected.

I repeated that I could not go back.

'There is very little that we cannot do if we are obliged,' he said. 'And besides, Mr. Lockesley will never leave me in peace at Gulley's Farm. I should only be taken again, and if you are not there poor Mary will have no friend.'

This was true. Half mad as I was, I saw it to be so.

'There is nothing for it,' said I, 'but to get that writ before daybreak, if I can. It is a full moon and a fine night. I shall instantly take a boat to Dawlish. If the judge is in bed, I'll have him out of it.'

'And supposing he will not give it to you ?'

'In that case I shall return here and go in your stead. I shall insist upon doing so. I am not as helpless as you think. You may have to leave Gulley's Cove, but you shall go back to Mary and I shall have kept my promise. But he shall give it ! He must give it ! I must lose no more time !'

I started up in such haste to be off that I scarcely bade him farewell.

At the water front I engaged a boat for the night and we set off for Dawlish. We passed close under the bows of the sloop. She lay dark upon the water; her rigging swayed gently against the clear night sky. I looked up at her and told myself that I should sail in her tomorrow, if there proved to be no other course. By tomorrow evening William would be again in Mary's arms, and he could take her 'home to Marblehead' — that 'sweet town' of which he could remember so little, but of which he always spoke so fondly.

'There are trees there,' he told me once. 'A great many trees, and the houses are of wood. 'Tis not like your fishing towns, that have no trees and are built of stone, — at Torhaven a man might be already at sea when he walks in the streets. But at Marblehead you may smell the earth and the trees. The land there smells stronger than the sea.'

My resolve filled me with exaltation, as though I had cast off fetters which had strangled me. I almost longed to sail in that ship, — to slip away from Pronto, who must be sleeping unawares in his snug bed at Dover Street, since he raised no word of protest. Hardship, exertion, rough usage, had no terrors for me. I believed myself equal to them all. William and Mary had been happy as I should never be; the best that I could do must be to preserve that felicity for them.

It was an exquisite moonlight night, with just such a gentle breeze as took us swiftly towards Dawlish. The lights of Exmouth, which had twinkled in the water, faded in the distance, but the riding light of the sloop stood out for a long time, as if beckoning to me.

We rounded Dawlish Head and came upon the town. It was growing so late that few lights were burning there.

I leapt ashore, bade the people in the boat await my return, and hurried off to find an inn. A drowsy ostler saddled me a horse and gave me the direction to Millstock House, where the judge lived.

Now that I was fully resolved how to act, and certain of saving William in any event, I had grown much calmer. All did not depend upon my getting the writ, although I was determined to get it if I could. I was able to consider what I should say, and was less afraid of saying too much ; I felt that I should cut a better figure with the judge than I had with the Sheriff. I rather hoped, however, that I might find him in bed and too sleepy to ask many questions.

Millstock House lay some two miles from Dawlish. I observed, as I rode up, that there were still lights in the lower rooms, as though the household had not yet retired. I hitched my horse to a ring by the door and rang the bell. Some time elapsed before it was answered, and I could hear a kind of clamour within, as though several people were shouting or singing. At length a servant appeared, none too sober, to whom I gave my card and explained my errand. When I asked to be taken to his master directly he looked doubtful, but he admitted me into the hall, where I waited while he went into an adjoining room, whence all the noise and singing came. There was plainly a drinking bout in progress. Some person was endeavouring to bawl a ballad whilst others were shouting him down. Presently the servant returned and said that he was very sorry, — his lordship was unable to attend to me.

'But he must do so !' I cried. 'Here is a case of false imprisonment. The laws of this country oblige him to attend to it.'

'I am afraid, sir——'

'Does he know that I am a Member of Parliament ?'

'If you will please to come in the morning, sir——'

'That will be too late. Take me to him instantly, or
it will be the worse for you ! British Justice must not be
denied in this manner !'

Shrugging his shoulders, he opened the dining-room
door and stood aside to let me pass.

My eyes were dazzled by a blaze of candles, my ears
confused by a babel of raucous voices, and my nose
assailed by the nasty stench of a debauch. Five or six
voices were shouting out a song, but were unable to com-
pete in volume with another which continually bellowed
for a jordan. When my vision cleared I could see a
number of men sprawling about a table. One of them
had risen and was staring at me.

'Here's Pronto !' he exclaimed.

I knew him slightly, — a very dissolute young fellow
called Wortley, whom I had met once or twice with
Crockett. He had but lately come into a fortune and was
getting through it as fast as he could. When sober he
would scarcely have had the assurance to call me Pronto,
but he now turned to the others and informed them that
I was his particular friend.

I asked for his lordship and was greeted by a yell from
the entire company :

'Down among the dead men !'

It was but too true. At the head of the table there
was an empty chair and under it was the master of the
house. Two or three of his guests were with him.

I looked to see if anybody there was sober enough to
understand me, and addressed myself to an old fellow
who still seemed able to pour his liquor into his glass
rather than down his waistcoat. To him I explained the
situation, imploring him to help me in bringing our host
to his senses, but he must have been drunker than he
seemed, for he answered not a word and continued to
stare pensively at the candle flames, as though he had not

heard. The rest meanwhile were demanding a song from me, for Wortley had informed them that I was a capital singer. I turned to the servant and assured him that his master would incur the most frightful penalties if he were not sufficiently revived to attend to me within the hour. I think that my manner really alarmed the man. He promised to do what he could, and staggered off in search of a colleague. Presently the two of them returned with a bucket of cold water, which they threw over his lordship without disturbing his slumbers in the least.

Much against my will, I was obliged to sing for the company and drink with them, for they were growing unfriendly. In a short time I was almost as drunk as they were. I did not take much, but I was exhausted with fatigue, hunger and anxiety. I lost all sense of time and do not know how often we tried, vainly, to revive the judge. We poured several gallons of water over him, hoisted him into his chair, and slapped his face ; but he remained completely insensible and slipped to the floor again as soon as we let him go.

At one time all the company appeared to be ardently interested in my cause. They were as determined to rouse him as I was, and repeatedly cried that :

'He mush do Brish Jushtish elsh why do we pay th' old shod ?'

I must have told them some part of the story, for I can remember Wortley drinking a toast to Mary Hawker and howling a maudlin song about her :

' Remember the vows that you made to poor Mary !
Remember the bower where you promised to be true !'

And I recollect that I was weeping and telling them that we might all be happy if we could go home to Marble-head, because there were so many trees there. I can hear my own voice, sobbing this out, in a room which had

grown more silent, since most of my company had passed
into oblivion. At last I must have joined them.

I wakened with a start. The candle flames were
guttering out and the grey of early daylight struggled
through the windows. All my companions were now
upon the floor amid swimming water, wine, broken glass
and vomit.

I rose and reeled round the table to take a last look at
the judge, in case he might show signs of coming to. He
lay upon his face. I touched his hand and thought it
uncommonly cold, though, to be sure, he had been
drenched in water several times. Trying to pull him
over, I found him stiff. He must have been dead for
some hours. I suppose he had had some kind of seizure,
and had probably been dead when we set him up in the
chair and slapped him.

This discovery completely sobered me. I tried to
summon the servants, but neither shouts nor tugs at the
bell-rope had any effect. They must have been sleeping
off the night's carouse in some distant part of the house.

The day was breaking fast and I was in haste to
return to Exmouth. I thought that I might leave them
to make the discovery in their own time, since there was
nothing to be done for the old man save carry him from
that pig-sty and shroud him decently. I could not risk
any further delay. I let myself out into the cold dawn,
mounted my horse, and fled from Millstock House.

The sky was turning red as I reached Dawlish. I
paid for the horse and got back to my boat. My thoughts
were clear and decided, and my head ached. I intended
to take William's place, though I felt none of the exultation
which had sustained me the night before. I did not fear
the fate before me. No quarters could be more disgusting,
no company worse, than those in which I had spent the
night. But I had no hope, either for myself or for any

other human being. The happiness which I had pictured for my friends now appeared to be an illusion, — insubstantial as the rosy clouds of dawn which had glimmered for a short time, and then sunk into the greyness of a rainy morning. I could not feel that it signified very much whether I stayed or went. But I had made a promise and I intended to keep it.

The wind was up and the sea grew choppy as we rounded the head. A great mass of rain clouds had come down over Exmouth and obscured the wide gap of the river estuary. The little boats at anchor in the bay were bobbing up and down. I looked about me for the sloop and could not find her.

I thought that I must have been mistaken about her position. I could not believe that she was gone until I landed at Exmouth and was assured by the people there that she had sailed at dawn.

Newsome

I was half-way back to Ullacombe before I discovered that I had, during the night's debauch, lost the letter which William had entrusted to me for Mary.

This circumstance gave me more pain than anything else, — a greater sense of failure. I had not even done what he asked me to do, which was far less than what I had promised. And I could not remember half his directions about the farm.

It was dark when I reached the Parsonage, for I had been obliged to sleep for a little at an inn at Exmouth, before setting out. Kitty and Newsome hurried to meet me and saw, by my face, that I brought no good news. I asked at once for Mary and learnt that she had returned to Gulley's Cove, for her children were there and she could not leave them for long. Almost mechanically I began to mount my horse again, meaning to go to her, but Kitty prevented me.

'You cannot go tonight,' she said. ''Tis past ten o'clock. Mary won't expect you. And you are wet to the skin.'

'I must not leave her waiting through another night.'

'If you had good news there might be some sense in your going on. What you have to tell may keep.'

So I came in and sat by a fire that they had lighted, for they expected me to come home cold and wet. They brought me food and mulled wine. Presently I began to feel warm again. Kitty's eyes were red, as though she had been crying, and, when she left the room to warm my bed, I asked Newsome if anything was amiss.

'Nothing,' said he, 'except this business of poor Mary Hawker. She has been crying over it for two days. She went to Gulley's Cove yesterday; I am afraid that poor woman quite believes that a Member of Parliament may do anything. Kitty tried to warn her that you might fail, but she refused to believe it.'

Kitty returned just then, and I was so much moved that I rose and kissed her. I loved my sister very much for her kind heart. She burst into fresh tears. Her disapproval of the Hawkers was all forgotten; she could think of nothing but Mary's grief. I gave them a brief account of my efforts, suppressing the fact that I had intended to sail in William's stead, for I knew that they would think it extravagant.

'As to disposing of the farm,' said Kitty, 'we will help her with that. It will give her a little money in hand. But I think that she had better get out of this neighbourhood; there is such a strong prejudice against the Hawkers. Yet she must not go wandering off among strangers. She should be near friends who will read William's letters to her and advise her. If we could but get her to Bramfield! My mother would care for her. In the old days the Chadwicks would have found some cottage — but one cannot hope that from Mrs. Ned. Perhaps we might get her a place as lodge-keeper at some great house. You must keep your eyes open, Miles, for something of that kind, among your grand friends.'

'I cannot think so far ahead,' I replied. 'What am I to say to her tomorrow? How am I to tell her?'

'You had better let me come with you. She will need another woman about her at such a moment.'

'Kitty! Could you bear to come?'

'To be sure I shall come. And so will Boo.'

She, also, refuses to call Newsome Augustus. Why he should be *Boo* I know not, but she vows that it exactly suits him. He said that he should certainly come. I realised that, in their quiet way, they were both as indignant as I was, and as shocked by Lockesley's vindictive abuse of power. I went to bed a little comforted, and in the morning we all rode over to Gulley's Cove.

Where the lane turned down to the farm, Kitty dismounted. She said that she would walk to the cottage and that we were to wait for half an hour before joining her. She went off, looking very pale. I realised that she was going to tell Mary before we came and that the worst was to be spared me.

Newsome and I sat upon our horses and gazed out over the sea. I told him that I was resolved to go to Portsmouth. I thought that I might still make some effort on William's behalf. Henry Dawson, who had been Caroline's husband, was at Portsmouth. He was now a Captain, and had lately married again, but we still saw something of him, for Caroline's little boy remained in my mother's care at Bramfield. I thought that Dawson might be able to tell me if there was anything further to be done.

'Not a bad idea,' agreed Newsome, 'but I should say nothing of it to Mary, if I were you. It would be cruel to raise her hopes, unless something comes of it.'

I said that I should not, and sat silent for some time, wondering if I should tell him my real reason for going to Portsmouth. I had not now very much hope of getting William out of the Navy, but I was resolved to join it myself. His look was hard to forget, — the look which he gave me when I asked him why he should fight my battles. To return to Pronto and Dover Street, after these scenes, was impossible. If such men as William were to be forced into the fighting, I should know no peace until I had joined them. That appeared to be the only kind of amends which I could offer to Mary. In all else, especially in the matter of practical help and advice, Newsome and Kitty were worth ten of me. *They* led useful, happy and contented lives. My own, just then, struck me as being singularly worthless.

I looked at Newsome and thought how little he had altered since I first made his acquaintance, at thirteen years old, and he had laughed when I asked if his father did not consider himself a gentleman. The men we were to become might already have been discerned. I was still wondering how to consider myself, while he had never wasted two thoughts upon such a topic.

Words were not easy in which to tell him of my intention. I knew that he would think it foolish. As a sort of preparation I gave him fuller particulars of the scene at Millstock House than I had thought fit to mention when Kitty was by. I described the drunken debauch and then asked Newsome whether he did not think the life of a bluejacket infinitely preferable to that led by some gentlemen.

'Sailors can get as drunk as gentlemen,' said he, 'and can be quite as nasty. Pray don't begin to think all sailors heroes because Hawker has been pressed.'

This was so near to the knuckle that I was silenced. His next remark, therefore, surprised me:

'Though I have sometimes thought it a pity that you did not enter the Service yourself. I believe that it would have suited you very well.'

'Do you indeed?' I cried.

'Why yes. I think an active life would have suited you. Your father thought you a scholar, but you are not, you know. You have no strong bent and you are inclined to mope. You would not do so, if you lived amidst danger and exertion.'

'I am inclined to agree with you,' said I. 'And I don't see that it is too late to change.'

I would have said more, but he remarked that half an hour was gone and that we should proceed to the cottage.

We descended the hill and tethered our animals by the gate. Before entering the house Newsome surprised me by drawing on, beneath his hose, a pair of red flannel knee-caps, explaining that he always did so, by Kitty's desire, when visiting people in trouble. He was inclined to rheumatism in the knees and Kitty believed that this malady might be aggravated by prolonged kneeling upon cold stone floors.

'And very often it is damp as well,' he said. 'Poor people will scrub their floors before the Parson comes.'

I asked if he meant to pray for Mary, feeling a lively repugnance at the thought of witnessing such a scene.

'I might have occasion to do so.'

'If she should ask for it, you mean?'

'I don't always wait to be asked. I must judge for myself. The solemnity of prayer often has a calming effect upon people who are distracted by grief. The mere repeating of familiar words will recall them a little to themselves. But when the sufferer is perfectly composed I try to acquaint myself with his state of mind before offering the consolations of religion.'

The cottage door was open and Kitty's voice called to us to enter. She had flung off her bonnet and was seated upon the hearth-settle with her arm round Mary's waist. The two little children were in a kind of pen which William had made to keep them out of the way of the fire; they stood unsteadily, holding to the rails of this pen, and watched the scene with solemn eyes.

Mary lifted her head from Kitty's shoulder and looked at me. There was no reproach in her eyes. I had dreaded that above all things, but there was none, and I immediately wished that there had been. Resentment is a protection; it shields some part of our minds, so that we are not entirely exposed to the full blow of calamity. When we can blame this or that person, we are not feeling the worst pain. But I saw that she had forgotten my rash promises. She was aware of nothing save her loss.

She was deathly pale and she looked very much surprised, as though she beheld something which she could not completely credit. I have, since then, caught sight of this pale astonishment upon other faces. I pass it in the street continually. Despair, mute and surprised, goes quietly about its business, unrecognised, save by those who have once been obliged to scan it fully. *They* must see it for ever. It dogs them all their lives, with a promise of what we must expect when we meet at compt.

Newsome advanced, and sat beside the women on the settle.

'It must be of the greatest comfort to William,' he said, 'to know that he can be certain of your fortitude. What pangs he would suffer, if he could not rely upon you! And how glad you must be that there is this, that you can do for him.'

'Yes indeed,' cried Kitty. ''Tis in such times that a man may bless himself that he has got a good wife.'

'And he knows,' continued Newsome, 'that you have good friends about you. Mr. Lufton was able to assure him of that.'

I found myself obliged to come forward, still tortured by the thought of that lost letter and the messages that I had forgotten. I said hastily that William desired her not to lose heart, for that he would come back, safe and sound, when the wars were over.

'And when will that be, sir?' asked Mary faintly, as though she depended upon us to tell her.

'Very soon, I daresay,' declared Kitty. 'A tyrant is never permitted to live for long. And then, you know, William will write to you and you may write to him.'

'Ah, Ma'am, I can't read or write. He was teaching me——'

'I will write for you, — anything you bid me say. We will tell him how cleverly you are managing.'

Mary shook her head and murmured that she should not know how to manage without William, that she was very ignorant and had had no schooling. She had looked to him for everything.

'You may overcome all trials,' said Newsome, 'if you look to our Heavenly Father. If you please, we will pray to Him now, that He may give you strength.'

We all knelt and he repeated the Lord's Prayer. Kitty and Mary joined with him, but I could not. I was suffocated with a needless anxiety lest he should repeat the prayer for Those at Sea. I might have known him better; he was not likely to increase Mary's sorrows by reminding her that William was not only gone, but gone into danger. He proceeded to the prayer for All Sorts and Conditions of Men. Then, raising Mary up, he seated himself again beside her upon the settle. I thought that she did look a little more collected. He began to talk to her in a low voice and she seemed to be attending.

Kitty and I went over to talk to the quiet little children in the pen. The younger had fallen asleep upon an old sack, but the elder was inclined to whimper. I lifted him up and sat with him on my knee, upon the old bench by the lobster-pots. He was a fine little fellow, with Mary's eyes. He knew me well, of course, and sat there, contentedly enough, playing with my watch and seals.

I could only catch a word or two of Newsome's discourse to Mary. He seemed to be reminding her of the forlornness of her condition before she married William, and pointing out that her lot, in spite of this temporary trial, was a thousand times better. She seemed to listen very earnestly, but I think that she took more comfort from the tone of his voice than from the sense of what he said. Newsome's voice in the pulpit is nothing extraordinary. He is not an eloquent preacher. But in conversation it has a friendly warmth which is heartening.

It was with some stupefaction that I remembered my own proposal, five years before, to take Orders and be Vicar of Ullacombe. I had thought myself equal to tasks of this kind! I had, in fact, always supposed that I should make a better parson than Newsome, since I might have preached a better sermon.

Kitty, meanwhile, was unpacking a basket that she had brought with her. She took out a bottle of wine and a fowl, ready cut up. Moving quietly about the room, she set a meal upon the table. I was reminded of the meal that I had watched Mary set, on my first coming to the cottage, when William sat, where I sat now, mending his nets. The whole anguish of it broke over

me afresh, as I thought of the haven which this little
house had seemed to me then.

'When Boo goes, you should go with him, I think,'
murmured Kitty, coming up to me. 'I shall stay with
Mary for a little and make her eat a good meal.'

'But we have given her no advice about the farm,'
said I. 'William thinks that she should sell it.'

'That must wait. 'Tis too soon to speak to her of it.
She cannot comprehend much more today.'

Mary suddenly sprang up in a wild burst of sobbing,
whereat I heard Kitty give a low exclamation of relief.
The little boy slipped from my knee and ran to his mother.
Newsome and I hurried from the house.

'Best leave her to Kitty now,' he said.

Before we mounted our horses he methodically removed
his red flannel protecters and advised me to brush the
sand from my knees.

We rode away from Gulley's Cove. I suppose that I
shall never see it again. A farmer at Gulley's Cross
bought the land, but the cottage remains empty. Few
would care to live in so secluded a spot. In time it will
fall down and become a ruin.

'I imagine,' said I, as we went home, 'that you are
accustomed to such scenes?'

'Pretty well. This was not so painful as some. Mary
won't starve, and William may some day return to her.
One can offer some rational consolation. But sometimes . . .'

He broke off and shook his head.

'I wonder then,' said I, 'that you can endure it.'

'Why, Miles, I believe what I tell them. Without
religion, I do not see how human existence is to be
supported. If there is to be no hope of another, and a
better world, — but I have that hope, and would wish to
impart it to others.'

I had never before heard him speak so warmly of his calling. I had thought that he took Orders merely as a means of livelihood. And so, I daresay, he did; but his heart was in his work.

He and Kitty appeared to lead so placid and cheerful a life that I had imagined this distressing part of his duties to weigh but lightly upon his mind. I had always regarded myself as being the more sensitive to human suffering. I had taken it for granted that all clergymen must pray in cottages. My father, I know, did so without any very painful feelings; he was confident that he relieved poor sufferers. But, for Newsome, I could see that it had been a considerable effort, both of mind and spirit. He looked pale and tired.

'Does it appear to you,' I said suddenly, 'that we are more humane? That we feel for others more than our fathers did?'

'Possibly. What of it?'

That is just like Newsome. If one propounds an idea to him he will always ask: *What of it?* He never muses. I replied that if we had really become a different people we should, perhaps, set about managing our affairs in a different way.

'What affairs? Do you propose to abolish suffering by Act of Parliament?'

'I suppose that the burden of suffering might be more equally distributed. The poor might be better protected against it than they are, if all were determined that it should be so.'

'Well! That is your business, not mine. When you have made every labourer in the country as happy as your friend Chalfont I will engage a curate for all the praying that I shall have to do.'

Kitty joined us at Ullacombe late in the afternoon, bringing a good report of Mary. The cow had calved

and Mary had attended the creature with signal success ;
she was not a little proud of herself, since William had
formerly undertaken such tasks.

Both Kitty and Newsome were as cheerful as usual
that evening, and I knew that they did not think the better
of me for my continued low spirits. But I felt that I
should not know an easy moment until I had taken some
decisive step. They had done what they could, and were
entitled to peace of mind. I had done nothing. I was
not content to allow that William's misfortune was of a
common sort which could be deplored and forgotten. It
appeared to me that the emotions which had governed me
during the past three days must lead me to some definite
conclusion. *Our feelings must ever be our best guide*.
Guide to what ? *What of it ?* I hoped to find out at
Portsmouth.

Captain Dawson

THESE memories still have power to agitate me beyond
what I could have thought possible. For some days I
have been unable to continue my memoir.

My health is much improved. I am, in fact, quite
well enough to get back to town. But whereas, a month
ago, I was eager to be off, I am now tempted to linger. I
have made no effort to arrange my progress of summer
visits, although it is now June.

Pronto keeps very quiet and does not plague me to be
up and doing. I suspect him. He has deceived me before
by this sham quiescence. Has he given up all hopes of
a place ? Does he mean to devote himself henceforth
entirely to conveyancing ?

I wish that I were certain he does not mean to turn
his coat ! To be sure, our Tory friends may have done

as much for us as they will ever do, but what interest does Pronto hope to secure among the Whigs? He has, I know, assurance enough for anything; he is *capable de tout*. But I don't see how he hopes to manage this somersault. I suppose that a few years of purification, during which we attend to our legal practice, might be the first step in such a course. It must, in any case, be several years before the other fellows have anything to offer us. Pronto is no rat, to desert a sinking ship. He transfers himself to fresh quarters in a manner which smacks of integrity and principle, while the fatal rocks are still a great way off. I believe it to be Pronto's opinion that Reform must come within the next dozen years. He is not so sure, though, whether it will be the work of Whigs, who have got in, or of Tories, who are determined not to be thrown out. And she who might have told him is no more.

The countryside is very lovely at this time of year. I am able to ride again and I went yesterday with Sukey over to Ribstone. The dog roses are blooming and the hay as good as ever I saw it. Please God we have a good harvest! Two bad ones in succession have come hard upon our people. How the poorest make shift to live I don't know, with bread the price it is. Wheat is double what it was two years ago. There is trouble everywhere, riots, rick-burning and the like. I suppose that it must always be so, after a long period of war, but it must be felt most sharply in such places as Bramfield where the Squire has no conscience.

Sukey was delighted with her outing. We talked much of old times and she reminded me of many little particulars which had slipped my memory. I have never felt myself so much in sympathy with her. She reminded me that our mother had her own names for many wild flowers, —

not the names common among the country people here. She must have learnt them from her Irish mother. We passed by Ribstone Pit which was full of the weeds which, round here, are called dandelions. Sukey remembered that our mother called them 'golden lads', and the seeds, which are here sometimes called dandelion clocks, she called 'chimney sweepers' on account of their likeness to the brushes which are used for that purpose.

'In a few weeks,' said Sukey, 'Ribstone Pit will be a sea of chimney sweepers.'

I believe that she might be a very agreeable companion, could she but escape from the penance of her life here. Some provision must be made for her when my father dies. I must see to it. She shall not be left to live with George and Anna. I have already provided for her in my Will, but I must consider a nearer future than that. I think it possible that she might do well, and be very happy, as housekeeper for me when I get to Troy Chimneys. She would be her own mistress and could do as she pleased, so long as she made me comfortable. A grateful sister is more biddable than a wife. She has a good mind and would, with a little encouragement, read more. She can talk amusingly. But she must learn to keep a good table. Upon that I should insist. Here she takes no trouble and, of course, has not the money to lay out that I should give her. I dropped a hint of this scheme to her and she was overjoyed. It is very pleasant to think that Troy Chimneys may bring unalloyed felicity to *her*. For me it can never be what I once hoped, but I shall feel that I have not laboured all these years in vain. My mother would have been pleased at this plan. She would have allowed that I am not entirely selfish.

We came home by Ridding's farm and I stopped to call to Harry over the hedge. I had not seen him for a great while. He now has the farm which his father had

before him, and he married, some years ago, a girl from
Chipping Campden. It is a snug place; the best farm, I
think, upon the Bramfield property.

I was surprised at the black look that he gave me,
though black looks are now pretty common hereabouts.
He came up with an unwilling air, as though angry at
being taken from his hay-making. I asked him how he
did and he scowled.

'What's wrong, man?' cried I. 'Is anything amiss?'

'You should know. You gentry should know if there
is anything amiss when a man is turned out of his farm.'

It did not occur to me, at first, that he could be
speaking of himself. I thought that he was indignant on
behalf of some neighbour, and asked who the man was.

'Myself, to be sure,' said he. 'I am to be flung out at
Midsummer. They have got the law against me.'

Our exclamations of surprise and indignation soon
convinced him that we knew nothing of it and he became
a little more civil. He came out into the lane and told us
some of the particulars.

I think that it is the worst thing they have done yet.
It is all that woman's work, of course. She is so stupid
that she cannot even understand her own advantage;
she will never get another tenant so good.

It is not only the bad harvests; he has had singularly
ill luck in other ways, pest among his cattle, and a flood
at Ribstone brook which ruined his haystacks. And then
he spent too much of his savings upon a new barn, having
reason to understand that half the cost of it was to be
borne by Ned. That is the work of a rascally attorney,
employed by Mrs. Ned as an agent; he is continually
playing tricks of that sort, I believe. Harry says that
Ned told him to build the barn and said that he would
pay half. Now this Simmons, this agent, denies that
there was any agreement and asks for evidence!

Be that as it may, poor Harry has got behind with his rent, has forfeited his lease, and is told to quit. I am sure that he could pull round, were he given time. But Simmons wants the farm for his son, a half-witted creature who never ploughed a furrow in his life. I urged upon Harry to see an attorney of his own, — I gave him the name of one in Tewkesbury. Although he has nothing written, he has witnesses of Ned's spoken promise about the barn. And they are cheating him in other ways; they are turning him out at such short notice that he will have to sell his stock at a disadvantage. I daresay Simmons hopes to buy it at a bargain. But he declares that attorneys are all scoundrels together and that he will get no justice among them, though they will take what is left of his money. He is a pig-headed fellow and too ignorant to look after his own interests.

Sukey, as we rode home, asked me if I could not remonstrate with Ned. But that I cannot do; I must keep out of Ned's affairs. Remonstrance would be useless. Any person supporting Harry Ridding must join battle with Mrs. Ned. A stranger might do that, but I cannot. For me she is too dangerous an antagonist.

Yet I hate a tyrant, and I feel almost as indignant for Harry as I did for William Hawker. Ten years have not taught me to take these things in a philosophical mood. They rouse in me a passion of rebellion. But nothing comes of it. My passion blows away, like the chimney sweepers.

I had best get back to Portsmouth and the set-down I got from Captain Dawson.

Every incident of my ride to Dawlish, and my return to Ullacombe, is printed for ever upon my memory. But I can recollect nothing at all of my journey to Portsmouth, — how I travelled, or when I reached it. This is not

surprising ; I am often astonished that I should remember
as much as I do. Miles has this retentive capacity, I
suppose, because so very little has happened to him in
the course of thirty-six years. Pronto's powers of recollection are of a different sort. He has facts, names and
dates at his command. But he is not plagued by 'the
inward eye' as Ludovic would call it. No scenes are
printed upon *his* memory for ever, and that is one thing
for which to be thankful ! Were I burdened with *Pronto's*
memory—

I suppose that I must have travelled post to Portsmouth, for I intended to go on to London after. I had
not seen Dawson for some years nor had I met his new
wife. They had visited Bramfield, and the family had
reported her to be well enough, if one did not remember
that she succeeded Caroline. She was, I think, anxious
to be upon good terms with us, for it was highly convenient
to her that we should have the care of little Frank.

My first recollection of Portsmouth is of dining with
the Dawsons at their lodgings, in a large party, and of
feeling that dismay which always comes upon me when I
must be Miles to some of the company and Pronto to
others.

To Henry Dawson I was Miles ; he had only met me
at Bramfield and our closest acquaintance had been in
those happy days when he was courting Caroline, before
Edmée came to the Park. But with Mrs. Dawson it was
otherwise. In her eyes I was an M.P. and a man of
fashion. She knew all about me, knew with whom I was
generally seen when in town, knew at what houses I
habitually stayed. She had, so she said, quite longed to
meet me, and I was forced to rattle away to her in a very
Pronto-ish style which caused poor Dawson to open his
eyes. She was an elegant, pretty woman, but too fine for
a sailor's wife. She could not endure Portsmouth and

was uneasily aware that her husband merely commanded a sloop, while my brother Eustace was captain of a frigate.

Dawson, meanwhile, was talking eagerly to his brother officers and, when I could attend to them, I found myself unable to understand a word that they said. For the greater part of the meal they talked of some French and Dutch prizes, then refitting in the dockyards. When the ladies left us they endeavoured, out of courtesy to me, to change the subject; they brought up one which they imagined must be within my comprehension. I might be excused for not knowing the difference between a mizzen course and a driver, but the whole nation must be disturbed by the strength of the American fleet, especially by their 44-gun frigates, and must be asking how we should come off, should we ever be called upon to engage them. Some of those present insisted that we must cut down our own seventy-fours to the clamps of the quarter-deck and the forecastle, to make what they called *razée* frigates. Others maintained that we should build new vessels with a complete spar deck to carry thirty guns.

'You will see,' said Dawson, 'that we shall have both, soon enough, if ever we have to fight the Americans.'

'Ay and that will come!' cried another. 'For they hate us worse than the French do.'

But Dawson was talked down by another fellow who had served on the *Endymion* and declared that ships of this class could engage any frigate upon the seas. He was by far the most persuasive talker and convinced me that he must know best. I had no very great opinion of Dawson's ability, but Dawson turned out to be right, I believe. Not long ago Eustace told me that the *Leander* and some other ship had been built to meet the American forty-fours.

They kept up this talk, without intermission, for about two hours. My head went round, though Pronto (who turned out to be there all the time *incognito*) listed some facts and figures which were useful to him later.

Dawson and his friends had been at this work for the best part of their lives and had thought of little else since they were twelve years old. As I listened, I began to perceive that I could never be of their company. 'Exertion and danger' might be all very well, as a cure for my *moping*, and I could fancy myself at sea, taking part in an action, but I could never, when on shore, take part in this kind of conversation. To be a sailor, one must think a great deal about ships.

Yet some obstinate part of my mind still enquired why William should be taken and I not. I determined to go through with the business, so soon as I could secure a private interview with Dawson, trusting that there might prove to be some way in which an active and healthy man of six and twenty might serve his country upon the high seas.

We eventually adjourned to the dockyards where a ship was building which Dawson wished me to see. She was modelled upon a Dutch vessel, the *Hippomenes*, captured at the surrender of Demerara, in which business he had taken part. He discoursed to me at some length upon the merits of this kind of craft. By the time that he had done I was so much exhausted that I returned to my inn and went to bed.

The morning found me still more reluctant to confide in him. It was clear to me that I was totally unfit to hold any position of responsibility upon a ship of war; it would be years before I had learnt a tenth part of all that I should know. And, if I meant to volunteer as a rating, I need take no advice from Dawson. I had merely to offer myself to the first recruiting party I might meet.

Why then, thought I, am I here? I must, to be sure, make some enquiries on William's behalf, but how can

Dawson help me to settle with my own conscience?

When setting out for Portsmouth I had intentionally rejected any rational consideration because I feared that it would work against my purpose. I knew perfectly well that mine was a lunatic scheme, — to break off so promising a career in favour of one which had never possessed the least attraction for me. But I believed that this lunacy might save me. The Christian martyrs — all, indeed, who follow conscience at the expense of self-interest — might be described as lunatics. I had entertained a confused notion that Dawson might take me in his ship and find a use for me, or might recommend me to some friend, — in what capacity I could not imagine, but I had been content to set this vagueness down to my own ignorance and to hope that Dawson might have some suggestion.

Waking in the sober light of morning, with all my wits about me, I perceived my own folly. However strong might be my determination to quit my present course of life, I had been already in it long enough to impair my fitness for any other. My capabilities had been for years entirely concentrated upon the grand task of making my fortune; they were now, to some extent, contracted and modified by the usage that they had received. I had, in Newsome's company, perceived my unfitness for Orders. I now doubted whether I should ever make a capable sailor. The mere desire to be useful was not enough; I was deficient in those qualities which might make me of use, qualities which Dawson and his friends, though they were nothing out of the ordinary, most certainly possessed. They had a passion for their profession which kept them talking of open timber heads by the hour together. Ambitious they might be, greedy of advancement and prize money, envious of one another, but their hearts were in their ships.

I had invited Dawson to breakfast and he duly appeared. He was a good deal altered since I had known him at Bramfield, and not altered for the better. *Then* he had been a handsome young fellow, in whom every virtue had been aroused to the full by his strong attachment to my sister. And his prospects, at that time, had been excellent, for he had an uncle or cousin at the Admiralty whose interest might secure him early promotion.

But Caroline was no more, and he had not got on as he deserved. His great relative had died or forgot him. Five years of exposure, hardship and disappointment had extinguished all that prepossessing ardour, nor was his second marriage as happy as his first. He had been continually in action, but action of that commonplace and useful kind which continues from day to day, and which we are inclined to forget in favour of those few great engagements which are all that the world knows in the history of a war. He had been passed over, again and again, and would probably never rise higher than the command of a sloop.

In my mood of humility I respected him and felt him to be a better man than I, but I was also obliged to think him very dull.

As soon as we had set to work upon our bacon and eggs I opened the case of William, but had some difficulty in getting his full attention. He began by thinking that I hoped to secure William's release and interrupted me with an assurance that he had no influence in that way. I would do better if I applied to Eustace. Set right upon this point he fell into a bitter complaint upon the policy which sent these malcontents into the Service. Your *reading fellows*, said he, were the plague of every commander and at the bottom of every mutiny. The trouble at the Nore had all been got up by rascals of that sort. Their leader had been a schoolmaster, if you please, and as rank a Jacobin as ever graced a gallows. Your reading fellows will bring politics into everything. I might see as much, if I would consider how differently matters went in what he called 'the breeze at Spithead.' *That*, he maintained, was no mutiny; it was but a little noise made by honest bluejackets who had grievances enough, God knew, but who put the blame where it belonged, — not upon their officers, but upon a Pay Office ashore, which robbed them. At any hour they would have put to sea directly, if the French had been troublesome. They would never have failed their officers.

It was some time before I could manage to convince him that William, though a reading fellow, was sensible, well disposed, and unlikely to lead a mutiny. I believed him determined to make the best of it, and I merely wished to know how I might get news of his welfare and whereabouts.

Dawson, when he had grasped this, grew more attentive. He listened to the whole story and ended by getting up quite a regard for William, saying that he wished he got more men of that temper on his sloop.

'You may depend upon it he will do well,' he said, 'and may soon expect to be made a petty officer. We are short of men fit for that work, and it does no harm if *they* have had some schooling. As for his wife, he will be able to send her a letter from the Depot Ship, when he knows to what vessel he will be drafted.'

He also asked me to let him know these particulars, as soon as I had got them, in case it should ever be in his power to do William a good turn. He might know something of William's commander, and be able to drop a word to him. He mentioned some vessel then at Plymouth, the name of which I forget, but it began with a B, and might have been the *Boyne*, the *Bellona* or the *Blenheim*, — upon which he hoped that William might serve, for she was, he said, a very good ship. It was a thousand pities that Eustace was in the Mediterranean and that I could not have gone to him, 'for I am sure he would be very glad to get hold of such a man, and *he* might have some chance of doing it. As for me, if I got such an one, I daresay I should lose him. You would not credit the shabby tricks that have been played upon me.'

He wandered off into a disconsolate account of the intrigues whereby commanders got away each other's men, complaining that brisk young fellows, with a turn for the sea, never came his way, — that he got none but cripples and jail-birds, and he might count himself lucky if he put to sea with a crew that had arms and legs. There is that side to every profession, — the jealousies, the feuds and the shabby tricks.

By the time that we had finished with Dawson's grievances we had almost finished breakfast, and I had still said nothing of what was uppermost in my mind. I looked at his stolid red face and wondered how to begin.

'It appears to me that these things are managed very unjustly,' I said at last. 'Here is a fellow like William, taken from his wife and children, and from a farm which will run to ruin without him, while gentlemen like myself are left in peace.'

'Why,' said Dawson, 'we don't want for officers, you know.'

'I suppose not. But I think I should have chosen the Navy as my profession, had I been able to foresee what dangers my country was going to encounter. I don't like to sit snug at home whilst others are forced to fight for me.'

He gave a start of surprise and stared at me a little thoughtfully.

'Would you not feel it so, in my place?' I asked him.

'Why, you don't sit snug alone,' he said. 'Most

Britons do the same. And some fellows must be in Parliament, I suppose, else we should have no British Constitution to defend.'

He thought this a capital joke and laughed heartily as he repeated :

'Ay, ay! We need some fellows to be sitting in Parliament.'

I repeated that I disliked that occupation and asked him outright if it was possible for a man of my age to join the Navy. At that he seemed thunderstruck, but was not, when he discovered that I was in earnest, as derisive as I had feared. There was, indeed, something almost apologetic in his manner, as he assured me that my plan was impossible.

'To be of use in the Service, you know, a man must have been bred up to it.'

'William Hawker was not.'

'Ay, but he is a bluejacket. I speak of officers. There is no way but to start at the beginning. A man of your age could not well take service as a midshipman, amongst boys of twelve years old.'

'But is there, then, no way in which I may fight for my country ?'

'Well, to be sure, you might join the Army. For *that* you need know nothing in particular. You have but to purchase a commission.'

I objected that the Army did not fight. Nor did it at that period. The danger upon the seas had been averted by our Navy, but the great military campaigns had not begun. We had not yet met Buonaparte upon land and some of us doubted whether we should ever do so. It is difficult now to recall our want of faith in our armies, ten years ago. When heard of, they were in retreat, and the unsuccessful expeditions to South America and Egypt had still further depressed our spirits.

'There is to be fighting now in Portugal,' said Dawson. 'They say that Wellesley is sailed from Ireland with a large force and that Moore is called back from Sweden.'

'It will be over in a week or so,' said I. 'Depend upon it, we shall be thrown out of Portugal. We are not sending forces sufficient to meet the French in Spain.'

'When did we ever send forces sufficient to meet the French? Were I a soldier I should be glad enough to serve under Wellesley.'

'I know that Castlereagh is all for him, but I believe that he is not to command.'

'What? Is he out? We had a cutter came in here, two days ago, that was at Cork when he embarked. 'Twas said on all sides that he was to command.'

'When he reaches Lisbon,' said I, 'he will find, if he does not know it already, that Dalrymple and Burrard have been put over him.'

Pronto had received this information, just before quitting Ullacombe, in a long letter of gossip from a particular friend, which told him of the recent squalls in Downing Street, and how pressure, brought by the Duke of York on behalf of Burrard, had ousted Castlereagh's man. It is exactly like Pronto to know that a general has been deprived of his command before the poor gentleman knows of it himself.

'Dalrymple does not intend to fight very much,' I asserted. 'I hear that his great scheme is to entertain the Duc d'Orléans in Lisbon, if His Highness can somehow be brought there. When they have dined together, the expedition will come home. Wellesley would not have been content with a dinner-party, I daresay, but he is out.'

Dawson swore that it was a pitiful business.

'But that is ever the way,' he complained. 'We must be down to hard tack and in danger of invasion before they will give command to an admiral who *likes* putting to sea, so one must not expect that they will appoint a general who *means* to fight, if they can help it. 'Tis enough to make a man turn politician ! No offence intended !'

This he added hastily, as though fearing it might sound insulting.

'Yet you advise me to join the Army,' cried I.

'I advise nothing of the sort. I merely say that you might find work in the Army but, as for us, you must be bred up to it. I am very sorry, Miles. I honour you for your feelings. Indeed I do. I had not thought . . . 'tis very strange . . . I believe that I did not do you justice . . . the fact is, that I had an argument with my wife last night . . . I thought her a little too partial to you political fellows, you know, and I thought that she had slighted Captain Spaulding, who sat t'other side of her, for she would not talk to him . . . I might have spoken unjustly . . . some fellows must sit in Parliament . . .'

He broke off in confusion. I could well imagine the argument. His wife had slighted his friends and would talk only to Pronto ; he had retorted by some contemptuous criticisms of political fellows.

He shook me warmly by the hand and took his leave. But at the door, he turned to exclaim :

'There is the Marines, you know !'

'The Marines ?'

'They might take you. And it is not work to be despised, since Nelson set them properly to the guns. Before that, nobody could be sure what they might be supposed to do. There is the 4th Division at Woolwich might take you. That is an idea ! They are all picked men, trained in the use of artillery. You might consider of it. But I must go now, for I have to meet a fellow.'

This time he really did go. Crestfallen though I was, I could not help laughing as soon as he had closed the door, for it was a most ridiculous end to my exalted project.

The Marines !

I am sure that there is no finer body of men in our services, and I don't know why there should be a universal tendency to laugh at them.   Perhaps it may be because the improvement in their condition is so recent ; the old prejudice against them has not yet been overcome. Eustace had often told us of the tricks that were played upon them, aboard ship, in the old days ; there is a saying among the common people : *Tell that to the Marines*, — implying that a Marine is so ignorant that he will believe anything.

I had been able to imagine the countenances of my family and friends at the news that I had gone for a soldier or a sailor.   They might be shocked, puzzled, disappointed, even contemptuous, but they would not laugh.   The news that Pronto had joined the Marines would keep half London in convulsions for nine days.

And that was the end of my trip to Portsmouth.

Lady Amersham

A DAY or two later found me at Colesworth, the country seat of Lord Beaumont, who had married Ludovic's sister.

She and I had always been good friends.   In the old days at Brailsford she had been a plain, good-humoured girl, who did not expect me to flirt with her ; we had often laid our heads together in schemes to restrain Ludovic and bring him into better accord with his father.

Her husband was a very pleasant fellow.   There was but one thing amiss with the Beaumonts, — a fault which I have frequently observed in Good Society.   They did not seem to suffer in the least from the vulgarity, the stupidity and the inferiority of the company which they were often obliged to keep. They were themselves well bred and intelligent, but they were not repelled by a Duchess who picked her nose or a Marquess who believed that Cape Horn was in Africa. They would not have dreamt of choosing their friends upon the score of compatibility; to them the Peerage was a family handbook and all in it some kind of relative with whom, however repulsive, they had closer ties than they could have with any commoner, however agreeable. It is this capacity for enduring one another which preserves our Aristocracy, I think, in an age of change. We commoners are too squeamish. If a man stinks we avoid him. They are made of sterner stuff; their noses are subservient to their sense of rank.

I had a reason for pausing at Colesworth on my way to London for I hoped that Lady Sophia might help me in the matter of Mary Hawker. Kitty's suggestion of a post as lodge-keeper was a good one; could I find any opening of that sort at Colesworth it would ensure that Mary would have friends at hand to read William's letters to her.

As I drove up to the house I saw Ludovic at an upper window, hanging over the sill in a limp manner resembling a punchinello at a puppet show, the effect being heightened by a tasselled white night-cap. I had not known that he was to be there, and I waved gaily. He responded with a lugubrious flap of one hand before vanishing from the window. I saw that he was in one of his black moods and the reason for it was explained by his sister as soon as she saw me.

'Do go up to Ludovic,' she said, 'and tell him that he must come out of his room. He has been there for three days, and all because Lowestoft is staying here.'

'Ah, they were at Eton together, I believe.'

'He cannot go through life like this. Everybody has been at Eton. Make him go out riding with you.'

I went up to Ludovic and found him in his dressing-gown, although the hour was noon. His room was in its usual state of confusion, — his man busy with some travelling bags which were either packing or unpacking. This was always the way with Ludovic. He can never settle. Even at Brailsford he will daily order this or that portmanteau to be packed for him, although he has no intention of going away.

He greeted me with another melancholy flap and told the servant to 'bring something' for me, leaving the interpretation of this command to the poor fellow's native wit. Nothing annoys him more than to be forced to explain his vague orders, for that obliges him to remember what time of day it is, and if one has come far, and how long it will be until dinner-time. The man departed and found out, from my postillions I suppose, that I had been travelling since an early hour, for he returned with a luncheon of cold meat and wine.

'You need not put those things up after all,' Ludovic told him, 'for I shall not be going today.'

When we were alone he said :

'I had intended going to the Isle of Wight, but, since you are come I shall stay, because I must take you to see Troy Chimneys. It is a house, some ten miles from here, and it would be just the house for you.'

'But I don't want a house.'

'I shall call you out if you don't want this one. It is the very thing for you, — not quite a manor-house and yet not quite a farm. I believe that it must have been built by a man who intended to be happy in it ; and there are very few houses of which one could say that.'

'But what a nonsensical name !'

'I grant that. One does not imagine chimneys upon the topless towers of Ilium. But you may change the name, you know, when you have got it.'

'My dear Ludovic, I have no intention, at this stage——'

'Oh, I know! I know! But it is to be sold and you might not have the chance again. You may buy it and let it for a while.'

I did not argue with him, for the prospect of showing me this house had clearly dispersed his fit of melancholy. As I swallowed my meal he rapturously described this latest dote, which lay, so he said, upon the banks of the Avon, a little to the north of Laycock. Although very secluded it was not difficult of access, since three lanes met there, one of which led, in less than a quarter of a mile, to the Bath road. I might, at small expense, improve and widen this lane, so that all my friends could visit me at their ease.

'If you have finished eating,' he said, 'we will go there now.'

I asked if we could get there and back before dinner, which I knew to be at four o'clock. This is the sort of question which always irritates him, for he hates to think of time and distance. He gave an impatient groan and tugged at the bell rope.

'What does it signify?' said he. 'We may dine upon the road. Oh Mason! Tell them to have horses ready for Mr. Lufton and myself immediately, and unpack my riding-boots.'

I returned to Lady Sophia and reported that I had got Ludovic out of his chamber but that I doubted if I could produce him for dinner. She was delighted, and declared that our presence at dinner was not of the least consequence, — we might dine where we chose. I changed my dress and we set out.

We had not ridden very far before Ludovic asked if the cliffs at Dawlish were not of a very strange red colour. The question startled me. I asked what had put Dawlish into his head.

'Because you have come from there, have you not?'

'I was there lately. But how could you know?'

'Somebody or other at Colesworth said that you had been there. I have forgotten who it was.'

Greatly disconcerted, I questioned him, but he declared that he could not remember. He can at times be very malicious, and is not near so unobservant as he pretends to be. I was dismayed at the thought of my Dawlish adventure getting out. To have been involved in a party of that kind would do my reputation no good; I had already heard it reported that all the worst rakes in Devonshire had been present when Hyde was found to be dead. I feared that Wortley had not been too fuddled to remember having seen me, and that the story must have been spread by him. But I could not imagine him as a guest at Colesworth.

'Who is staying at Colesworth?' I demanded.

'My mother.'

'And who besides?'

'Don't pester me like this. You will find out soon enough. I have not seen any of them except Spencer Perceval.'

'WHAT?' cried I. 'Is *he* here?'

'He has been, and still is, I believe. But I think he goes off tomorrow.'

Pronto, roused to sudden and violent life, gave a cry of anguish. To be staying for a night in the same house with the Tory leader and to miss him at dinner was a crushing mishap. Pronto's acquaintance with Perceval was not near so close as he could have wished; here was an opportunity for improving it clean thrown away!

'I wonder your sister should say it was of no consequence if we were away for dinner!' cried I.

'Nor is it.'

'It might be for me. You seem to forget that I might have reasons for seeking Perceval's company. I should like to know him better than I do. This is just such an occasion when— 'Tis too bad of you not to tell me before! I am sure that your mother would think it very strange if I did not take the opportunity to— Can you never think of anybody but yourself? Because you don't care to meet Lowestoft, you take me upon this wild-goose chase.'

'And that is all the thanks I get for saving you from a dinner with Crockett!'

'Is Crockett here, then?'

'To be sure he is. And what's more, I remember now,— it was he said you had been at Dawlish. Did you not get very drunk at Dawlish and beat a judge to death?'

'Does he say that?'

'Something of the sort, I believe. Sophy said that he had entertained them all at dinner yesterday with some great story about you at Dawlish.'

'Before Perceval! I must return instantly and contradict it. I cannot think how Lady Sophia came not to warn me, why she sent me out of the way! She knows my position.!'

'Your position, so far as she is concerned,' said Ludovic, 'is to act dry nurse to me. She does not care a fig for you otherwise.'

This was perfectly true, and I knew it. But the insolence with which he proclaimed it put me quite beside myself. I turned my horse abruptly and galloped back to Colesworth in such a rage that it was touch and go whether I did not gallop straight on to London and join the Marines. The arrogance of these people was too much. I could endure it no longer. A dry nurse! That was how they thought of me, — a kind of valuable upper servant to be rewarded with tit-bits. My career, my future, was nothing to them in comparison with their own convenience.

If I had seen Lady Sophia again, and she had scolded me for leaving Ludovic, I really think that Miles might have won the day. But nobody seemed to be about, when I reached the house. I could not go off without a word. A servant told me that her ladyship might be walking down beside the lake. So off I went, and by the lake I encountered, not Lady Sophia, but her mother, who was very composedly feeding some swans. She waved her hand in greeting, smiled her smile, and said:

'What a talent you have for turning up at the right moment! You can carry this basket for me.'

Pronto bowed and took the basket.

Miles could not have done less, but he would not have done it with so much alacrity.

We fed the swans and then sauntered for a while by the lake. Lady Amersham asked if I had yet seen Perceval, and shook her head at me when I said that I had been riding with Ludovic. I excused myself by saying that Lady Sophia had bid me go.

'Oh, Sophy does not understand these things,' she said. 'I am particularly anxious that you should talk to him, for we have been speaking of you, and I believe that it may soon be in his power to do something for you.'

She said nothing of Crockett and I came gradually to believe that Crockett's great story had done me little damage. He tells too many scandalous stories; his malice defeats itself. Ludovic had been teasing me, and I had been caught, because he teases so seldom.

Lady Amersham took me more into her confidence, upon this occasion, than she had ever done before. She told me that, in her opinion, Portland might soon resign, that his health was far from good, and that another twelve months might see Perceval at the head of the Government. She expected that he would make great efforts to secure a coalition with Grey and Grenville, and that he would not easily give up hope. He would therefore reserve some very good places for their friends, should they consent to come in. These places would not, meanwhile, be given to leading Tories but would be offered to young men like myself, who would later be expected to resign them, if they could be filled by Grenvillites. She prophesied that Croker, for instance, might get astonishing advancement, and mentioned the post of First Secretary to the Admiralty, which that young man eventually did get. And she believed that something equally good might be forthcoming for me, if I put myself in the way of it.

'You may think it is uncertain,' she said, 'and not worth while to take a place that must be given up. But I don't believe that he will succeed with Grenville, and if he does not, you may stay for years. I expect this to be the kind of government which staggers on and on, while all expect it to collapse in a matter of months. My counsel to you is that any offer of this kind would be worth taking, even though some uncertainty is attached to it. I should not expect it before next year, but it might happen sooner, so it is best to be prepared.'

Prime Ministers have been known to change their minds after a saunter with Lady Amersham. By the time that we returned to the house Pronto was in an assured ascendancy, for if Croker was to get £4000 p.a., Pronto did not see why he should not do as well.

At dinner everything fell out capitally for him. Mulgrave was there, and he had also been at Portsmouth, and the conversation took a dockyards direction ; Pronto was the only person present who knew anything about *razée* frigates, and the number of guns carried by American ships of war. Pronto created an excellent impression; only a very serious and hard-working young man could have contrived to learn so much during so short a time.

Crockett kept very quiet. He would have liked to trip Pronto up, but he had the sense to see that he must hold his fire. He, Lowestoft, and some others, did most of the drinking at one end of the table, whilst serious conversation carried on at the other. They stayed when the rest of us went, — Perceval and Mulgrave to their despatches, Beaumont and Pronto to join the ladies.

Pronto

THE weather was warm and we all strolled out upon the terrace to admire the sunset, which was remarkably fine. We stared and exclaimed at the splendours of the western sky which cast a deep glow upon the whole front of the house, turned green lawns to bronze, and the women's white dresses to rose.

I have said that Miles and Pronto never communicate. That is true in a sense; they have no overt debate. But there is an infernal sort of coalition between them, all the same. It is entirely to Pronto's advantage. He draws upon Miles' credit and does nothing in return. His experience and his address are never at his victim's disposal, as I have shown in the case of William Hawker. But Miles' talents are unfailingly at his command. The confounded fellow can look like Miles, and talk like Miles, and read *Comus* as feelingly as though £4000 a year were of no consequence whatever. He never listens to the nightingale, but he can talk as though he did.

I think that he never showed to better advantage than when he admired this sunset. All the ladies were in a romantic mood. Even Lady Amersham smilingly declared that she could not go indoors just yet, and sent for a warmer shawl. The younger members of the party, braving the dew, wandered down to the temple by the lake, where they might see the sky reflected in the water. They stayed there until the last red was gone, and the trees stood up black against a yellow afterglow. One by one, the few small stars of summer made their appearance.

'I think,' said Lady Lowestoft, 'that Pr—— that Mr. Lufton should sing to us.'

There was a murmur of assent. Pronto was quite ready to oblige and chose a ditty of Lyttelton's which should give point to the conversation that had gone before, since all the company had been laughing at a young lady who complained that she *could* not fall in love. The air needed a harp, but he managed it pretty well without an accompaniment.

> Say Myra, why is gentle love
> A stranger to that mind
> Which pity and esteem can move,
> Which can be just and kind ?
>
> Is it because you fear to share
> The ills which love molest ?
> The jealous doubt, the tender care,
> That rack the amorous breast ?
>
> Alas ! by some degree of woe
> We every bliss must gain :
> The heart can ne'er a transport know,
> That never feels a pain.

Soft voices called applause, which was mingled with laughter, because some swans had swum up close to the shore as if to listen. Lady Sophia accused Pronto of being a second Orpheus. He was pressed for another air but, before he could oblige, there was a halloo! from Lowestoft, who had come from the house with Crockett and was standing a little way off, throwing pebbles at the swans.

'Hey Pronto! Is that the famous song you sung at Dawlish?'

An awkward silence fell. Pronto perceived that all were looking at him through the dusk; there was, after all, some hidden curiosity concerning his reputed exploits at Dawlish. He replied very calmly :

'No, my lord. It was another song altogether took me to Dawlish. But I shall not sing it when you are here, for I am sure that you would not care for it.'

'No, indeed,' cried Lady Lowestoft. 'He hates music. Go away, you horrid creature. Crockett! Pray take him away.'

Lady Sophia also told them to go away and play billiards. I heard her say in a low voice to Mrs. Madden, a Wiltshire neighbour who was dining there, that if Crockett could not be depended upon to prevent that sort of thing she did not know why one should ask him to the house. It was Crockett's business to keep drunk men quiet, just as it was Pronto's business to amuse the ladies. He took the hint and walked off, dragging Lowestoft with him.

Pronto hoped that the incident was over, and so it might have been had not the young lady who could not fall in love been so inexperienced in atmosphere as to ask, very innocently, what he *had* sung at Dawlish. This enquiry was maliciously taken up by Lady Lowestoft, who pressed to hear the ditty. He saw that he must either explain Dawlish with some credit to himself or allow it to be for ever a source of scandalous speculation.

He sighed and told them that Lord Lowestoft had

touched upon a tragical little business in which he had recently been concerned. They might have heard of the death of Mr. Justice Hyde? A faint stir among them advised him that they certainly had.

'Upon the night of his death,' continued Pronto, 'I called upon him in the hope of saving a friend, a humble friend, from disaster. The business was of the utmost urgency, — I dared not stay till morning. I arrived . . . too late! His lordship was dead . . . in circumstances . . . but I need not go into that——'

'Oh, pray do!' murmured Lady Lowestoft, but Pronto managed not to hear her, and hurried on:

'Had I reached him but a few hours earlier . . . but I will, if you please, tell you the whole story, for I think that your kind hearts will feel for poor Mary Hawker.'

'*Mary* Hawker!' cried several voices. 'Was your friend a woman?'

Women will not listen to a story unless another woman comes into it. By now he had aroused their curiosity. He told his tale very well indeed, heightening all that might appeal to the sensibility of his audience and omitting anything that might offend them. He softened William's rough pride, emphasised his enthusiasm for poetry, but mentioned no books of a controversial sort. William was pictured as a loyal Briton who had fled from America rather than raise a parricidal hand against his king. That it was William's father who made this choice, and that William himself did not approve of it, was not allowed to appear, nor was the true story told of William's independence at the hustings.

Pronto appeared as the patron rather than the friend; he mentioned that he had stayed a night with this poor couple, but not that he had shared their bed.

Concerning Mary he was more frank. She needed no touching up. She made a most pathetic figure as she was, with her sweet singing, her forlorn situation, and her devotion to William. As he told of his frantic efforts on her behalf, and his hopeless return to Gulley's Cove, many of his fair listeners were in tears.

'"Tis as good as a novel!' said Lady Lowestoft, wiping her eyes. 'But pray, what is to become of her?'

Pronto begged their help in deciding this, and got a thoughtful enquiry from Mrs. Madden as to Mary's proficiency in the care of poultry.

'For she might,' said that lady, 'be the very person for me. I have some rare pheasants, and I have recently begun to breed Muscovy ducks. I am looking for a reliable woman to take care of them. There is a cottage she could have, behind the old stables.'

Pronto was able sincerely to praise Mary's skill in poultry-keeping. He declared that nothing could be more delightful, so long as Mary should have some friend at hand who would read William's letters to her.

'Oh I will do that,' promised Mrs. Madden, 'and write hers for her too, if she likes. It will be amusing to hear what such people have to say to one another.'

This happy sequel to a pathetic story was felt by all to furnish a good end to the evening. If tears had been excited, benevolence now dried them. But Lady Lowestoft was insatiable:

'You have not yet sung your Dawlish song,' she complained. 'I suppose it was one of Mary's songs. Do pray sing it!'

Pronto objected that it was but a country ballad and not fit for such company. They bore him down, assured him that he should not be criticised, and reminded him that he was not in a drawing-room. A country ballad would just suit the occasion. He was most reluctant and would have sung another, could he have thought of a likely substitute, but his wits deserted him and he was at

last obliged to give them the air which Mary had sung so
often at Gulley's Cove.   Darkness had quite fallen and he
was glad of it.   If they smiled he would not see their
faces.   Never has he exerted himself more than he did
then, hoping to sing so sweetly that the faults of the song
might be forgotten.   In a room, among lights, it would
have been impossible ; under the faint stars, beside the
lake, he had more confidence.

> Cold blows the gale at Hallowtide,
> And coldly falls the rain.
> The dead man rises from the flood
> And seeks his earthly love again,
> And seeks his love again.
>
> Well met, well met, my sweetheart true !
> How come you to my bed ?
> Your sighs have drawn me from the sea,
> Your tears have raised me from the dead,
> Have raised me from the dead.
>
> Oh bitter is the salt, salt sea,
> And chill the ocean deep ;
> But salter yet those endless tears
> That nightly break upon my sleep,
> That break upon my sleep.
>
> And if my tears can bring you back,
> They shall for ever flow !
> They hold me from the Port of Heaven,
> Where fain, and fain am I to go,
> Where fain am I to go.
>
> Ah weep no more, no more for me !
> When shall you let me rest ?
> When acorns fall from the mulberry tree,
> And the sun rises up in the West, my dear,
> And the sun rises up in the West.

In the little silence which fell, as the last notes died away over the water, Pronto knew that he had escaped ridicule. After a short pause he began to talk briskly in favour of such old songs, saying that they should not be despised, for that Shakespeare often used them. A lively discussion arose as the party returned to the house; all were glad to pass from feelings which had threatened to be too painful. Other old ditties were remembered, heard from nurses and people of that sort; it was agreed that they should be collected and set down before they were quite forgotten.

On his way upstairs, Pronto looked into Ludovic's room to see how matters stood there and to make his peace, if possible, for having deserted before dinner. Ludovic was playing upon his flute. At the sight of Pronto he waved it angrily, exclaiming:

'Don't come here, if you please! I wish never to see you again. You will find a letter from me upon your dressing-table.'

The letter proved to be long and abusive. It accused Pronto of caring for nobody but himself, of using all his friends as stepping-stones, and of hiding the 'pangs of conscious truth' which, in his case, could not even be described as *struggling*.

Ludovic occasionally flew into these rages but they never lasted for long. Pronto went to bed in high good humour. He believed that he had impressed Perceval. He had got himself out of the Dawlish scrape. He had foiled Crockett's malice. He had pleased Lady Amersham. And he had found an excellent opening for Mary Hawker, — had done more for her in a quarter of an hour than Miles had done in a fortnight. Best of all, he had so much outraged Miles, in doing it, that the wretched fellow was not likely to give any trouble again for a great while.

I recall that evening as a more innocent and respectable man might recall a sensual debauch. Mingled with our shame and remorse, at the memory of any excess, there is always the sense that some other person has been guilty of it.

Not I! Not I! It was Pronto!

Troy Chimneys

BUT I had bad dreams that night. I should not now remember this if I had not, next day, recounted one of them to Ludovic, who made me write it down. He is as superstitious upon this subject as any housemaid. He writes down all his own, and any which his friends may mention, believing that some great secret is hidden in our dreams.

I dreamt that I was in the House and about to speak upon some very important subject, but unable to remember what it might be. I sat hoping that I might recall it, when a voice moved the order of the day for going into Committee, and I saw that Henry Dawson had taken the chair. He said: *We will now examine some of your reading fellows!* I started up, with a sense of extreme urgency, but was embarrassed by Lady Amersham's basket which I held. As one does, in dreams, I hoped nobody would notice it. I began to speak upon the export of Jesuits' bark, though I knew that this was not what I had to say. Voices began crying: *Who is this man?* I told them that I was Prefect of Hall, but was interrupted by a loud crash and by Maria Cotman, who pulled at my sleeve, with a sly smile, and whispered: *He is dead!* The debate continued amid persistent crashes and other voices echoing: *He is dead!*

Four years later, when I had totally forgotten this dream, Ludovic sent me a copy of it with the date, jubilantly claiming that it had been prophetic. I cannot agree with him. If a man writes down every dream he has, some can always be found which will fit future events. I was in the House upon the day of Perceval's death; we had gone into Committee upon the petitions against the Orders in Council, and Stephen was cross-examining a witness, when we heard a report in the lobby, and a whisper went round that 'somebody was shot,' followed by a stampede for the door. But I do not believe that the *he* in my dream was poor Perceval, and the crashes were not shots, but a repeated hammering at my door which eventually woke me.

I started up, supposing the house to be on fire, and called out something, whereat Ludovic rushed into the room, talking very fast and with even less than his usual coherence. I heard sentences like these:

'. . . Have never been myself obliged to work for a living and forget that others are not so free . . . no business to expect my friends to be always at my disposal . . . particularly ashamed of the expression *stepping-stones* . . . could wish that my mother had less power with you . . . if you can ever forgive me . . .'

In short, he had come to beg pardon for his letter and to ask very humbly if I would not accompany him to Troy Chimneys.

'With all the pleasure in the world,' said I. 'When do we start? Instantly I suppose?'

It was scarcely daylight, but Ludovic embraced this suggestion with enthusiasm and summoned the unfortunate Mason to bring us breakfast. As we ate, I recounted my dream and he wrote it down.

'But why,' said I, 'should I dream of Maria Cotman? Dawson and the basket are explicable; they have been recently in my mind. But I have not seen her, or thought of her, for years.'

Ludovic asked very seriously if any striking passage in my life had been connected with this young lady. I was bound to admit that she had been present when I received a great blow. Then, said he, I might depend upon it another blow was coming; I should soon hear of bad news. He was a little crestfallen when the weeks passed and I did not, and now insists that Maria turned up, four years too early, to warn me of Perceval's death.

I asked him if he had a Maria Cotman of his own, who foretells disaster. He nodded and presently muttered: *Candle snuffers!* He explained that, where one particular person or image would be too dreadful, a deputy is sent; he says that Maria Cotman and the candle snuffers are deputies for something much worse. But the instances of his own dreams, which he gave me, do not quite bear him out. It is true that he has often dreamt of candle snuffers before trouble, but I should say that it is always trouble of his own making; he *has* made a blunder from which ill consequences *will* ensue. Were he to dream of snuffers, and then be hit by a thunderbolt, I might allow his theories. But, if these 'deputies' come to mock at us for our sins and mistakes, they are more comprehensible. Maria Cotman might well grin at me that night at Colesworth.

Within an hour we were off upon our excursion, and had a capital ride over the downs. Ludovic was in spirits, as he always is after one of his black fits, and I was happy enough to be galloping so swiftly through the fine air, in the sunrise.

A little below Calne we came to a rough lane which led us to a ford over the Avon. Ludovic said that this was one of the three lanes of which he had spoken. After crossing the river we went at a walking pace, for the ground was rutted. The lane, pleasantly shaded by trees,

ran between flowery banks. Presently we came to the
corner of a high stone wall, with a dovecote in the angle.

'Is this Troy Chimneys?' I asked, as we rode along
beneath the wall.

He said that it was, and I knew at once the kind of
house it would be, for I have seen several, in that part of
the country, built upon the same plan. To tease Ludovic,
I began to describe it, though we could not see it over
the wall, assuring him that I had never been there before,
and pretending those supernatural powers with which he
was so anxious to endow me.

'There is a square enclosure,' I said, 'a little court in
fact. Two sides of it are composed by this high wall, and
two by the wings of the house, which is of a greyish brown
stone, with a steep pitched roof, and gables for the second-
storey windows. It has a square porch and a flagged
path leading from that to a white gate in the wall. The
enclosure is all grass, very closely shaved, with a fine old
mulberry tree.'

'But this is sorcery!' cried Ludovic, much excited.
'You have got it all exactly, except that there is no
grass and no mulberry tree. The court is merely a rough
farm-yard. But you certainly *will* have grass, and a
mulberry tree, for nothing could suit the place better.
Here is your white gate!'

I laughed at him, but was pleased to find how well I
had guessed at the house. Opposite the white gate our
lane joined two others, one going towards Bath and the
other towards Salisbury, the three meeting at a little
circular space which would, so Ludovic said, be very
useful for turning round a carriage.

Once inside the gate we seemed to be secluded from
the world, for the high walls hid all save the foliage of the
trees. The principal part of the house faced the gate,
and had a square porch, as I had said, with a date, —

1620. This wing was clearly of later date than the other, which ran at right angles and had much smaller windows, set at irregular levels. But the two harmonised very well.

Ludovic had a key and proceeded to unlock the great oaken door in the porch. We passed straight into an immensely long room which ran the whole length of that part of the house. It was lighted by six windows and there were great fireplaces at either end, with stone chimney-hoods. This room was panelled with fine linen-fold. I thought it a noble apartment but a trifle sombre. I was better pleased with the two parlours behind it, for they faced east and were full of the morning sunshine. I was immediately struck by a rippling play of light upon the ceilings, made by the sun catching the river below the house.

'It is set high enough that you need not be afraid of floods,' said Ludovic. 'Though the river runs in so near, there is quite a steep slope of grass down to it. We were coming a little way uphill, all the time, in the lane. And as you see, the prospect upon this side is very open. A clear day will give you a fine view over the meadows to the downs. These rooms shall be your parlour and study. The great room in front must be your dining-room; it is something large, but one very large room is a necessity. There are moods when one must have space. And there is a door from it to your kitchens, which will be in the other wing, where you may lodge your servants. These are the stairs, through this door. I don't like a boxed staircase, but at least it will prevent draughts. There are five or six bed-chambers above. The barns, stables and cart-houses are beyond the kitchen wing, and there is a very pretty cottage. You must look at the orchard; you will like it extremely. There is some good farm land goes with the property; you may let it, or put a man into the cottage to farm it for you.'

I let him chatter, whilst I sat in the window-seat of the larger parlour and watched the slow, liquid play of the sunlight upon the ceiling, with its reminder of the constant current passing below. This particular has always delighted me in Troy Chimneys. I try to go there upon a sunny morning, so that I may see it. The passing of time never presents itself in a more agreeable fashion ; I like to think that when I am dead, as long as the house stands, the sun and the water will write these chronicles upon the ceiling, — the same sun, the same river, — only the current gives an illusion of change. I already saw myself living there and beholding it daily. I might some day get the Hawkers into the cottage. William could have the farm, and the stream of time, rolling ever past us, might carry away all that I wished to forget.

We went through a door, from the smaller parlour, to the slope of grass down to the river. Ludovic said first that this must be shaven. Then he changed his mind. I must let it grow and plant flowers in it, daffodils and snake-bells.

Suddenly he turned and faced me :

'Admit that you could be very happy here and that you are wretched as you are.'

'My dear Ludovic ! I could not afford to buy this house.'

He began to speak and checked himself. I knew that he had been about to offer me the money and then, recollecting his insults of the previous day, doubted the delicacy of such a suggestion.

'Besides,' said I, 'the man I mean to put into the cottage will not be available, I fear, for some years yet.'

'But you may not get another chance for such a house. And soon you will not want it, if you go on as you do.'

I knew what he meant, and felt the truth of it.

'If I thought,' he said, 'that you were happy . . . if

I thought your heart to be in a political career . . . I blame myself that I ever brought you to Brailsford. There is a blight upon it, I think. And I cannot endure to hear people call you Pronto!'

I started. It was the first time I had heard him use that name. I said that I was not called so at Brailsford.

'No. But it is my fault that you live among people who do.'

'You are mistaken. I was extremely ambitious, even at school. And it is all very well for you, Ludovic, who were born at the top of the hill, to censure ambition. What would you have me do? I am not, I think, without talent and ability. Am I not to exert myself? Am I to spend my whole life at the bottom?'

He shook his head and declared dolefully that it was the wrong hill, but he was unable to indicate a better. Later, when we were inspecting the orchard, he resumed the argument:

'But your passions? Your passions?'

This he pronounced in so shrill a voice that I nearly laughed. I knew what he meant,—that our principal exertions should always be inspired by some passion. I agree with him, if, among the passions, may be included such propensities as Henry Dawson's enthusiasm for open timber heads.

I told him that I had none. Then, remembering my recent gallopings over Devonshire, I qualified that by saying:

'Only one thing in the world has power to transport me; the spectacle of tyranny and the sufferings of helpless people.'

At that he gave a kind of groan and said that I had better buy a desert island.

'Helpless! Helpless!' he cried. 'That indeed is insupportable. If you feel it to be so, you must seclude yourself, as I do. What could be more secluded than this spot ?'

As we rode homewards he attacked me again :

'I cannot conceive how you come to prefer my mother's guidance to yours.'

'My mother,' I replied, 'is too good for this world. She can't give one advice. She believes that we shall always act rightly if we feel as we ought. If I were to purchase Troy Chimneys, for example, she would merely ask what feelings prompted me to do it.'

'The pursuit of happiness ! Sure she cannot censure that !'

'I fancy she might. She would call it an escape from feeling. She believes that our feelings should rule us, and that our search in life must be for a duty which we are happy to fulfil.'

'I never observed so austere a strain in her.'

'No. All you see, all that anyone sees, is the Paradise made by one angel upon earth. Her goodness seems to be so easy and natural that one is scarcely aware of the inflexible principles upon which it is based.'

This mystified him. He knows nothing of moral principles. He grew up among people who had none, and was not enough of a philosopher to have discovered them for himself.

I had actually a sum put by sufficient for the purchase of Troy Chimneys, though such an outlay would leave me very short. Before leaving Colesworth I bought the house, — exactly why, I cannot tell, except that I wanted it very much, and felt that such a deed might count as a challenge to Pronto. But he made no objection. It has turned out to be a good investment and 'property in Wiltshire' sounds well.

I found an excellent tenant, almost at once, who took

it upon a ten years' lease, with the understanding that I might wish to live there myself at the end of that period. I have spent a good deal, since then, upon various improvements. Dr. King, my tenant, is a middle-aged clergyman and he keeps a little school there. Half a dozen lads, too delicate for a public school, board with him. They live very happily, I think, for Mrs. King is an excellent woman and cares for them like a mother. Poor Ned would never have caught the ringworm in the Kings' establishment. I go there often and I like to see these rosy lads about the house.

King has been of the greatest assistance to me in my improvements. Between us we have put the front court into grass, and have planted a mulberry tree, which comes on very well. But we have never got snake-bells to grow upon the river slope.

For some years I cherished my project of getting the Hawkers into the cottage, but I don't think now that it would answer, even if they were willing to come. William has done very well in the Navy; I have had several cheerful letters from him. He seems to have become entirely the sailor, and I suspect that he is a good deal altered. He has made the best of his lot with a vengeance. I daresay that he gets little time for reading. He writes that he would like to remain in the Navy, were it not for the separation from Mary. As it is, he does not despair of taking her to America some day, though he has been very busy fighting the Americans since 1812. 'We sail under the Jack and they under the Stars and Stripes,' he wrote to me once, 'so what else can we do, when the gentlemen at home bid us send one another to the bottom ? They tell us the cause is just. But *That's more than we know*, as the soldier says in *King Henry the Fifth*.' This is the only occasion upon which he has quoted anything out of a book, when writing to me.

I see Mary sometimes, when I go into Wiltshire. She succeeds very well as poultry-woman to Mrs. Madden, but she too is greatly changed. She has put on flesh and lost her rosy cheeks. She says little. That surprised look is still there. When I think of the lively girl who laughed at William as she clambered into bed, and meet the blank stare of this stout, pale, silent woman, I feel that she is a stranger. I once asked her if the children did not delight to hear her sing. She said hastily that she never sings now.

If they came to Troy Chimneys, I doubt if our old intimacy could be resumed. We are all changed. Perhaps they never were quite what my fancy painted them. I suppose that I may have once been a little in love with *both*, if such a thing is possible, — I mean in love with that composite creature which is a happy couple. To feel a warm friendship for such a dual person is not uncommon. Most men have an attachment of that sort, my feeling for Kitty and Newsome is an example of it. The love I have for each is enhanced because they are united to one another. But with the Hawkers it was more romantic, as though I shared something of their felicity, — shared William's tenderness for Mary and Mary's pride in William. I may have overlooked many shortcomings, little rusticities, for the sake of the charm which they exerted upon me. I am sure that all I have said of them is true, but it may not be the whole picture.

In any case, time will not run back. Not even the river at Troy Chimneys does that, where time runs at his gentlest. Elsewhere he tramps forward.

KAI CHRONOU PROUBAINE POUS!

INTERLUDE: 1879–1880

INTERLUDE: 1879–1880

Cullenstown, Dec. 27, 1879

DEAREST FRED,

We have found three letters, which I enclose. They were in a drawer labelled 'Miscellaneous' and must, I think, have been written by Cousin Ludovic. I daresay they were with the Lufton papers originally, but there is nothing to identify them, and whoever put them into the library (I think it was Aunt Honoria) did not connect them with the others.

Forgive this hasty scribble. We have still our Christmas house-party on our hands. I am afraid you must have been very dismal at Brailsford — I *wish* you could have been here. Please to tell me how you are, when next you write. You never do.

Yours affectly,
EMILY

Enclosures

I

Can you dine with me in Town on Thursday? At A. House of course. I shall be there to see Woodward who is very hopeful about *Tito*. I believe that we may hear it in London next year. If we do I shall cry *Nunc Dimittis!* for the efforts of a lifetime will have been rewarded. Pray don't tell me that you would rather have D.G., for it is indubitably inferior. You never heard it in full, only some airs which I agree to be very fine. But I heard it, as you know, when my father was in Vienna and I can assure you that opera Buffa was not in M's vein, nor should he ever have stooped to the comic. He excelled in the solemn and the sublime. Come on Thursday.

2

Your insulting note has just arrived. I waited dinner for *at least* five minutes before deciding that you never got mine. What keeps you in Gloucestershire? Oh, I remember! One of your sisters is to be married. An Irish baronet, did you not say? Pray wish her joy from me.

I could not believe that you were not in Town. Everybody here is in the greatest agitation and I should have expected you to have 'catched the contagious fire.' Canning, Castlereagh, Wilberforce, and some saints, deserted last night; the Gvt. defeated 226-213. So much has even forced itself upon *my* intelligence, and you know how ignorant I manage to be. No quarter is expected from C. House. Perceval however is quite calm and grows almost witty, for he said: 'I do not think there are many rats, only a few mice.' My mother, also, refuses to disturb herself. She believes that the K. will get well and we are having all this trouble for nothing. She also says that: *Les ministres Jacobins ne seront pas les Jacobins ministres*. I believe her to mean that a Prince Regent will not be the same as a Prinney. Perhaps you take the same view? But I wonder you a'nt here, mouse hunting.

What do you mean by my fantastic precocity? I will allow that I was but five years old when I heard D.G. My opinions upon every subject were formed at that age, and I have seldom found reason to change.

3

Thank you for your letter. To your question: Did my mother suffer much during the final stages of her complaint? I must answer that she did. She bore it with the fortitude that you might expect of her. The end was so dreadful that I could not wish her life prolonged by a single instant. I should have prayed for her death, had intercession with the Being who ordains such agony struck me as a rational proceeding.

What you say of her is very just. She was genuinely fond of you and your progress gave her as much satisfaction as anything in her life. In a way, you were the son I *ought* to have been. Her disappointment in me was not so bitter when she was making plans for you.

My father feels it more than I should have expected. I hope that his strongest emotion is one of remorse. He is at Colesworth and at present behaves as he ought. I hope the Beaumonts may keep him in order, for if a certain person is now brought to live openly at B'ford I shall quit the place. I shall not remain under the same roof with one whose existence, so flagrantly recognised, was for years an insult to my mother.

I cannot but compare my family with yours, that knew a like loss but a few months ago. I think often of *your* father, and of his desolation. And I envy you, for you can have none save happy memories.

Brailsford, Jan. 5, 1880

DEAREST EMMIE,

Thank you so very much for sending those letters, and for hunting them up. They must certainly have been written by Chalfont to Lufton; the first two I put in 1810-11, the last must have been written in 1816, when his mother died.

I am getting on famously with Jim's great-uncle. He has just bought Troy Chimneys. The papers give me some invaluable information about Chalfont. I feel that

I quite understand the poor little man. It is a wonder that he was not much madder than that, with such a father. I once read a description of breaking on the wheel, and it gave me nightmares for a week.

Cunningham is now here with me and is enthusiastically wrestling with the Chalfont boxes, some of which are too heavy for me to lift. We have done wonders in the last day or two. We have waded through a ton of recorded dreams, tailors' bills, sketches of cottages which he never built, and letters from poets, some famous, some now forgotten. We have kept our eyes open for the name of Lufton, but have found nothing yet.

Cunningham is now reading the Lufton memoir, the early part. He says that Lufton should have been a Whig — that he would have been perfectly happy if he could have got up a hero-worship for Fox. It was a piece of bad luck that the Amershams were Tories. If he had struck up a friendship with the son of a great Whig family, it would have suited him much better.

But I don't know. I imagine that *Pronto* would have been pretty much the same among the Whigs, though he could have spouted more about Emancipation and Reform. There was that kind of climber on both sides.

Cunningham says he might have gone in with humanitarian reformers, and instanced Romilly and Whitbread, who were much ahead of their age. I told him that he had not selected very happy examples, for they both succumbed to melancholy. One cut his own throat, I believe, and the other shot himself. Castlereagh was not the only man in public life to commit suicide during the Regency.

It was a *melancholy age*. Everything I read convinces me of that. To survive it one had to be thick-skinned, or a fanatic, like Wilberforce, able to hammer away at one point and overlook the rest. Reforms of every kind were overdue, but it was the less sensitive, the men who did not suffer from too much imagination, who took the first steps. The poets secluded themselves, or got out of the country, and the humanitarians blew out their brains.

I thank heaven that I was born in 1850! So much has been accomplished, that we may be sure the rest will follow. We have got rid of oppression, injustice and tyranny. Another fifty years may see the whole Continent as far advanced as we, and then we may hope to 'Ring out the thousand wars of old, — Ring in the thousand years of peace!' There's a New Year message for you!

Your loving brother
FRED

THE LUFTON PAPERS
(Concluded)

JOURNAL

THE Present obtrudes upon the Past in a manner which I had not foreseen. I had thought Miles to be quite finished and waiting submissively by the Styx until Pronto joins him. But he grows unexpectedly lively, — as troublesome as ever, else he would not have got the business of Harry Ridding put right. Few though his good deeds may have been, he has at least that one to his credit. Harry and his farm are safe.

The Past, moreover, obtrudes upon the Present. Things dead and done with don't lie easy in their graves. A note which I wrote to Edmée fifteen years ago (I had forgotten it, but I must have sent it on that morning when I went to Brailsford to ask for the Ullacombe living) has turned up, or rather been brought up, in a way which might have ended in wigs on the green. If Ned had not chosen to take my word rather than hers, he must have called me out. The sight of those few hurried words, dashed off so long ago by an earlier Miles, affected me so much that I never considered this aspect of it until later. I don't know if Madam wished us to fight, but she certainly meant us to quarrel.

My indignation over Harry's wrongs so grew upon me that I was unable to remain a passive spectator. I went over to Ribstone again and saw him, and offered to pay the arrears of his rent and the next half-year in advance, if we could get some document from Ned accepting this payment, and waiving the forfeiture clause in his lease. Harry refused in a very surly manner. He said that it was as bad to owe money to one gentleman as to another and that, if he was to be ruined, he would sooner be so without accepting charity, etc. I could feel for him. A man used so ill, cheated out of his rights, must cling to his pride. But he probably talked it over with his wife, who is a sensible woman, for he appeared at the Parsonage next day in a different frame of mind. He owned that he would be very grateful for the loan from me, and told me of his hopes for a gradual repayment. I know that he will do his best. If he fails, I tell myself that I can well afford the loss.

I set off at once for the Park and had the good luck to meet Ned upon the way. He greeted me quite cordially, and I told him my errand without any preamble. He made fewer difficulties than I had expected. He seemed to be uneasy himself over Ridding's case, though he did not understand it very well, and had been misled by Simmons over the terms of the lease. I explained that there would be no need to make out another, a task which he obviously dreaded, in face of the opposition he might expect. A letter, signed by himself, accepting the money and waiving the forfeiture clause, would suffice. He asked me to come with him to the Park and to write the letter 'in a way no attorney fellow can upset.' We were in the library, at work upon this, when Madam burst in upon us, demanding to know what we were about.

Ned, looking more frightened than I could have wished, began to explain. She said angrily that Ridding was not a desirable tenant, a poor farmer who could not pay his way, and that they owed it to themselves to put in a better man.

I was determined not to interfere, and kept silence while Ned valiantly brought out some of the arguments that I had used with him, — that Harry had never failed with his rent before, that he was honest and industrious, and that his family were old tenants on the Bramfield property.

'My father and his father——' said he, but he was not allowed to continue further.

'Your father, Mr. Chadwick, did his best to ruin his family. We should be beggars if we continued as he did. Farms are not almshouses, nor parsonages neither!'

This was a hit at my father, as we both knew. She thinks that it is time he died, so that she may be able to dispose of the living. Ned began to look promisingly obstinate.

'We shall not be the losers in this transaction,' he began, 'we are to be paid in full. Miles has——'

'Oh I know that it is all Mr. Lufton's doing! If he likes to frow his money away he must please himself, but he should not saddle us with a bad tenant.'

(I used once to be charmed by her inability to say *thr*.)

'Harry Ridding is an old friend,' continued Ned doggedly. 'We used all to play cricket together, when we were boys.'

'A fine reason for allowing him to ruin your land!'

'I say that he does not ruin it.'

'I say that he does.'

I suppose I should have walked out of the room. It is intolerable to witness bickering of this sort between a husband and wife. But I was unwilling to go until I had got that letter in my pocket, and I feared his resolution if I deserted him just then. I put in a word or two, since I could not stand by in silence.

I said that Ned and I had learnt a great deal from playing with the village children and tenants' sons. Ignoring her exclamation of disgust, and her assertion that village children are nasty, dirty creatures with whom her own should never be suffered to associate, I said that in this way gentlemen's sons may learn how villagers think, how they talk among themselves, how they regard their betters, what are their difficulties, hopes and fears. We had learnt, in that little democracy of childhood, lessons which differences in station might have withheld from us later on, for we should never again be met with such frankness.

I don't think that she listened. She stood (we were all standing, since she would not sit) gazing at me contemptuously, not for what I said, but for being what I am. She is a formidable creature, one can't deny it. There are no two sides to *her*; she is all of a piece and that is why she always gets what she wants. Nobody could call her a beauty now. She wore a morning wrapper and a strange tall cap, none too fresh; if she had washed herself recently the fact was not apparent. But she is — powerfully *female*. One cannot talk to her, or look at her, without being aware of it. Repulsive as she is, there is but one thing to be done with her; she knows it and despises those who expect anything else. She thinks me a fool for not having made better use of my opportunities in the avenue that night, long ago. She thinks Ned a fool for marrying her. I daresay she may have some respect for Pinney, if, as I believe, he took her measure, enjoyed her, and got clean off.

Ned, during my little homily, had been whipping up his courage. When I had done, he said that he was resolved to let Harry Ridding remain at the farm.

'If you do,' said she, 'I shall never forgive you. The farm is promised to Mr. Simmons for his son.'

'I made no such promise, and I don't mean to change my mind. You had better leave us to get on with the business.'

Huzzah! cried I to myself, pretending to look out of the window. The next sound that I heard was the door

slamming and a sigh of relief from Ned. The enemy
had retreated.

We continued with our letter. Ned had signed it and
I was just putting it into my pocket when she reappeared,
carrying a sheet of paper. My heart sank. I thought
that she might previously have got his signature to some
other document which could cook our goose.

'You force me to show you this,' said she, putting it
into his hand. 'I have kept silence, Mr. Chadwick, only
because I did not wish to cause ill feeling in your family.
I have been accused too often in that way. You must
know that Mr. Lufton is not to be trusted. If you knew
all, you would have forbidden him the house these many
years, for at one time he persecuted me with attempts
which he knew to be odious to me, nor would he desist
until I freatened to tell you. Will you please to read
this?'

This proved to be my confounded love letter. Ned
looked at it, stared, swore, demanded what the devil it
meant, and was at last persuaded to let me see it.

That it was my hand I could not deny. It was undated
and the ink was faded. It said that I was off to Brailsford
but hoped to return in a couple of days, and that I would
then say all that I had been prevented from saying 'when
Ned stumbled upon us, and you ran off.' There were
some sentences of tender apology for my own want of
restraint. I hoped that she was not angry, — I had not
been able to help it — I loved her too well. She would
forgive me, she must forgive me, for I was all hers and
would behave better next time.

'I suppose,' said I, when I had collected my wits,
'that I must have written this at a time when I believed
myself engaged to — Edmée de Cavignac.'

'I was never engaged to you,' said she coolly.

'I beg your pardon, Madam! I never said that you

were. If you had thought yourself engaged to me you would not have married my cousin. But I made you an offer, and misunderstood you so much that I believed myself accepted.'

'When was this?' asked Ned, who was staring suspiciously at us both.

'Very soon before — before your marriage, Ned.'

'That is a lie,' stated Edmée. 'He never made me an offer. He used every art to seduce me, both before and after I married, but he never made me any honourable proposal.'

The effrontery of this so confounded me that I was speechless. I saw that it was her word against mine. She meant to get rid of me, and my interference on Harry's behalf, by getting up a quarrel, — any quarrel. I was to give her the lie in Ned's presence, an insult which no husband can allow. She hoped to provoke a burst of indignation which would betray me into doing this. But, fortunately for us all, I felt none just then. I could only feel very sad, for myself, for Ned, even for her. When I spoke, it was with a mildness which startled both of them.

'Our memories tell us different things,' I said. 'It all happened a long time ago. I remember that I loved you once, and told you so, and asked you to be my wife, before I ever dreamed that you would marry Ned. I am very sorry indeed if you did not understand me and believe that you have cause to remember otherwise.'

I turned to Ned and added:

'You have known me all your life. I cannot be quite sure when I wrote this letter. I can only ask you to consider whether you think me capable——'

He interrupted me with an oath.

'I'll be damned if I think it. You were always a good fellow, Miles. You were after her too. I knew that. But you would always have been above-board, and once she was my wife you would keep off.'

'You say that I lie? You insult your wife?'

She advanced upon Ned as though about to strike him, but he pushed her roughly aside exclaiming :

'I have had enough of your tricks. I know them. Come along, Miles! If you are going to see Ridding, I think I will come too.'

As soon as we were out of the house he said that women are all the same and that one cannot trust a word they say. They are never satisfied until they have got a man hugging them and squeezing them in some snug corner, and then they cry out that it is all his fault. He was not by any means as shocked or as embarrassed as I was. Fifteen years with her have, I suppose, rid him of what little delicacy he possessed. But it was intolerable to me that she should so have exposed herself before us both, — that we should be obliged to admit what she is. I had an impulse to excuse and defend her, and said that it might have been difficult for her to understand us, coming amongst us as a stranger and unused to our way of thinking.

'Ay! That's what she says. They are all against her, because she is a foreigner.'

I suggested that, for this very reason, she should not play so great a part in managing his affairs. She might mean well, and, with such a family, it was but common sense that she should watch every penny. But she could not be expected to understand the management of a great property, and I was sure that Simmons imposed upon her. If he would but get an honest steward, and attend to these matters himself, a heavy burden would be taken from her.

He listened moodily, but he did not disagree with me.

We went to Ribstone and settled the business of the farm. Before we left I had the pleasure of seeing Harry grasp Ned's hand with something of the old cordiality. This part of the affair I can never regret. Neither Edmée nor Simmons can get Harry out now, unless he has very bad luck.

My spirits rose upon the journey home. I dared to hope that this might be the turn of the tide and that, having once asserted himself, Ned might continue. He is very stupid, but I think that he could manage well, with a good steward to advise him. His family life must always be wretched, but in the world, would he but exert himself, he might be useful and respectable. He looked more like his old self, when we were at Ribstone, than I have seen him for many a year. But I noticed that his face grew longer and longer as we approached the Park. When we came into the village he burst out with :

''Tis all very well, Miles ! *You* are not married.'

Since it was dinner-time I suggested that he might come to the Parsonage, when we had stabled our horses. He accepted with alacrity, poor fellow ! Had I suggested that he remain for the rest of his life at the Parsonage, I believed he would have jumped at the offer.

All the family had known of my errand, when I started for the Park that morning, and were upon the watch for my return. The sight of Ned with me assured them that the news must be good, and they welcomed him with all the affection which we have missed for so long. By good luck we had an eatable dinner ; Nanny had dressed some ducks and we had a side of beef.

Sukey pleased me by putting aside all her grievances against the Park ; she could not have been more pleasant and civil to Ned. When at her best, as she was that night, she can be very charming. She is the cleverest, the most amusing, of all my sisters, just as Caroline was the sweetest,

Kitty is the kindest, and Harriet the most beautiful. My
father and George both displayed their unqualified
pleasure in this settlement of Harry's business and even
Anna managed to smile. It was the pleasantest evening
that we have had since my mother died ; something of
her spirit seemed to have returned to us.

Ned stayed late, though I knew that they were all
wishing him gone, that they might learn how I managed
to circumvent Edmée. When, at last, he was forced to
move, he did so very unwillingly. I took him to the door
and watched him slowly cross the lane and let himself
into the Park by the little gate. His day of freedom was
over and now he must spend the night with Edmée.

A thousand questions awaited me when I returned to
the parlour. I merely told them that Edmée had been
outrageous, — so outrageous that I should not repeat
what she had said. I daresay they all supposed her to
have said something insulting about my father. He
looked a trifle grave when he heard that I had carried my
point in face of open opposition from her, and said that
he was sorry I should have taken part in a conjugal
dispute. Nobody, said he, is justified in coming between
husband and wife.

'Would you have had me desert Harry's cause ?' said I.

'No. But I would have had you avoid an open dispute
with her. You could have waited until you could get Ned
alone.'

'That would have been never. She would have seen
to it.'

'Poor Ned,' cried Sukey. 'She will make him pay for
this piece of independence.'

'He must stand up for himself better. Since he has
begun, he had better go on.'

Sukey shook her head at this and doubted whether
Ned could keep it up.

'But we shall know if he does,' she said, 'because in that case, he will come here again quite soon. He knows that we all support him. If he keeps away from us, that will mean that he has hauled his colours down.'

We did not see him again until church on Sunday. What he must have suffered in the interval defeats imagination. He gave me a baleful, furious look, more like the glare of a baited animal than of a human being. I daresay he is now angry at me for getting him into this scrape. I fear that all may now be over, in the way of friendship between us. But, if I had not stood my ground, it would have been all over with poor Harry. I cannot regret what I did.

But I must record that I dreamt again, that night, of Maria Cotman, — in what connection I cannot remember. The fact would not have struck me had I not recently recorded my former dream. In fairness to Ludovic, I have written to tell him of it. But I do not see what reason she has, upon this occasion, to triumph over Miles.

Not that I am quite satisfied at the way in which I managed the business. I believe that I should not have tried to excuse or defend Edmée, as we rode to Ribstone. I should have let him speak out, which I believe he would have done, had I not checked him. We could have agreed that he has married a horrible creature, but that all women are much the same. In that way we could have formed a kind of brutal male alliance which might hold against such assaults as she must have made since then. Once again, we were harassed by the wish to behave and speak like gentlemen. What is a man to say about such a woman, if he may not describe her in ungentlemanly terms ?

I believe that it is upon account of creatures like this that men most usually fight. 'A woman's honour' is a cant phrase. It is a total lack of it in some women which engenders violence. If a man cannot describe his wife without disgracing himself, he must relinquish reason and become a fighting animal. Swords and pistols are his escape from the truth. We are lucky, Ned and I, to have come out of this as well as we did.

MEMOIR: 1808–1818

Lingshot

LADY AMERSHAM was seldom wrong. All that she had foretold at Colesworth came to pass within a twelve-month. Portland resigned. Perceval succeeded him. Pronto got his place, and stuck to it for eight years.

Respectable and hard-working years were they for Pronto. He was able to drop some uncongenial acquaintance and he grew very steady. When visiting in the country he spent more evenings at his writing-desk than in the drawing-room. He was no longer obliged to sing for his supper or to put up with people who called him Pronto to his face.

Miles did not care for all this work, but otherwise had no quarrel with him. Money was laying by, Troy Chimneys grew more charming every year, and the door-way to escape stood ever open. So, at least, thought Miles. That it had been slammed, and barred, by Pronto before the house was even bought — but I must go back a little in order to explain how that came about.

Pronto, in those first years of struggle, never neglected civility in certain quarters which a less thorough fellow might have been liable to overlook. He knew that great people will often forget a promise, or a friend, unless there is someone at hand to remind them at the critical moment. This *someone* need not be a person of any great consequence so long as he or she is certain to be there when need arises; a poor relation, a spinster aunt,

even a confidential servant will do, — any of those permanent fixtures in great houses which rate almost with
the furniture. If chairs and tables could be grateful for
polite attention, and could express gratitude by crying
out : PRONTO ! whenever his lordship is about to dispose
of a piece of patronage, — then Pronto would have been
very civil to the chairs and tables. He would, of course,
make no parade of it, but he would pay some pleasant
little compliment to the table as he took his seat at it,
suggest that it has been frequently in his thoughts since
he saw it last, and enquire with concern after the great
scratch it got last year.

Universal geniality is so much a habit with him that
he continued in it long after he had no need to do so.
'Mr. Lufton has a kind word for everybody !' says the
housekeeper. 'Mr. Lufton never forgets to ask after my
rheumatism,' cries the poor old cousin. 'Mr. Lufton
made a snowman for us,' remember the children. With
so many voices in his favour, Mr. Lufton is less likely to
be forgotten.

No ally is more useful, in this way, than one of those
supernumerary gentlewomen who sit in corners making
fringe, who write notes, run errands, wash lap-dogs, play
country dances, and ride backwards in the carriage. They
are immensely important, and their good word should
always be secured. Pronto never forgot their names and
took pains to discover their tastes. If one pressed flowers,
he would always contrive to bring some for her when he
took a country walk ; they might be the commonest of
weeds, but she was pleased with the attention. If another
netted a shawl, he always knew for whom it was intended
and never failed to enquire after its progress. He was
seldom so busy dancing that he forgot to thank the lady
at the instrument.

It was as an ally of this sort that he first took notice

of Miss Caroline Audley, in the early days of his servitude
to fortune, when he was obliged to look very sharp about
him. She was the half-sister of his friend Frank Morrill
of Lingshot, in Surrey, with whom Pronto stayed a good
deal about the year 1806, before he got West Malling.
Morrill had two seats in his pocket and Pronto hoped to
get one of them.

Miss Audley was at that time about five and twenty,
but seemed older in comparison with a bevy of blooming
half-sisters in their teens. She was tall, above the middle
height, with light-brown hair which she wound into a
grecian knot at the back of her head. Her eyes were
hazel and her complexion clear, but too pale. There
was nothing in her to strike one, in that house full of
handsome girls. Her manner was grave, although she
smiled often enough to contradict any suggestion of
melancholy. Her voice, low and very clear, was seldom
heard ; but when she spoke all listened, for she spoke
only when applied to for her opinion.

Pronto noticed that she had a good deal of influence
with her half-brother. He therefore lost no time in
acquainting himself with her circumstances and history.
He is very adroit at getting information without seeming
to ask ill-bred questions. He learnt that Captain Audley,
her father and Mrs. Morrill's first husband, had left her
no fortune, that she had been engaged, seven years before,
to a naval officer who had fallen in action, and that since
then she had refused an offer from a clergyman. (Most
of this information must have come from Louisa Morrill,
a prattler of sixteen who never knew the meaning of
reserve.) She was no favourite with her mother, for
whom she slaved without complaint. Mrs. Morrill's
affection was entirely reserved for her second family.
Gentle, pensive Caroline had always been regarded by
her as, in childhood an encumbrance, and later as an

unpaid servant. The half-brothers and -sisters were all
fond of her, but they had been brought up to regard her
as of no consequence, — her comfort or wishes were
seldom considered.

Her good graces might be valuable to Pronto, and he
set himself to secure them. He paid her a good deal of
attention, — not so marked as to arouse expectations, he
was too sharp for that, — but he certainly took more
notice of her than other people did. It was no unpleasant
task, for she was very conversible and a good musician,
the best accompanist he ever had. He *may* have indicated
a little more admiration than he felt ; most women expect
that and like it. And he had a genuine regard for her,
so that Miles was not entirely banished from the scene ;
she had, obviously, enough taste to prefer his style to
Pronto's.

After securing West Malling he saw less of the Morrills
for some years. But the intimacy revived when Perceval
was succeeded by Liverpool, and Vansittart went to the
Exchequer. Morrill was a connection of Vansittart and
had gone into Parliament himself ; he and Pronto were
thrown together a good deal in their joint support of
Vansittart, and from 1812 onwards Pronto was a constant
visitor at Lingshot.

Mrs. Morrill was now dead and her son married. But
Miss Audley was still there, doing for young Mrs. Morrill
everything that she had formerly done for her mother.
All the Morrill girls were married except Margaret, the
eldest, but it was not to be expected that Caroline Audley
would now marry ; she was past thirty and an old maid.
Pronto was pleased to see her again, to resume their
pleasant chats and to sing to her accompaniment.

The Morrills were well-bred people of the sort now
cultivated by him. They never called him by that odious
name and, in fact, the protean creature least deserved it

when in their house. Though possessed of considerable influence, they did not move, never aspired to move, in the highest circles. They were a good old respectable county family. Since they were not in the peerage they could be nice in their choice of acquaintance; they were not obliged to entertain a Lowestoft or invite a Crockett to keep him in the billiard-room. They only asked that Pronto should behave like a gentleman and for this Miles was grateful, though he thought them a trifle dull. The Pronto of Richmond Hill, the Pronto who sang Mary Hawker's song at Colesworth, never showed up at Lingshot.

He was a particular favourite with young Mrs. Morrill, who hoped to make up a match between him and Miss Margaret. The sisters-in-law did not hit it off very well, and Pronto in 1813 was far more eligible than Pronto in 1806. He had a brother an admiral, a sister married to a baronet, he was earning £4000 a year, had property in Wiltshire, a place at the Exchequer and a promising future. It was high time that he married. Many of his fair friends were agreed upon that. In houses where, seven years earlier, he would never have been tolerated as a suitor, he was now encouraged to admire those daughters who had hung too long upon the family tree. Had he wished to marry, he could have got a wife with a larger fortune and greater connections than Margaret could bring him. He was, however, in no hurry. He did not care to subject himself to the influence of any one set, and he was also, perhaps, aware that Miles might give trouble if he took a wife. Miles had kept quiet, all these years, because it was understood that he might claim his freedom some day. He had submitted to Pronto's domestic arrangements, including the villa at St. John's Wood (which was given up in 1814), but a wife of Pronto's choosing was not to be imagined at Troy Chimneys.

This long truce came to an end at Easter last year. I was staying with the Morrills, and one morning I took a stroll before breakfast. Whenever I am in the country it is my habit to rise early and take a walk before Pronto comes on duty. My path took me through a beech wood ; the bluebells were particularly fine that year. Pronto had taken that path the day before, with Mrs. Morrill and Margaret, and had said as much as they required in praise of so lovely a sight. But Miles could not fully enjoy it until he was alone.

Walking some way before me, down the noble aisle made by the trees, I caught sight of a young woman whom I did not recognise as staying in the house. I presumed her to be young, although I could not see her face, because of a *something* in her walk. How shall I describe it ? Few women walk so, after the age of one and twenty. They may move with conscious grace until they are ninety, but they are marching in step with Time's heavy foot, and they know it. Only the young, who never heard that tramp, walk as easily as the light flows on my ceilings at Troy Chimneys, can muse while skipping along, and never know that half an hour's walk will bring them thirty minutes nearer to the end of all. This girl did not skip ; she was walking slowly. I thought for a moment of my mother, who also had a something in her walk which I have already likened to the gliding of some beautiful ship. But this other, thought I, evokes a different image, — her progress is more solitary, more mysterious — one does not know whence she comes, or whither she goes — she does not appear to know it herself — she is like a cloud which floats slowly onward, not of its own will, but carried by some quiet wind unfelt upon earth. '*Lonely as a cloud.*' I must find out who she is !

I quickened my pace so as to catch up with her. As I drew nearer I recognised, with a pang of disappoint-

ment, that grecian knot of hair. This mysterious stranger
was but my old friend, Miss Audley. I had never seen
her before at a moment when she thought herself alone.
The enchantment dissolved and I was about to turn off
into a side avenue, for I was in no mood to sacrifice my
solitude, when she heard my footsteps and turned.

I hastily summoned Pronto, who was delighted at the
encounter and convinced that she must find it equally
gratifying. A stroll through the woods with so universal
a favourite as himself could not displease her. He offered
his arm and she took it. But they had not proceeded
very far before he became aware that he was *de trop*.
This meeting was unwelcome, and he knew it because he
is very sensitive to atmosphere. She was tranquilly
pleasant, as ever ; in fact she was too much as ever.
They might have been walking with a dozen people. The
tone, the pace, the glances, suitable to a *tête-à-tête*, were
missing. Miss Audley also was, apparently, in no mood
to sacrifice her solitude.

But there was no way out of it. Good manners con-
strained them to walk together until they were out of the
wood. But when they reached the Lingshot garden
Pronto thought that he might escape. He invented a
sudden errand to the stables, explained it, and took his
leave with becoming grace :

'Such a delicious walk as we have had ! I shall *never*
forget it !'

The hazel eyes rested upon his for a moment. She
half smiled and said :

'Oh, Mr. Lufton ! How hard you work ! Are you
really obliged to say such things *before* breakfast ?'

In any other woman this might have been flirtatious,
but it was impossible to imagine Miss Audley as a flirt.
Raillery, in a friend of eleven years' standing, is permis-
sible. Yet Pronto felt a little foolish.

'You are very severe!' he complained. 'I fear you don't approve of compliments?'

'Oh, yes, I like them after ten o'clock in the morning. Before that, I think we should all say and do exactly as we please.'

'I am very sorry,' said Miles. 'I knew that you would rather have been alone in the wood. But I did not know how to dispose of myself. I ought to have climbed the nearest tree. I am afraid that I spoiled your ramble.'

'Not more than I spoiled yours. We both, I fancy, had gone out alone to gaze at the bluebells, without all those Ohs! and Ahs! and endeavours to ascertain *how* blue they are. And now we have prevented one another, because we are altogether too polite.'

'Exactly. But I am the worse sinner, because I told you that they were like the sea, and you did not irritate me by likening them to anything.'

'Oh! I don't mind the sea very much. They may be as blue as the sea for all I care, since I never saw it.'

'What? You have never seen the sea?'

'Never!'

'Ah! you have missed something.'

'I believe so. Everybody tells me that I should admire it extremely but nobody offers to take me there, and I have so little spirit that I have not yet set off in search of it myself. Is it really the colour of bluebells?'

'Not at all. But I cannot believe that you *never* saw it!'

'Can you not? I have never been away from Lingshot for a single night, you know, since I was two years old.'

'Good God!'

My horror amused her. She does not laugh when she is amused, but her eyes become lighter in colour. They have a kind of golden glow. I had not noticed it before. I wondered that I had not. And, while I was still pondering over this, she nodded to me and walked off.

I felt that the conversation was by no means finished, but had no chance to resume it during the day. I went into the drawing-room at least half an hour before dinner, however, in the hope that she might be early too. She generally was down and dressed before the others, in case there should be some last-minute duty or emergency, — the fish not come or the dessert to be arranged.

I was rewarded. She was there, reading by the window. I took the book from her, ascertained that it was Crabbe, and was making some remark about his work when she objected, with a trace of impatience, that we had been discussing Crabbe for eleven years. I suppose that we had, and it was ridiculous to begin upon the subject as though we had just met. But I could not explain that Pronto's discussions did not count.

'I will tell you something about him,' said I, 'which you never heard before, from me at least, because I only learnt it lately myself. I hope you don't know it.'

I told her how Crabbe had taken the manuscript of his poems to Edmund Burke and was then unable to leave the spot where his fate might be decided. All night he paced up and down in the vicinity, watching a light in a window of Burke's house, and playing with the fancy that the great man might be sitting up, reading his poems.

'And so it was,' I concluded. 'The light was in Burke's room. He did sit up all night. He was reading the poems.'

I got another golden look.

'I wonder if we should like it,' she said, 'if the world were always as well managed as that ! I believe we might think it dull. Such a story is pleasing because it is rare. Tell me another.'

' 'Tis your turn to tell me one.'

Footsteps were heard crossing the ante-room.

'Some other time I will.'

'*Before* breakfast?'

She smiled and shook her head as Mrs. Baddely, young Mrs. Morrill's mother, came in. But after dinner, when she was to play for me and we were looking over some songs, I contrived to whisper that I should walk early in the wood and that, in honesty, she owed me a story.

'And to which of you am I to tell it?' she asked, selecting a song.

'To which? Ah — you don't know me — you must not judge me by——'

'Nonsense! I have known you both for eleven years.'

She walked across the room and sat down at the pianoforte. Pronto sang less like an angel than usual.

Miss Audley

IT was with some trepidation that I set forth upon my early ramble next day. She had not exactly forbidden me to join her, but she had given me to understand that she liked to be alone at that hour. I was determined, however, to find out what she had meant, and I knew of no other time in the day when I might be certain of a private interview.

I did not above half like it. Miles and Pronto were not near so distinct in my mind *then* as they are *now*, but I was keenly aware of some inner conflict and had thought that nobody suspected it save Ludovic. It was most disagreeable to suppose it common knowledge, — to imagine that jokes could be made as to 'which' of us might be expected to dinner. Such a fancy kept me awake for half the night.

I went towards the beech wood and found her waiting
for me by the gate out of the garden. She came forward
at once, more agitated than I had ever seen her, and burst
into a frank apology:

'Oh! I was hoping that you would come! I must
ask your pardon for my intolerable impertinence last
night. I cannot imagine what prompted me to speak so.
If you have ever, yourself, talked nonsense, and regretted
it, then you must forgive me!'

'My dear Miss Audley!' said I, drawing her arm
through mine and leading her into the wood, 'you can
never in your life have talked nonsense. I can only accuse
you of obscurity. Pray explain! Who are these two
gentlemen whom you have known for eleven years?'

'Oh, it is nothing — a ridiculous fancy of mine. I
meant the *private* Mr. Lufton and the *political* Mr. Lufton.
There is some such distinction, I imagine, in anyone who
must sustain a public character.'

'And are they really so distinct? Can you always tell
them apart?'

'I think so. The private Mr. Lufton likes solitude and
hates the world. The political Mr. Lufton never forgets
his duty, and will pay compliments before breakfast.'

'I see. I was aware of the distinction myself, but I
had not thought it so obvious to my friends.'

'Oh but it is not!' she exclaimed quickly. 'I assure
you that nobody save myself, so far as I know, ever thought
of anything so foolish.'

At this I grew easier, for it was impossible to doubt
her word. I asked if she had any particular names for
these two creatures, for I still feared that the hateful
name of Pronto might be used at Lingshot, behind my
back. She parried the question, but at last, perceiving
that it had some real importance for me, confessed that
she called them *Lufton* and *The M.P.*

'But I was not an M.P. eleven years ago!'

'No. But I was sure that you would soon become one.'

I blushed a little, remembering how determined I had been to secure one of Morrill's seats, and realising that she must have seen through my manœuvres. I felt that we were in an awkward situation, as though we had been dancing in a masquerade which had lasted for eleven years. Now that the masks were down, *I* was a little out of countenance. She was not quite what I had always supposed. I could have wished that her surprise should be equal, — that she should make some discovery concerning me. I decided that she had better learn to know Miles better ; she had guessed at his existence but she could know little of his more amiable qualities.

As we sauntered through the wood I made several observations which were quite worthy of Miles but which sounded as though they came from Pronto. At every step I expected her to ask how the M.P. came to be out so early. But she listened and assented very demurely. At last, in despair, I asked for the story that she owed me, reminding her that she had promised one.

'But I don't know what kind of story you prefer.'

'Something, if you please, in the style of my Crabbe story. Something with an unexpectedly happy ending.'

She reflected for a while and then she said that she would tell me the story of Billy Thatcher, a foundling, brought up by the Parish at Lingshot.

I prepared myself for a pathetic tale, for her manner was grave. It remained so throughout the whole history of Billy Thatcher, which was as unedifying a fable as ever I heard. Billy, it appeared, was a rustic rogue, drunkard, poacher and thief, who possessed a miraculous faculty for disconcerting his betters. The final episode ran something like this :

'We therefore decided to put Billy in the stocks, as an

example. But he did not remain there for above half an hour, because the London coach came in, garlanded with laurel, and drew up at the inn. It does not do so generally, you know. Everyone knew that there must have been a great victory and ran out to hear the news. Whereat Billy set up a bellow that he was a Briton too, and had as good a right as anybody to hear about *his* victory. It was universally allowed that he had, so the beadle was fetched, and Billy let out and brought to the coach, where he might hear the guard read the newspaper. This was a great blow to our morals at Lingshot, for nobody had ever got out of the stocks so quickly before, and all the little children were more struck by this circumstance than by any other, upon that historic day. Indeed, I am certain that when Dr. Dowling referred in his sermon, upon the following Sunday, to "the hero of Waterloo" every child in the church believed him to be talking of Billy Thatcher.'

I was lost in amazement, for I had always thought her to have little sense of the ridiculous. I remembered that I had, but two days earlier, beheld her reading Law's *Serious Call* to Mrs. Baddely, who slept profoundly during the exercise but was liable to rouse if the reader desisted. The contrast between her great snores, and the austere exhortations read out to her, was one which nearly capsized my solemnity. What a good thing, I thought, that Miss Audley is not easily struck by the ludicrous ! For I had not then learnt to recognise that golden glow which signified secret amusement. I am now sure that she was enjoying herself very much.

After that I met her and walked with her every morning. I have said that the Morrills, though pleasant, were a trifle dull. One could always be certain of what they would do in any circumstances, — of what they would say upon any subject. I sometimes found myself quite

suffocated by this, although I liked them. I wondered
why they ever troubled themselves to talk, since it was
but to repeat what they had said a thousand times already.
Miss Audley was never dull, one could never be quite
certain of what she would say, and conversation with her
was a most refreshing kind of entertainment.

These early rambles were no secret from the rest of the
family, but nobody, I think, thought them surprising.
We were old friends, we both liked to walk before breakfast ; it was but natural that we should walk together.
To suppose me her admirer would not have occurred to
them. She was an established old maid in their eyes,
and I an eligible bachelor with a very good opinion of his
own deserts in the way of a wife. I myself was so much
aware of this that I sought her company without fear of
raising expectations or provoking comment. I knew her
to be far too sensible to suppose that I had fallen in love
with her, and I had no fear that she might fall in love .
with me. She said things occasionally which no woman
would say to a man in whom she hoped to inspire tender
feelings. She was too calm, too candid. There were
none of the little pauses, the evasions, the altered tones,
which betray hidden feelings of that sort.

Her solitude was the circumstance which, at first,
struck me most forcibly, as I came to understand her
character. She had spent the whole of her life at Lingshot,
had met no company, read no books, heard no conversation, save what that house afforded, yet she was completely unlike all the rest of them. She had never known
a parent's indulgent tenderness. She had been of first
consequence with nobody, save for those few weeks when
she had been courted by her sailor. She was then but
seventeen and he one and twenty, — the nephew of a
neighbouring squire. They danced together a good deal,
but had, I imagine, few conversations alone. 'A pitiful

little engagement' was her mother's description of it. I think that he was dear to her chiefly because she was dear to him. He departed, never to return, and she, for twenty years, had been learning how to make the best of solitude. I remarked to her once that Lingshot was not, surely, the place which she would have chosen for life, had she been free to choose. She owned that it was not and that she had, at one time, suffered pangs of rebellion.

'But then, you know, it would have made a whole family miserable, and me no happier, had I allowed myself to become a tiresome creature. It is one's duty to be happy, I think, — as happy as one can.'

She had been equal to this duty because her principles were firm and because she had worked out for herself a strange kind of philosophy which enabled her to extract a good deal of entertainment from a life which most would have thought intolerable. She took great pleasure in observing everything minutely and in musing over what she saw. She had deliberately fostered her own solitude, — her independence from her surroundings. She once said that nothing can be truly appreciated 'unless one withdraws oneself from it. Our preferences must always blind us.' It was clear to me that great suffering had gone to form this philosophy, but I did not wonder, when I thought of what her life had been.

Her greatest pleasure was in the strange, the unexpected and the paradoxical, — all those elements which were least in favour at Lingshot. She had also a taste for irony; in the 'stories' which I told her, it was always the ironic which most struck her fancy. I quarrelled with her a little for that. Irony makes me uneasy. But she liked it. She thought that it modified the sadness of the human lot; 'since so many stories seem to be but part of some other story which we do not quite understand.'

I was sorry to have so little to tell her, for Pronto's

adventures supplied very few anecdotes of the kind that she liked. She was eager to hear of my visit to Paris, two years before, for she would have liked to travel and read all the travelling books that came her way. But I had nothing to tell her of Paris that would do, save my meeting with Princess Czerny, and those old stories of Rome and my Aunt Gussie. Of Peel, Wellington, Castlereagh and Fitzgerald, whom I had constantly met while there, I had only the most commonplace Morrill-ish tales to tell. She preferred to hear about Ullacombe and Bramfield and Ludovic reciting Wordsworth to the cows.

She, in turn, told me the history of every person in Lingshot village. Her stories were full of spirit and character. Not all of them were as cheerful as that of Billy Thatcher. She told me once that the trouble and sorrow she had witnessed among the poor had struck her so forcibly as to make her ashamed of rebellion against her own lot. One incident in particular brought tears to her eyes when she spoke of it, — a natural child sold to a man who was taking a party of children northward, to set them to work at cotton spinning.

'I saw the little boy's face as he was led away,' she said. 'I shall never forget it. So helpless! So helpless!'

Those words reminded me of Ludovic and his *helpless!* For a moment a great pang went through me, a kind of despair, as though some giant wave were breaking over the world, and in my ears were millions upon millions of voices sighing: Helpless! Helpless!

'I went to my brother,' she continued, 'and told him that I thought we had abolished slavery upon British soil. He explained to me that it is not slavery; he said the lad would be paid for his work and could leave it if he chooses, and that I might be sure these children would be well cared for. He said it was for the boy's own good to be taken where he could get employment. But how can we be sure? The man that took them had a dreadful face. And how could a child of seven leave his work, if he was ill treated? He looked at me, as he was led away — like a dying person — and I could do nothing. But after that I thought: What is *my* lot? What are *my* wrongs? And I think it changed me very much.'

She asked me earnestly if I thought that these children are well treated. I would not distress her by telling her that I am far from certain that they are. I tried to reassure her. I know very little about it, nor am I anxious to know more, for there is nothing to be done.

Over books we constantly fell out. She liked history, biography and travel, but she did not care much for recent poetry, although I think I might have converted her a little about that. She had never before met with anyone who understood it. But over novels she was obstinate; she could not like them. Edgeworth's *Castle Rackrent* pleased her and she admired Defoe, but she objected strongly to anything sentimental, nor would she listen to my pleas for my favourites: *Emma* and *Mansfield Park*, of which she complained that they kept her continually in the parlour, where she was obliged, in any case, to spend her life. A most entertaining parlour, she allowed, but:

'That lady's greatest admirers will always be men, I believe. For, when they have had enough of the parlour, they may walk out, you know, and we cannot.'

In her judgments of people she was very mild. I seldom heard her censure anybody. I was soon quite easy upon the score of Pronto. So acute an observer must have discerned his insincerities, but so merciful a judge would pardon them. And then, she had never seen what he could be; in that house he was a very respectable fellow.

I was the more astonished, therefore, at her displeasure
one morning when I spoke slightingly of 'The M.P.' and
of the political world in general. She appeared to be
genuinely shocked, and took me up at once, exclaiming
that the political career is the finest open to any man. I
laughed at her, and asked if she would have liked to be in
the Cabinet, and quoted the lines :

> Th' applause of listening senates to command,
> The threats of pain and ruin to despise,
> To scatter plenty o'er a smiling land,
> And read their history in a nation's eyes.

'Oh no, no !' she said. 'I know that you must spend
most of your lives preventing bad from getting worse, a
task for which you get no thanks, though it is the hardest
of all.'

'Then what is so noble in our calling ?'

'It is noble because you may speak for what is noblest
in us. Manners and morals are constantly improving.
We grow more nice in our notions of justice. When some
great measure is to be brought in, it is not the applause of
senates which signifies, it is the silent applause of a nation
which has come to understand and desire it.'

She had, in fact, as exalted a notion of politics as my
mother had of the Church. Her seclusion, her confinement in the narrow life of the parlour, had given her a
heightened admiration for all those activities in which
she, as a woman, could not share. I thought of Lady
Amersham, and smiled. 'Great measures' had not been
much in her line. But the ladies of Lingshot were not of
the Brailsford sort, who had a finger in every pie. They
knew little of politics and cared less. I never saw one of
them reading the newspaper ; it was always taken to the
men's quarters as soon as it arrived. They never joined
in our discussions ; politics, indeed, were avoided in their

presence, and young Mrs. Morrill complained if they
were not :

'If I hear anything more about the State of the Nation,
I shall be obliged to muzzle you men !'

Miss Audley would have liked to hear more. She
once, a little diffidently, asked me to explain the Sinking
Fund to her, for she had heard me speak upon it at
Guildford, and had listened, awestruck, but unable to
understand what I said. I cried for mercy and insisted
that I should pay compliments before breakfast, if I were
not let off the Sinking Fund. I had no idea, at that
time, that she really wished to know ; I thought that she
asked out of civility. It took me some time really to
understand her.

She credited her brother and myself with immense and
disinterested zeal for the public good, the more so because
she could not understand what we did, and was perplexed
by the Sinking Fund. As far as Morrill was concerned,
she may have done him no more than justice. He had a
large fortune and was not obliged to take up any career.
I think he only went into Parliament from a sense of
public duty. He is an excellent fellow, but very stupid.
I daresay he believes that England would be lost without
a Tory Government. There is, at Lingshot, none of the
cynicism to which I was accustomed at Brailsford, — a
cynicism so pervading that the Amershams themselves
were scarcely aware of it. For them there was but the
one question : How shall we keep power in our hands ?

I was surprised at Miss Audley's *naïveté* and simplicity ; but I thought them touching and would say nothing
to disillusion her, once I knew the nature of her enthusiasm. It pleased me to know that there *was* a trace of
enthusiasm in a character which, upon the whole, inclined
a little too much the other way. She was aware of her
own faulty education, and diffident in proposing an

opinion upon any topic outside a woman's sphere. While admiring 'great measures,' and wishing to see them introduced, she was too humble to argue with her brother when he told her, as I heard him do, that Whitbread's scheme for National Free Education was fantastic nonsense.

It was not unpleasant to me that she should think so well of the M.P. and admire him for toiling at finance, as though he had gone to the Exchequer for the most laudable motives, rather than for an income of £4000 p.a. It must be so dull and dry, she once remarked, and yet so necessary !

Superiority of character and intellect in a woman may rouse our admiration ; it is seldom likely to subdue our hearts. The better I knew her, the more I found to admire. The more I found to admire, the less likely was I to love. I valued her as a friend. I wished that she had been my sister. I delighted in her wit and in the odd, original turn of her mind. But I felt none of that enchantment which unlocks the door to passion. For one moment it had whispered to me, when I saw her walking in the beech wood and did not recognise her. That whisper was not repeated, during my Easter visit at Lingshot, although I looked forward eagerly to our morning walks.

I have, in my time, listened to unutterable nonsense from women who had the power, like 'Circe and the sirens three,' to take the prisoned soul and 'in sweet madness rob it of itself.' I never objected to this kind of larceny. I resemble most men in preferring the sirens' song to the 'sober certainty of waking bliss' which we may enjoy in rational conversation with a superior woman. Nor is this preference perverse in us. Divine Providence has seen fit to make superior women something scarce, and the world, as Benedick says, must be peopled.

Miss Audley was thirty-six years old, and gave herself the freedom of a woman who has reached *l'âge canonique*. She accepted the world's view that she was now too old to be loved ; had she thought otherwise, she would have been more upon her guard.

Upon our last morning I told her how very much Lufton had enjoyed these rambles and reproached her for never having said two words to him before, in the course of eleven years.

'Tell me,' I said, 'why did you suddenly relent ?'

'Oh — I don't know that I did. But I was so rude to The M.P. that he has kept away, poor man !'

'I hope that you have learnt to like Lufton better ?'

'Yes. He is not as solemn as I thought.'

'There is not really such a very great difference between them ?'

'There is a great difference in age. Lufton is very young.'

'Possibly. He has fewer cares. At what age do you put him ? The M.P., you know, is five and thirty.'

'For Lufton I should subtract — thirty.'

'Five years old ! No, no ! That is too bad ! I thought you liked him better than that !'

'But I do. He is a most agreeable playfellow, — as people of five years old often are.'

'Has he always been as young as that ?'

'Always. He never changes. The M.P. has altered and aged considerably since I first met him, but not Lufton.'

Upon that note of raillery we parted and met again at the breakfast table. During the meal a small incident occurred which might be likened to the first tremor of a landslide.

She had, I knew, been greatly looking forward to a concert at Guildford that afternoon. Music was her delight and she had little opportunity of hearing it. During breakfast some casual change of plan deprived her of this pleasure. I forget how it came about — other people changed their minds — there would, after all, be no room for her in the carriage — I must have witnessed such occasions many times in eleven years, for nobody cared about her comfort. Now, for the first time, I was consumed with indignation. I knew how much she had wished to go ; she had spoken of it that morning. It drove me mad to see them treat her so, since not one of them would enjoy the concert half as much. But I could do nothing. My chaise was at the door and I had my adieux to make. I could only press her hand, at parting, with a look of silent sympathy.

Even as I jumped into the carriage, I was wondering if I had not once before parted from her thus, — silently pressing her hand, and rushing from the house in the grip of some strong emotion. I searched my memory and recalled the occasion, — eighteen months earlier I had been staying at Lingshot when news reached me that my mother was no more. How could I have forgotten it ? All the Morrills had been out skating except Miss Audley. I had stayed because I had letters to write. When the express from Bramfield arrived I had gone to find her, so much stunned that I knew not what I did. She ordered a carriage, sent a servant to put up my things, suggested and undertook various commissions on my behalf, and made me eat before I set out. I now remembered all her kindness and my bewilderment, — how she had given me a little flask of spirits, in case I should get very cold upon the journey, and come to the door with me with advice to my driver to avoid a certain road said to be under snowdrifts.

I supposed, I hoped, that I had thanked her. I could recall nothing save that I had pressed her hand and run

speechless from the house. And then I had forgotten!
I had taken her kindness for granted as the Morrills did.
I had no great right to be indignant with *them*, and it
appeared that she had some grounds for describing
Lufton as very young. I had turned to her as a boy
might turn to a parent, and I could remember now, with
shame, that I had actually spoken to her with angry
impatience when she tried to get some message clear,
that she was to give to Morrill. It was some paper that
was to be explained and I could do nothing save cry out :
  'What does it signify ? Oh what does it signify ?'
  The more I thought of it the more uneasy I became.
I wished that I could be of service to her in some way, so
as to atone for past neglect. I was to be at Lingshot
again at Whitsun. I found myself looking forward
eagerly to the visit. She should see that I did not forget.
She should see that I was not ungrateful.
  I thought about her frequently, during the next few
weeks.

Caroline

I DOUBT if it is ever safe to think frequently of a woman.
Perhaps if she be over seventy years old, a shrew, and
very plain, one might venture — but it would be wiser
not.
  When not obliged to think of other things, last summer,
I thought of Caroline Audley. She haunted my imagination. I fancied conversations with her, in which she
should revise a little her opinion of Lufton, — should
allow him to be more manly than she had supposed. In
these interviews he played the man in a very determined
fashion, and she most obligingly played the woman, —
refrained from those cool, friendly jibes which might

have brought him down to earth. This fancied Caroline was softer, more pliant, than the actual Caroline; her superiority, though warmly acknowledged, was not allowed to obtrude.

Whitsun arrived and I set off for Surrey in quite a fever to open this new phase in our acquaintance. The auguries were good; I had written to her once or twice and sent her *Christabel*, which was not likely to be read at Lingshot, and, when writing to thank me, she had owned to liking it but wished that I were by to explain it to her, for that its style was new to her and she did not understand it very well. I could ask for nothing better. I was ready to explain anything to her, except the Sinking Fund.

I took with me a great package of music and new books. I looked forward to many walks and talks which should lead us — somewhere — to some understanding which should satisfy me. I had not exactly asked myself what it should be. I suppose I should have said that I wished her to do me justice. But I must really have wished that she should think of me as often as I did of her, — not justly, but because she could not help it.

Disappointment awaited me. There were no walks, — no talks. The little Morrills had the measles and she was scarcely ever out of the nursery. It was impossible to see her alone. She joined us every day at dinner and spent the evening with us, but in the mornings she was invisible.

Walks and talks might have cooled my ardour; this thwarting separation fanned it. I could do nothing save watch her covertly, when she was in the room, and listen for her voice.

I had never thought her plain. I should always have described her as singularly graceful. But, in the past, I should not have compared her with the other women in the house, who were all of them exceedingly pretty. I now found them insipid, because they were *not* Caroline. Mrs. Morrill made too many grimaces. Margaret had an ugly voice. The brilliance of their complexions could not be denied, but so many women have brilliant complexions! And their conversation drove me frantic.

Had the weather been fine we might all have walked out after dinner and I should have secured the opportunity for some strolls with her. But it rained. We spent every evening indoors, at music or at cards. It rained during the whole of my visit until the very last day, when the sun burst forth as we sat at dinner. I immediately called the company's attention to the fact and suggested going out, in spite of Mrs. Baddely's objection that the ground would still be very damp. I insisted that I must get some fresh air and that I had not yet seen the roses.

'There are none to see,' said Margaret. 'They have all been dashed to pieces by the rain.'

'Still,' said I, 'I think I must take a little turn. Miss Audley! Will you not take pity on me and come too? I am sure that it will do you good, for you have been more shut up than any of us.'

She thought that she might venture, though the other ladies tried to dissuade her, saying that her shoes were too thin.

'I shall put on thick ones,' she said.

I sat for as short a time as possible with Morrill over the wine, and then made for the drawing-room. Mrs. Morrill and her mother were there alone; I heard them laughing as I opened the door, but they straightened their faces as soon as they saw me. There was, however, a spark of mirth in Mrs. Morrill's eyes as she told me that I would find Caroline and Margaret in the rose garden. Margaret had changed her mind and decided to go too.

Cursing Margaret, I made my way to the rose garden and was soon strolling round the confounded place with a lady on either arm. Caroline's eyes were golden ; she perhaps found this walk amusing. But she was too kind and too good-mannered to allow us to sulk in silence. She talked tranquilly, explaining her sister-in-law's plans for improving the garden.

Presently Morrill appeared with a message that we should all come in, as Mrs. Baddely desired to go to cards.

'I shall not go in just yet,' said Caroline, 'for I don't mean to play cards tonight. I have a little headache, and shall go to bed early.'

'Poor Caroline !' said he. 'You are wearing yourself out with those children. But don't stay long, for it is quite chilly.'

A guest must play cards if he is bid. I had to go off with Morrill and Margaret. But, as we reached the house, I had a happy thought.

'Your sister,' said I, 'should have a shawl or a cloak, if she means to stay out. Could I not take one to her ? You need not wait cards for me, as you will have four without me.'

He thanked me and sent a maid for a shawl. Within two or three minutes I was on my way back to the rose garden. The sun was setting and the birds singing, as they do upon an evening after rain. She stood listening to a thrush, among the sodden rose bushes.

'How did you get away ?' said she. 'Oh ! A shawl for me ! Clever Lufton !'

I put it carefully round her shoulders.

Pronto has shawled countless women, with that delicate solicitude which is almost a caress. For most of them he has cared not a pin. For some he has sighed in vain. One or two have been as much to him as any woman can be to Pronto. He can wrap them up with formal gallantry, with the respect that does not presume to hope, with the tenderness that speaks of conscious gratitude. But Miles had not made much work over a shawl since he danced with Edmée at Stokehampton.

Caroline looked absolutely beautiful to me just then ; I may have gone out to her with the intention of explaining *Christabel*, but a sudden and violent impulse now rose up within me, — a desire to break through this solitude, to catch her in my arms and kiss her back to warmth and life. For she must have been another creature *once*, thought I. She was not always like this ; not always *happy alone*. I hated the cold garden and the watery sunset, and the wet rose petals.

She stood still for a moment longer, listening to the thrush.

'What nonsense it is,' she said, 'to think a nightingale superior to a thrush !'

'Do you have nightingales at Lingshot ?'

'Why yes ! I wonder you have not heard them ! They shout all night, and keep one awake.'

Then she turned and took my arm, with the old frank friendliness.

'I have been so sorry,' she said, 'to miss our early walks. I had some amusing stories to tell you. When the measles burst out I was furious. But then it rained, so we could not have walked after all.'

'I was never more disappointed in my life !' cried I.

She looked a little startled, for this could not be taken as a compliment from The M.P. It was said with too much vehemence.

After a short pause she thanked me again for the books and music that I had brought for her, promising herself much pleasure from them as soon as the measles should be over. Her manner had no power to soothe me. I suppose I must have answered very absently ; I was more occupied by the light touch of her hand upon my arm than by what she said. Presently I broke out with :

'I never thanked you for your goodness to me — when my mother — when I had to go, on that dreadful day. I have been thinking of it. I believe that I never thanked you.'

She looked her astonishment.

'But that was the winter before last!'

'So much the worse, for I never thanked you.'

'Oh yes! Yes you did!'

'I wrote to you after? From Bramfield?'

'You sent me a note, enclosed in a letter to Mrs. Morrill. It is not surprising that you should forget. You were in great trouble and must have had to write so many letters.'

She was now, I could see, really puzzled and distressed by my manner. Perhaps she thought me drunk. We had come to a path leading to the house, and she turned to take it.

'You are not going in!' I cried. 'Not yet! Not after five days without a word! Stay a little longer — I have not said anything — we have not said anything yet!'

'I am afraid that we shall not say anything very entertaining tonight. I have a headache and you should be at cards. It is sad, but that is often how things fall out when one has been looking forward to them.'

'Entertaining — I did not come out for that! I have thought of you continually since I went away — you have been ever in my mind — you do not know, you cannot know, how much I admire you, esteem you——'

'Oh dear yes, I think I do. I don't suppose you have *quite* so good an opinion of me as I have of myself, but that, you know, is more than we can expect from any of our friends.'

This sort of thing might have done five days earlier. Now it could not check me. I rushed on. I told her that she had become inexpressibly dear to me, that I valued her friendship more than anything on earth, that I feared I had been careless.

As soon as she could, she broke in :

'Pray don't talk like this ! You have never been careless. I value our friendship too, but if it is to continue there must not be this sort of exaggeration.'

We were walking towards the house, for she was quite determined to end the interview.

If I do not exaggerate, thought I, then I love her and should say so. I did not know it before ; but now I must either accept her reproof or stand my ground.

'It is not exaggeration,' said I, 'for I love you, and I mean to tell you so.'

At that she cried out, in a kind of horror :

'Oh no ! No ! Impossible ! You forget — you forget !'

'What do I forget ?'

'We are not young now. I am not young now. I am changed. The time is gone over for——'

'You are not a twelvemonth older than I.'

'For me that is all quite over — any thoughts of — you cannot mean it ! You never meant to talk like this, but I provoked you by laughing at you. If you please, we will never refer to this again. Good night !'

She slipped from me and ran into the house.

To face the card-party, until I had regained some degree of composure, was impossible. I took a turn in the grounds, and rapidly made up my mind. I loved her. I must marry her, for she had become necessary to my happiness. I had not thought of it before, but I felt no hesitation, once the fact was clear. That I had made a fool of myself, and begun badly, troubled me a little ; I did not wonder that she had thought me drunk and run away. I had taken myself by surprise. Had I known my own feelings sooner I should have declared myself in a very different manner. I should not have addressed her

without considerable preparation ; I had given her no
warning, no grounds to suspect such an alteration in my
regard for her. All that must be set right.

Cards were over and the company was drinking tea
when, at last, I returned to the house. They looked at
me a little queerly, I thought, as I stammered out my
apologies, — that I had been tempted by the beautiful
evening and had taken quite a long walk — they must
forgive me — tomorrow would imprison me once more
in the noise and bustle of London, etc. etc. I don't
suppose that they believed me. They fancied that some
sort of scene had taken place between Caroline and myself,
which had agitated me so much that I was obliged to walk
it off. Why must people have such lively imaginations ?

After tea Morrill took me off to the library. He said
that he hoped Caroline had not stayed out too long, and
I assured him that she had returned to the house within
a very few minutes, having found it too cold, in spite of
the shawl.

'I am glad of it,' he said, 'for she might have caught
a chill. She is fatigued with nursing these measles.'

'She does too much,' I cried indignantly.

'Very true, but it is impossible to prevent. She has
got so much into the habit of considering others before
herself — however, we must learn to do without her
when she goes to Vienna.'

'Vienna !'

This was news to me. I had heard nothing of it. He
explained that she was to go in the autumn with Louisa,
now Mrs. Egerton, and that they would spend most of the
summer at Bath. Egerton was at the Congress, in some
advisory capacity, but his wife had remained in England
on account of recent ill health. When she followed him,
Caroline was going with her.

'Then she will see the sea !' said I, very stupidly.

That was the first thought which occurred to me. The second was that she should not see it upon this occasion, if I could prevent it. This Vienna scheme did not suit me at all.

Morrill was talking of the advantage which the change would be to her.

'She should be persuaded into a little laziness and self-indulgence,' he said. 'I have been trying to get her away from here ever since she inherited her fortune.'

He looked at me, in an enquiring way, and must have seen by my countenance that this too was quite unexpected. I had always believed her to be penniless.

'Since she is perfectly independent, it is nonsense that she should spend her life here, slaving for us,' he went on. 'We shall be sorry to lose her, and while I have a home it would always be hers if she wishes; but she should have a change. These measles for instance! Had she not been here we should have managed without her. But she is too good, — too kind. She has got out of the habit of ever wanting anything for herself.'

'I did not know — I had not heard—' was all that I could manage to say.

I longed to know *how much*, but could not ask. He, however, was equally anxious to tell me. A relative of her father's had died recently and left her fifteen thousand pounds. I expressed my pleasure and spoke warmly in praise of her. He responded with equal emphasis. For some time we sat there, extolling Caroline and feeling foolish, for it was obvious that the offer which he hoped I should make could not follow immediately. Delicacy must prevent me from going to the point within ten minutes of hearing about the money, especially after an acquaintance of eleven years.

This conversation decided me against addressing her again before I left Lingshot. There must be a decent

interval, and I must give myself plenty of time. I decided
to wait until the Summer Recess, when I could pursue
her to Bath and pay court to her, undisturbed by Miss
Margaret or the measles.

But it would not do, either, to let her suppose that I
had not been serious, or that I regretted my outburst in
the garden. I left Lingshot upon the following day
without seeing her again, but I wrote to her from Town.
I said that she must not be angry with me, that I had
been too precipitate, but that I hoped soon to have an
opportunity of making my peace with her, and explaining
myself.

It was not a letter which demanded an answer, and I
got none.

Pronto, meanwhile, was resolving to give up his place.
The Opposition, which had tried in vain to cut Croker's
salary, succeeded with him, and sheared him of £1500.
The remaining £2500 was not, in his opinion, a sufficient
reward for all the work that he did. He might make a
good deal more at conveyancing. Lady Amersham, had
she lived, would probably have counselled caution. But
that guiding hand was withdrawn, and Pronto, without
it, more liable to make mistakes. He resigned and sulked
within his tent, expecting his friends to do something for
him. A man who has not stood upon his dignity when
he ought will often mount that horse-block, in a lordly
way, when no steed is in sight. Pronto's friends thought
him uncommonly lucky to have got so far. He had held
a place which many of them coveted for eight years. Nor
was he so indispensable as he believed. Nothing was
done for him, and he began to think seriously of a return
to his legal practice.

This entirely suited Miles, who intended, as soon as
possible, to lead a life of leisure with Caroline in Wiltshire.

He had not quite enough laid by, though her fortune would bring the happy day a good deal nearer. He meant, during the next few years, to make as much money as he could at the Bar, living perhaps in a cottage at Hampstead, in order to retire to Troy Chimneys before he was forty.

It is a year ago today that Pronto resigned his place! That is strange, for the interval seems much greater. So many things have happened. Miles got his *coup de grâce* in August. Pronto fell off his horse in November. And, during the last few weeks, whilst I have been engaged upon this swan-song, I believe that a third event may have taken place. Miles and Pronto are both finished. Who then is writing this?

A long effort of recollection may have some strange results. I began in a mood of bitterness and self-compassion. But hope revives when I consider that there must be, hidden within me, some third person who is able thus to estimate the other two. Pronto could not have written this memoir, nor do I think would Miles have been equal to it. I know little of the fellow who writes, but I hope to know him better, for all cannot be over with him. He is but six and thirty; he has half the allotted span still before him, and he seems to be in tolerable spirits, in spite of the chapter which he must now bring himself to write.

It must be finished tonight, for I shall not have much more time for such things. The Cullens are here for a few days, on their way back to Ireland, and I mean to go there with them. We are very lively at the Parsonage. I dropped a hint to Harriet on Sukey's behalf which may, I think, bear fruit. She is, at any rate, taking a little trouble to see that Sukey has some amusement while they are here. There are parties and schemes every day, and on Friday we all go to dance at Chipping Campden.

I am glad to have James Cullen here, for I must rely upon him in this ridiculous business with Ned. I don't know what I should have done without him; there is nobody else in whom I could confide, or who would act for me. I told him as much of the story as was necessary, in the hope that he would agree with me, — that I need take no notice of such nonsense.

No man ought to take a fortnight before deciding that his honour has been injured; the Statute of Limitations ought to apply to such matters. Ned knows I have done him no wrong. I suppose he has been nagged and bullied and bedevilled into pretending to think that I have. Fourteen nights with a fury who will not let him sleep till he swears he believes her! But he could have sworn, and left it at that. He was not obliged to call me out. But very stupid people suffer from a blinkered kind of logic.

Cullen, unfortunately, is an Irishman and therefore does not think it nonsense. Nor is he shocked at the idea of such a meeting between kinsmen. He assured me that, in Ireland, cousins fight daily. I daresay they do; they fight daily and they are all cousins.

'Ah! Ye must meet um!' says he. 'If he sent ye a challunge there is nothing for ut. Ye must meet, to show ye've no bad feelings between ye. Wan shot, fired wide, will do to stop the ould mare's mouth. Say no more! Pinney and I will settle ut.'

(Cullen's brogue is not, perhaps, quite so pronounced as this. Harriet insists that he has none. But Sukey and Kitty both declare that my imitations do him no injustice.)

What Pinney thinks of the matter, I cannot imagine, nor how much of the story he knows, nor why he acts for Ned. If my surmises are true, *he* deserves to be a principal rather than *I*. There seems to be no way out of it, but I will not take such nonsense solemnly, I mean to do my best to make us all look as foolish as possible. It is the only protest that I can make against a custom which I think as barbarous as Hamlet thought his uncle's kettle-drums. If only I could make old Ned laugh when we get there — how shocked Pinney and Cullen would be! But I am afraid he will not laugh. I am afraid that he is violently angry, — because he has been bullied into doing me an injustice, and knows it, because I got him into a scrape over Ridding and robbed him of a fortnight's sleep, because he is obliged to be furious with somebody. It would be worse for the poor old fellow to tell himself the truth; his honour has been pretty well mauled, but not by me. I daresay he wishes me dead, rather than know that he ought to be fighting Pinney.

I must remember that Cullen, though he constrains me to go through with this ridiculous farce, is also constraining Ned to satisfy his rage with 'wan shot, fired wide,' instead of trying to kill me. All customs have had their uses. I can understand that this one may have played its part in taming man.

I am giving them as much trouble as possible. I quite refuse to have a surgeon brought into it. Cullen is such a stickler for etiquette, he was for getting one, but there is none to be had save old Hankey, from Ribstone Priors, and he could never keep his mouth shut. The story would be all over the country in twenty-four hours. And in any case, what is a surgeon to do, if we are not to be hitting one another? To be sure, if we take to firing wide, we might hit Cullen or Pinney! A bow at a venture is ever perilous. I mean to wear my blue coat for the occasion. It is thoroughly unsuitable.

What a tale this would have been to tell my Caroline! I must call her mine, for nobody knows what she is,

better than I. And how the end came I must now set
down, in spirits so altered that there seems to be no
resemblance between the story I set out to tell and that
which I have told. I had expected this last chapter to be
blotted with tears.

> Seared in heart, and lone, and blighted,
> More than this I scarce can die !

There should have been pages upon pages in that
strain.

But truth is healing. The effort of recollection has
forced me to do justice to her, and, in doing it, there is
such balm, such freedom of the spirit, that I could almost
call myself happy, were I not obliged to remember what
she suffered. I may have deserved my whipping. She
never did. The story may be a sad one, but the sadness
is for her. There is in it some of the irony which she
found to be a solace ; she may have been right. Our
story may be 'part of another story which we do not
quite understand.' Some other person, reading it many
years hence, might interpret it better.

Manet Sors Tertia

WHEN Parliament rose I set off for Bath in the best of
spirits. I was pretty sure that Caroline would take me,
though some persuasion might be necessary. I might
have to overcome some scruples on her part, for which I
honoured her, in consenting to so unequal a match. For,
in the world's view, it was unequal. Younger, handsomer
and richer women were very ready to have me. Upon
the whole I was glad that she had but fifteen thousand
pounds ; had it been fifty, Pronto would have been

accused of marrying an old maid for her money. As it was, he might be exposed to some ridicule, and she would shrink from that.

She must be made to understand my real views, my true tastes, my contempt for the world that I was quitting. To live with her at Troy Chimneys, amid books, friends and music, to listen to the nightingale and watch the river, — I could imagine no purer happiness. Our tastes just suited; I felt that we were made for one another, and it seemed impossible that she should not feel it too, once she understood my plan.

That she should immediately love me, with the ardour which I now felt for her, I did not expect. I had promised myself that she should, when she was my wife. Had I married for ambition only, and without passion, I should not have been content unless I could excite it in my wife. No woman, so far as I know, has ever had cause to complain of my address, if I set myself to win her.

Very few misgivings beset me as I drove westward. I foresaw no difficulties which might not be overcome, although I did not hope to be accepted immediately. I must not bring down upon myself a definite negative at the outset; persistence after an outright refusal is inconsiderate and ill-bred. It should not too soon appear that she was my first object in coming to Bath; I was to be there, ostensibly, to settle some business at Troy Chimneys, and I meant to go to work very cunningly. She had had my letter, written after Whitsun, and I hoped that she had reflected upon it. So far as I was concerned she might go on reflecting for a little while longer. It would do her no harm to wonder if, and when, I meant to reopen the subject. A little suspense, some fluttering of the spirits, would be good for my calm, sensible Caroline.

I should, in the meantime, gradually unfold my plans

to her. I should apprise her fully of the kind of life which I meant shortly to lead, before inviting her to share it. If possible, I should get her to Troy Chimneys, for I was certain that she would be delighted with the house.

Much must depend upon the tact and good-nature of Mrs. Egerton. I hoped that Morrill might have dropped a hint to her ; he knew of my hopes, for I had confided them to him before I left town ; he had been delighted and had evidently thought it an excellent match for Caroline.

Upon arrival I dined, took a turn by the river, and then, having nothing better to do, went to the play. The piece was *King Lear*, and my thoughts flew instantly to Caroline, for she and I had once discussed this work. (Ah, Caroline ! When did my thoughts not fly to you ? The most unlikely objects could evoke you. An old man in the Haymarket crying : *White Sand ! White Sand !* thrilled my heart, because one day, during that frustrated visit at Whitsun, I heard your voice upon the staircase desiring a servant to bring white sand.) She had never seen *King Lear* upon the stage, but she reprehended the custom of uniting Edgar and Cordelia in the last scene ; she insisted that Shakespeare's original intention should be respected and that Cordelia should die. I maintained that this conclusion is too barbarous for the refined taste of our age, to which she replied that the whole play is too barbarous for our age. She might be right. But some parts of it are so fine that I should be sorry never to have heard them upon the stage.

I came late and Lear was cursing Goneril as I took my seat. The theatre was insufferably hot and the candlelight dazzled me, after the cool dusk of the streets. Ludovic has an impracticable notion that plays should be acted in the dark, — no lights save upon the stage. This, says he, would force the audience to watch the actors and prevent them from looking at one another. But, apart from the impossibility of continually extinguishing and relighting candles, I should not think much of acting which depended upon such a device. An actor of genius should *oblige* his audience to watch him. If they may look at nothing else, it is putting him to very little trouble.

This Lear was inferior, — a ranting, spouting fellow who nearly blew the feathers from Goneril's head. I am glad, I thought, that Caroline does not see this. Immediately after, I caught sight of her, sitting in a box with Mrs. Egerton. Her eyes were fixed upon the stage.

My heart did all those things that are proper. There is an exquisite pleasure in watching a woman one loves when she is unaware of it, — her thoughts far away. I had never been able thus to watch Caroline since I saw her wandering in the beech wood and began to love, without knowing that it was she.

The house appeared to like Lear better than I did. When he got to the '*serpent's tooth*,' loud applause broke out, which he acknowledged before he *away! awayed!* himself off. Caroline, who had been all stillness and attention, frowned a little and changed her posture, as though she did not like the interruption. Her sister also turned, looked about her, and caught sight of me. She started, smiled, acknowledged my bow, half glanced at Caroline who was still watching the actors, and then smiled to me again. Thirty seconds assured me that she knew all and was my ally. Lear came ranting on again a moment later but, as soon as we had got rid of him for that scene, she beckoned to me to join them in their box. I went immediately, for Goneril and Albany were unable to hold the house, — a buzz of talk had broken out and several people had set off to visit their friends. Nothing could have been better for me; things were arranging

themselves charmingly. I was spared the awkwardness
of a first call in Devonshire Crescent, and hoped now to
go there by invitation.

What Caroline's feelings might be was not apparent.
She had got command of her countenance by the time
that I reached their box. They had risen to curtsy to me
upon my arrival but we all sat down immediately and
Mrs. Egerton whispered to me that we must not talk,
since her sister preferred to listen to the play. I said that
I was always happy to be guided by Miss Audley's taste,
and for the rest of the piece remained as silent as I could,
without incivility to Mrs. Egerton. I knew that any play
must be a treat to Caroline, for she had seen so few.
This improved as it went on. The recognition between
Lear and Cordelia was truly affecting; it cannot help
but be so. Mrs. Egerton had recourse to her pocket-
handkerchief. Caroline, I could see, was quite trans-
ported. At the words : *You do me wrong to take me out
o' the grave* she gave a great start and after that sat as
though she held her breath ; whereat I must uncon-
sciously have held my breath too, for at that last *Forget
and forgive !* we both drew a long sigh.

We did not stay for the farce, but walked out together
into the warm summer night, where I took my leave,
happy to know myself invited to dine upon the following
day. I felt this easy opening of the campaign to be a
most favourable augury. I had been able to explain my
presence in Bath, and to express the hope of seeing them
as often as they would allow it.

Dinner next day went off with equal smoothness. Mrs.
Egerton made no attempt to thrust us upon one another ;
she treated me as her brother's friend rather than as
Caroline's suitor. She could not have entered into my
views, or understood my tactics, more thoroughly had I
explained them to her in so many words. I think, though,

that she thought it diverting to act chaperon to a sister so much her senior, for whom she could never have expected to perform such an office.

Nothing happened, during the next day or two, to advance or retard matters. Mrs. Egerton encouraged my visits. Caroline was her usual calm friendly self, though she talked more than I liked of her pleasure in going to Vienna. I began, indeed, to regard Vienna as my chief obstacle ; she had so much wished to travel that she might sigh a little at relinquishing such an opportunity. I felt that seclusion at Troy Chimneys might not strike her as a great improvement upon seclusion at Lingshot, unless I could take her to see the house and to fall in love with it as I had. To get them both there became my principal object. The school was closed for the summer holidays, but I had been over to see the Kings, who had begged me to bring my friends to dine and spend the day, whenever we might please. Mrs. Egerton forwarded the plan, declaring herself devoured with curiosity to see my house.

I insisted that we should set off very early. I wished the morning sun still to be upon the river, so that they might see the reflection in the house, though I had not mentioned this beforehand. It was a surprise which I was saving for Caroline. The ladies were driven and I rode beside them, ecstatic in the prospect of seeing my beloved girl walk into my beloved house. For some reason I pictured her walking all alone up the path to the door, and vanishing into the shadows of the long room, — walking some way before me and unconscious of me, as she had walked in the wood. She was to be so much enraptured with the house that she could think of nothing else. Where Mrs. Egerton and the Kings were to be I did not ask. They were obligingly to vanish and Caroline, 'lonely as a cloud,' was to walk up the path to her home.

But of course that could not be. The Kings came out to meet us at the gate. We walked up the path in a chattering group, made the more boisterous by a couple of dogs which leapt and yapped and were reproved by the Kings.

The house is now delightful; my improvements have been well set off by Mrs. King's good taste. They use the long room as a schoolroom, and reserve the two parlours on the river side of the house for their own use. King took me through to his, at once, to show me some letter that he had had about tithes. When we returned to the other, we found Mrs. King and Mrs. Egerton absorbed in the amazing discovery that they were both acquainted with the same Mrs. Rylands. Caroline sat in the window-seat, her eyes upon the ceiling. She had discovered my secret. I went over to her at once and said, in a low voice :

'You know now why I bought this house ?'

'How clever of you not to tell us beforehand !'

'Your sister has not yet found it out, I think.'

'What if the sun had not shone ?'

'I should have hanged myself.'

Mrs. Egerton's bonnet ribbons nodded closer and closer to Mrs. King's cap. This Mrs. Rylands must have been of extraordinary interest to them. What experts in intrigue all women are ! They were keenly aware, I am sure, that Caroline and I were whispering together. I will engage that Mrs. King's opinion was half formed before I had handed the ladies from the carriage ; she only waited to find out which was Miss Audley and which Mrs. Egerton.

Later she took us over the whole house. Mrs. Egerton was loud in her praises. My girl said less, but I could see that she was charmed. I grew very happy. I determined that I would take her a walk forthwith, by the river, and let her know the chief of my plans, — that I meant to be living there entirely in a year or two.

After a luncheon, we set out upon this walk. Mrs. Egerton declared for sitting in the shade of my little mulberry tree, which has come on very well, though it is not yet the great old tree that I fancied when I first pictured the house. Mrs. King sat with her, and King, who at first proposed to walk with Caroline and myself, was somewhat peremptorily despatched by his wife to look for some books. I took Caroline through a door in the wall beyond the old wing, which led us into the orchard. Here I showed her the fruit trees that I had planted, and got her approval for leaving some old cherries, which were too large to net from the birds, but which I had preserved for the sake of the blossom.

We then sauntered on to the path which leads through the meadows by the river. I now began upon my revelation.

Caroline was slow to understand me. She seemed to have great difficulty in believing that I genuinely meant to throw up my career. When convinced of it, she made no attempt to conceal her dismay.

Perceiving that her response was not quite what I had expected, I asked her outright if she did not think that such a change would be a happy one for me.

'You cannot mean it!' she exclaimed, in obvious distress. 'This is one of Lufton's sudden impulses. I am sure that you will think better of it. It is a little set-back that you are out of a place, and this has discouraged you. But you are certain to get another; you will go on and go higher. You cannot mean to throw it all away at five and thirty!'

I assured her that I could, — that I had never cared for politics save as a road to fortune, that The M.P. was abhorrent to me, that I meant to be Lufton for the rest of

my life, and that she should applaud me for it, since she
and Lufton were very good friends.

'But I could not like a permanent Lufton,' she objected.
'Is he not very idle ?   Forgive me if I am being too frank,
but you have asked for my opinion.'

'What ?   Would you have me toil at politics all my
life ?'

'I cannot believe that you would be happy for long
with no serious occupation.   Perpetual leisure may look
tempting when one is over-tasked.   But when you have
it you will weary of it.   What should you do here all day
long ?   "Sit upon the ground, and tell sad stories of the
deaths of kings" ?'

'Many men lead a life of leisure.   Why not I ?'

'Because it would not content you.   I am sure that it
would not, for you are very ambitious.   Indeed, I can
understand why you love this house, and you might
surely soon spend some part of your time here.   But to
seclude yourself completely now—   No, no !   Wait for
twenty years !   Then your mulberry tree will be so grown
that it will give shade to all these friends whom you mean
to invite.'

We were both of us, by now, not a little agitated and
perplexed.   Our saunter by the river had become a
strange, unequal sort of progress.   Sometimes we would
halt and then one or the other would make a sudden start
forward again.

I said, with some heat, that The M.P. was a scheming
fellow, insincere in his professions and seldom disinterested in his friendships.   To this she assented more
readily than I liked, though I wished her to assent.

'I daresay you have observed as much,' I said.

'I have,' she agreed, with something like a sigh, 'and
regretted it.   But I realise that something of that must be
a necessary evil in public life.   It is to be excused in a

man who must rise entirely by his own exertions, as you have.'

'You don't find it repulsive ?'

'You were obliged to secure interest — to get a seat,' she said hastily. 'You may have scolded yourself for making use of . . . for resorting to artifice which was something beneath you . . . for making professions which . . . but against that you must put your energy, — your usefulness, the high opinion in which you are held. There is so much to be done ! Now that the wars are over, I am sure that great measures will be brought forward, in which you must wish to play a part !'

'What measures ?'

'Oh, I do not know. It is for you to know that. A great many things seem to be very wrong; they could not be set right during the wars, but now there is an opportunity.'

'And you condone disgusting artifice in a man, so long as he is righting wrongs ?'

'Not entirely,' she said, after a slight pause. 'I merely mean that you are too hard upon The M.P. You censure his faults but you do not recognise his virtues.'

'And you, I think, are very hard upon Lufton, who is by far the better creature. You *must* agree that he is better. He has chafed under this bondage for years. He has made a thousand plans for escape.'

'I know that he resolves and re-resolves, "in all the magnanimity of thought." What else does he do ?'

The dispute continued. She would not yield. Gently, but firmly, she gave me to understand that she thought Lufton my bad angel. His sincerity and his fine feelings led to nothing. The M.P. for all his contemptible qualities, which she owned to disliking, was, in her view, the more respectable creature of the two.

I had asked for her opinion, and I am now convinced

that she went no further, in the way of criticism, than a friend is entitled to do, when consulted. But, at the time, I was mortally offended.

The shock was very great. I did not pause to consider how much must be unknown to her. She had never seen Pronto at his worst, and could not therefore perceive how much cause Miles had to revolt. I had myself allowed her to believe that my political ambitions were more disinterested than was actually the case. And all the origins of this conflict within me were hidden from her. They were, at that time, far from clear to me, — the part played by Lady Amersham, the effect of Edmée's betrayal, the young louts at Winchester who presumed to despise parsons' sons. I felt that she was shattering my dearest hopes, exalting all that was worst in me, and deriding all that was best. And I daresay that I should feel so still, had I not rashly ventured upon this memoir.

'If you really think all this,' said I, deeply mortified, 'I am sorry for it. It had been my hope to persuade you — I meant to ask you if you would not share my life here. I had no idea that you would consider it so despicable.'

A declaration in such terms deserved no reply. She turned away and walked quickly towards the orchard. After a moment I followed her and started upon some kind of apology. But my resentment was so great that I only made matters worse. I told her, almost in an accusing tone, that I loved her, could not be happy without her, had hoped that she would like my house but was willing to live anywhere she pleased, so long as she would marry me. If a husband in the Cabinet would content her, I would do my best to get there, though I could make no promises.

At last she turned to me and said :

'Mr. Lufton ! Pray let us have no more of this. I am very sorry indeed if I have caused you pain. But I cannot

marry you. Whatever feelings you entertain for me —
and they seem to be strange ones — I cannot return them.
It would never be in my power.'

'I begin to believe you,' cried I. 'If you loved me,
you would do me more justice.'

'Ah no! It is when one loves that one is unjust.'

'You say so, because you have never loved.'

I added other reproaches. Why had she treated me
with such encouraging friendliness, if she did not mean
me to love her?

'How could I suppose that you would ever think of
such a thing?' she cried. 'Why should I not have been
friendly? We had known one another for years, and the
difference in our situations — you were as fully alive to
that as I, until a very short time ago.'

The M.P. might have taken his rejection with more
dignity. But she had wounded Lufton, and he seemed to
be intent upon proving that he was 'very young.'

We were now got to the door into the front court. I
tried to pull myself together, to mount my high horse, to
end the scene in a more stately way.

'Madam——'

But at that I got a look from her which silenced me, —
a look between laughter and tears, so full of friendly
reproach, so *like* her, that my full loss burst upon me.
This was Caroline, my Caroline! She was not to be
mine! She had refused me!

We joined the others, dined, and returned to Bath.
Mrs. King and Mrs. Egerton talked at dinner with excessive animation. They must have guessed that all had
gone amiss and were covering up. We took leave of Troy
Chimneys. We got over the long miles of the homeward
road. I did not suffer any extreme pangs as yet, for I
had taken refuge in anger. Most men will do so, if they
have the choice between rage and pain. For rage, while

it lasts, can supply a kind of substitute for high spirits, —
a destructive glee which renders the sufferer immune
from any other sensation. As I rode home beside the
carriage I revelled in it. Very well, cried I to myself,
very well! It does not signify! I don't care! I shall
show that I don't care! 'I will do such things — what
they are yet I know not' — it is she who will suffer, not
I! She will be very sorry for it. Nobody else will marry
her. Thank God I discovered her true character in
time. I had thought her worthy of me; I was willing to
take her without a penny, though she is no beauty and a
year older than I. I gave her credit for soul and sensibility.
She has none. Worldly success — that she can understand, and nothing else. All women are alike.

We reached the house. I handed my ladies from their
carriage and saw the door close behind them.

Here the story should have ended, for we never met
again. Would — I was going to write: Would to God
that it had! But I will not say that. The events of the
following day have caused me months of anguish, but I
will not regret them, since they taught me to honour her
as she deserves.

This painful sequel I owe to Mrs. Egerton, who sent
me a note, early next morning, begging me to come and
see her, as there was something very particular which she
wished to say to me. She should be all alone; Caroline
was so much fatigued by yesterday's excursion that she
was remaining in bed for the day.

I could not very well refuse this request, although I
knew what it meant. Mrs. Egerton was going to try her
hand at reconciliation. I was determined not to relent,
but it suited my wounded consequence that somebody
should apologise for the treatment I had received, —
that somebody should placate and flatter me. She would

certainly feel that her sister had refused an unexpectedly
good offer, and she would give my version of the story
to Frank Morrill. I set off for Devonshire Crescent,
determined to play the injured man.

She received me with looks of sympathetic concern
and with that suppressed enjoyment which all women
display upon such occasions. I am sure that she was
sorry, but the opportunity of intervention did not displease her. She liked to be playing a rôle. Most women
prefer an unhappy love affair ; one that runs too smooth
does not interest them. In this they differ very much
from us, I think. They can positively enjoy a painful
situation, and will discuss it endlessly. Feeling, in their
eyes, exists to be dissected rather than obeyed. If a man
confides to his friend that his love does not prosper, the
friend is very sorry for it and gives what comfort and
counsel he can, but he does not enjoy the conversation
and wishes it over. To a woman the conversation itself
furnishes a pleasing interest.

Mrs. Egerton had something to tell me which she
could no longer keep to herself, though she had no
business to tell it. I am not at all sure if she even thought
that it would do much good, but she insisted that it
might, in order to justify such unreserve. If her object
was to make me profoundly miserable, she certainly
succeeded.

She told me at once that she knew all. She had taxed
Caroline with having refused me, and Caroline had
admitted it.

'But,' said she, 'I have sent for you, because I am
convinced that she does not know her own heart.'

Mine beat a little quicker at that. I was not softened,
but I wished that Caroline might feel some regret.

'She has loved you, I *know* that she has loved you,
for a very long time.'

'Her rejection of me yesterday could not have been more decided.'

'Oh, I daresay. But listen! I *know* that she fell very much in love with you when you first came to my brother's house — many, many years ago now. I really forget how many.'

At this my blood froze, and a pang of absolute terror assailed me, as though I had suddenly found myself stepping over a precipice. I knew immediately that it was true. Conviction seized me and would not let me go.

'Nobody perceived it except myself,' continued Mrs. Egerton. 'Nor have I spoken of it to anyone. But I was a sharp-eyed girl, and I flatter myself that I did not miss much of what went on about me. She could not conceal everything from me. Besides, at first, I really thought that you might be falling in love with her. You talked to her so much, and praised her playing, and took more notice of her than most of the men did.'

'I cannot believe that I ever——'

'Oh I don't accuse you of trifling with her. Your attentions were never marked enough for that. But I thought it odd that you *should* notice her so much, and I therefore watched you both pretty closely, and I could soon see that you were everything to her. I am not in the least surprised at that. You have a very taking way with you, as I expect you know. I don't suppose that she had ever met a man who talked to her so much, or considered her tastes, or entered into her ideas. That poor boy who courted her long before — I am sure he had not half your power to make himself agreeable. My mother always said that he only took notice of her because all the smarter girls had slighted him. But, if you will allow me to be perfectly frank, you were quite captivating in those days. I don't mean to suggest that you cannot be captivating now. But you are now more a man of the world.

and I think it would be a little bit more clear what your
feelings really are. In those days, you were so boyish and
impulsive and poetical — even *I* could not be sure that
you meant nothing until I noticed that you never went
beyond a certain point, — the point that would have
committed you. She should have noticed that too, of
course. It was very simple of her. But then, you know,
she understood little about flirtation. She did not go out
very much, and in the years when one flirts I suppose
that she had been mourning for her poor sailor. It only
broke upon her gradually that you meant nothing. You
ceased coming to us at one time, although you were
invited. And of course you would have come, if you had
cared for her. I forget what year it was, — that you were
to have come and did not ?'

I said that it was in 1807.

'Ah yes ! It was the year of Tilsit ! Because we heard
of that upon the same day that we heard you were not
coming, — my brother was so gloomy about Tilsit, and
we girls were all so gloomy at the prospect of a summer
with no Lufton, you cannot imagine how dismal we all
were, — well that is a very long time ago ! Ten years !
But Caroline became an altered creature. She cried
herself to sleep every night. I know, because we shared
a bedchamber. She would wait until she thought I
slept, and then the sobs broke out. I knew her better
than to say anything. But often I would pretend to be
asleep when I was not, so that the poor thing might be
free to cry——'

I broke out in protest, exclaiming that she had no
right to betray her sister.

'I only do it for her good,' said she complacently.
'She fell into a sort of melancholy, after that, from which
I think she has never recovered. Yet she would always
defend you, if you were criticised. My mother — I

betray no secrets, for I think you must have guessed that
you were no favourite *there* — my mother sometimes
said little things in your disfavour. But Caroline defended
you. I remember that once she said—'

Here Mrs. Egerton pulled up, aware that her indis-
cretion was running away with her. But I knew, without
being told, what must have passed. Frank Morrill's
mother had accused me of having come there solely in
order to secure the family interest ; once I had got West
Malling, I would not trouble to visit Lingshot. And
Caroline, on my behalf, had said that such expedients
are to be excused in a man who must rise by his own
exertions. I had already heard her excuses for Pronto, —
the excuses which her generosity had found for him,
after he had broken her heart.

I cannot bear this, I said to myself. I cannot bear to
think of it. I must not think of it. I shall go mad if I
do. I need not, for it is all over. She has refused me.
We have parted. I must forget her as soon as possible.
That is better than thinking about it.

'She would not have refused me yesterday,' said I, 'if
any feeling of that sort had remained.'

'Oh yes. It is very natural. Consider that for years
she has been forbidding herself to love you — telling
herself that she does not——'

'She is far too frank and sensible to deceive herself.
And too generous to bear a grudge. Had she still cared
for me, I think that she would have accepted me.'

'Ah ! You think so because you are a man. I am a
woman, and I understand her better.'

They always say this and we always swallow it. We
should get on with them much better, I think, if we never
allowed them to explain each other, for, when they do,
they lead us into a maze from which there is no escape.

I should not have listened to her. I should have

resigned myself to that frightful truth which gripped me, — that my chance with Caroline had come and gone long since, — that, in her exalted resolution, she had forgiven me far too well. The girl who had loved me ten years before was lost beyond recall ; the woman she might have become, had I loved her then, was lost too. The surviving Caroline had learnt to cherish solitude, — she was not for me, not for any man.

But I allowed myself to be talked into a kind of hope, against reason, against feeling, — since, between us, we settled upon a picture of Caroline which did her little justice. She did not know her own mind. She did not know her own heart. There might be a little resentment, it was very natural, which had prompted her to inflict pain upon one who had caused her so much. She had not meant what she said. She would soften when she knew of my remorse. With patience, I might still prevail.

I was the more ready to listen since this kind of reasoning did away with certain mortifying memories. I was able to forget those strictures upon Lufton, and set them all down to the reproaches of a wounded heart. We had a long discussion. We must have been closeted together for above two hours, for Mrs. Egerton had a great deal of very good advice, once she had prevailed upon me to listen. She thought it better that I should leave Bath for the present, giving Caroline a little time for reflection and regret. She herself would meanwhile be my constant advocate, and would engage to let me know when to return.

We were still in the midst of this sanguine conspiracy when Caroline's note was brought in.

The servant said that a boy had left it at the door, saying that a lady, travelling post to London, had given him a shilling to deliver it at Devonshire Crescent by midday.

'Travelling post to London!' cried Mrs. Egerton, breaking the seal. 'But this is Caroline's hand!'

She looked at it, turned pale, cried out and thrust it into my hand before rushing from the room. Bells were rung, maids ran up and down stairs, — the whole house echoed with cries and exclamations, as it became plain that Caroline was gone. She had slipped out, with a small travelling bag, while I was closeted with her sister, had hired a post-chaise, and quitted Bath.

Whilst all this clamour proceeded I stood in the drawing-room, reading and re-reading her note:

I am going to London. Pray send my clothes to Lingshot. You shall have my direction when I know what it will be. I choose to live by myself for a while.

Nancy tells me that you have sent for Mr. Lufton. I know you too well not to guess what you mean to tell him, and I cannot bear to see either of you again. You have no right to betray me, and no right to give him this needless pain. You do me wrong to take me out of the grave. Tell him to forget — forget and forgive.

I tried to forget, because I did not wish to forgive. I spent the autumn in a reckless, angry mood, refusing to think, determined to remember nothing.

Then came my accident, my illness, and the eclipse of Pronto, which left me no defence against memory.

But why should I have feared it? This long reverie of recollection has brought me more of good than evil. It has raised my mother from the shades, an image no longer dim, but as a light which shone like heaven upon my childhood. Hawker has returned to me, as I first knew him, I have seen Ludovic galloping over the downs, I have remembered why I love Newsome and Kitty so much. Beyond all other blessings, — my beloved girl has been restored to my heart. Where she may be now, I know not ; but wherever she is, God go with her.

Of Miles and Pronto this may be a sorry tale :

> But genuine love must prize the past,
> And memory wakes the thoughts that bless ;
> They rose the first — they set the last.

What shall I do now ? I do not trouble myself greatly over that. It will follow, — it will follow as the night must follow day. To know himself is the first thing that a man must do before he dies. It is not all, but it is the first.

There must be no more of these boyish starts, — no more dreams of going to sea, no more attempts to fly the world. Miles has compounded too often with Pronto in that way, and set a Harry Ridding against the pangs of conscience. I trust that this business of Ridding's may be the last of his exploits. The feelings which prompted these impulsive actions must, and shall, be put to a more effective use. 'There is much to be done.' I will no longer cry : Helpless ! 'A duty that I may be happy to fulfil.' I shall find it. I have still half of my life before me.

It was daylight when I began this last chapter. Now it is dark, and a young crescent moon has appeared above the trees in the park. Down in the lane I can hear voices and low laughter. Harriet, Sukey and Anna are strolling there ; I can see their white dresses glimmer among the shadows.

They have just spied me at my window and are calling to me to turn my money in my pocket and kiss my hand to the new moon.

FINIS

EPILOGUE: 1880

EPILOGUE: 1880

Cullenstown, Jan. 14, 1880

DEAR FRED,

I am afraid we are in hot water over the Lufton Papers. My mother, who is now with us, has just discovered that you have them. She is much distressed that we should have let them go out of the house, — so much distressed that I think you had better send them back, if you have got all the information you want about Chalfont. She talks of destroying them.

As I suspected, she did know something. After beating about the bush for a while she told me what it was. It is not much, — only what she had from my father ages ago, and she has a most happy faculty for forgetting anything she doesn't care to remember.

Lufton was killed in a duel. It was all hushed up. In my mother's words : 'The inquest said it was an accident, but your grandfather was there and he said it was sheer murder. Your uncle fired wide, but the other man, who was drunk and very angry, did not, which shocked everybody very much. Your grandfather had to be very careful what he said at the inquest.'

This last sentence is, I imagine, my Mama's euphemism for perjury ! But she doesn't worry on Grandpapa's account. *Wherever* he is now, they can't get him for it.

It is the man who did it (she swears she never knew who he was) or his children, that she thinks of. Some of them may be living still and might be distressed if this story got out.

Family skeletons !

I think she is making a fuss out of nothing, but perhaps you had better send those papers back.

Yours ever,

JIM

Brailsford, Jan. 18, 1880

DEAR SIR JAMES,

I am writing on behalf of poor Harnish, who has had a severe set-back, a bad haemorrhage a couple of days ago, which has completely knocked him up. He does not wish Lady Emily to know, as it might frighten her, and he is sure that it is nothing and that he will soon pick up. I hope he is right; the doctor seems to be fairly optimistic. But I wish some of the family were here. The only relative in England is young Chalfont, at Eton. I have written to let him know, and to the Amershams, in Vienna, of course.

He wants me to tell you that we are returning the Lufton Papers, and have enclosed with this a letter we found, not from Miles Lufton, but from his brother George, which confirms Lady Cullen's story. We found it before we had finished reading the memoir so we knew what the end would be; and, as the 'other man' concerned is clearly identified, there is some reason for caution. We have looked that family up in Burke, and find that he died in 1846, but his grandson still owns the Gloucestershire property. These things are better forgotten.

I will let you know how Harnish goes on.

With kindest regards,

Yours very sincerely,

CHARLES CUNNINGHAM

Enclosure

The Parsonage, Great Bramfield, Glos.

July 12, 1818

MY LORD,

I am in receipt of your lordship's letter of the 10th inst. and will do my best to answer your questions.

As to the *circumstances* of my brother's death, I think this question sufficiently answered by the findings of the Coroner's Jury. He died by *misadventure*, being accidentally shot by our cousin, Mr. Edward Chadwick, of Great Bramfield Park. Evidence was given by Mr. Charles Pinney, of Stokehampton, and by my brother-in-law, Sir James Cullen, who were both witnesses of the melancholy event. All four were shooting at rabbits in a disused quarry, locally called Ribstone Pit, having gone there very early one morning for the purpose. That they used pistols has occasioned, I believe, some comment, but it is not uncommon for gentlemen to amuse themselves at this kind of sport. Both Sir James and Mr. Pinney stated that my brother stepped unexpectedly into range when Mr. Chadwick happened to be firing. He was hit in the lungs and died within an hour.

As to his *state* and final moments, I was present at the end and will give as full an account as I can. I was still abed when a message was brought to me that there had been an accident. I hastened with the messenger, a labourer called Howes, to Ribstone Pit. Sir James was, by then, gone off to seek a surgeon ; the bleeding was so profuse that they dared not aggravate it by moving my brother until skilled assistance should arrive. I found him supported in his cousin's arms ; Mr. Chadwick, unable to believe that he was dying, repeatedly exhorted him to say that it was nothing, and that he was not really hurt.

Poor Miles, upon perceiving me, gasped out that it

was 'not Ned's fault' and that I must 'tell them so'.
After that he said nothing collected. His mind seemed
to wander. He murmured something which I could not
catch ; it sounded like : 'Missed the venture and hit
Ahab.' I suppose that he was trying to explain the
accident. I asked him if he was comfortable or if he
would prefer to be moved to the nearest cottage. He
replied : No. He should do very well among the chimney
sweepers. Perceiving that the awful moment was fast
approaching, I began to repeat the prayer for dying
persons, constantly interrupted by the sobs of Mr.
Chadwick ; Mr. Pinney and Howes kneeling beside us.
My brother cut me short with a whisper that I should
'Pray for the helpless — pray for all sorts and conditions'
— I accordingly began that prayer but had got no further
than *all who profess and call themselves Christians* when he
broke in again, to ask for Ridding, a farmer upon the
Bramfield property. 'Here are Bob, Ned and I, but
there should be four of us, you know. Where is Harry ?'
With that he fixed his eyes earnestly upon the labourer
Howes. I took no notice and continued the prayer. At
the words *the bond of peace*, he cried out suddenly, in a
strong voice : Begone ! He fell into a strange, wild fit of
laughter, which was strangled by a gush of blood, and all
was over.

He is buried beside our mother, in Bramfield church-
yard.

It is very kind of your lordship to enquire so particularly after my father. He is so much shaken by these
dreadful events that I doubt if he will ever again be equal
to his parish duties. While he lives I can remain here,
acting as his curate. At his death I am certain that the
living will be presented elsewhere, and I do not know
where I can expect preferment, unless I may depend
upon your lordship's continued interest in our family.

As regards the property in Wiltshire, it is not in my power to give any precise information, but I believe that it is to be sold to the present tenant. I may say that the whole of my brother's property goes to my sister Susan, in a Will executed by him this Spring. I will not criticise his action in thus passing over the claims of other relatives. My sister has chosen to remove from Bramfield and has gone to Ireland.

Your lordship's final question leaves me completely at a loss. I know nothing of my brother's dreams. If he received some warning of his end, I never heard of it. As to the particular dream which he communicated to your lordship, — I cannot see any connection between this sad fatality and my sister-in-law, formerly Miss Maria Cotman, now Mrs. Poole, and resident in Jamaica.

I have the honour to be
Your lordship's obliged, humble
and obedient servant,

GEORGE LUFTON

THE END

VIRAGO MODERN CLASSICS

The first Virago Modern Classic, *Frost in May* by Antonia White, was published in 1978. It launched a list dedicated to the celebration of women writers and to the rediscovery and reprinting of their works. Its aim was, and is, to demonstrate the existence of a female tradition in fiction which is both enriching and enjoyable. The Leavisite notion of the 'Great Tradition', and the narrow, academic definition of a 'classic', has meant the neglect of a large number of interesting secondary works of fiction. In calling the series 'Modern Classics' we do not necessarily mean 'great' — although this is often the case. Published with new critical and biographical introductions, books are chosen for many reasons: sometimes for their importance in literary history; sometimes because they illuminate particular aspects of womens' lives, both personal and public. They may be classics of comedy or storytelling; their interest can be historical, feminist, political or literary.

Initially the Virago Modern Classics concentrated on English novels and short stories published in the early decades of this century. As the series has grown it has broadened to include works of fiction from different centuries, different countries, cultures and literary traditions. In 1984 the Victorian Classics were launched; there are separate lists of Irish, Scottish, European, American, Australian and other English speaking countries; there are books written by Black women, by Catholic and Jewish women, and a few relevant novels by men. There is, too, a companion series of Non-Fiction Classics constituting biography, autobiography, travel, journalism, essays, poetry, letters and diaries.

By the end of 1986 over 250 titles will have been published in these two series, many of which have been suggested by our readers.